DAUGHTER OF ASHES

DAUGHTER OF ASHES

A Hannah Ives Mystery
Marcia Talley

Severn House Large Print
London & New York

This first large print edition published 2016
in Great Britain and the USA by
SEVERN HOUSE PUBLISHERS LTD of
19 Cedar Road, Sutton, Surrey, England, SM2 5DA.
First world regular print edition published 2015 by
Severn House Publishers Ltd., London and New York.

British Library Cataloguing in Publication Data

Talley, Marcia Dutton, 1943- author.
    Daughter of ashes. – (The Hannah Ives mysteries series)
    1. Ives, Hannah (Fictitious character)–Fiction.
    2. Dwellings–Remodeling–Fiction. 3. Public records–
    Fiction. 4. Detective and mystery stories. 5. Large type
    books.
    I. Title II. Series
    813.6-dc23

    ISBN-13: 9780727871824

Severn House Publishers support the Forest Stewardship Council™
[FSC™], the leading international forest certification organisation. All
our titles that are printed on FSC certified paper carry the FSC logo.

Typeset by Palimpsest Book Production Ltd.,
Falkirk, Stirlingshire, Scotland.
Printed and bound in Great Britain by
T J International, Padstow, Cornwall.

For Carol Chase
A good friend knows all your stories; a
best friend helps you write them.

ACKNOWLEDGMENTS

Ernest Hemingway once said, 'Writing, at its best, is a lonely life.' And yet, this novel would never have made it into your hands without the help and encouragement of so many generous people. I'd like to thank my amazing team:

My family – husband, Barry Talley and daughters Laura Geyer and Sarah Glass – who support me every day in every way, even when I'm completely lost in 'Marcialand.'

Crime writer, Kate Charles, for teaching the master class at St Hilda's College in Oxford, England, where the seed of this novel was sown.

Friend and colleague, author Sarah Shaber, who told me a story at the Sisters in Crime writing retreat in Charlotte, North Carolina that changed everything.

Wally and Hannah Pickworth, who let me hang out at their Eastern Shore cottage on Butcher Creek in Virginia where the plot for this novel was cooked up over crab cakes and wine.

Jeannine Wayson, realtor with Coldwell Banker in Annapolis, Maryland, who in no way resembles any of the characters in this book, but if she did, she'd be dangerous.

W. Edward Hudgins ('Judge Hudge') for help navigating and interpreting historic court records.

Linda Sprenkle, fellow adventurer, location scout and long-time friend.

My colleagues in the Writers' Circle in Hope Town, Abaco, Bahamas and to my partners in crime back in Annapolis, Maryland – Becky Hutchinson, Mary Ellen Hughes, Debbi Mack, Sherriel Mattingly, Shari Randall and Bonnie Settle – once again, for tough love.

And, as always, to Vicky Bijur.

Wandering oversea dreamer,
Hunting and hoarse, Oh daughter and mother,
Oh daughter of ashes and mother of blood,
Child of the hair let down, and tears,
Child of the cross in the south
And the star in the north,
Keeper of Egypt and Russia and France,
Keeper of England and Poland and Spain,
Make us a song for to-morrow.
Make us one new dream, us who forget,
Out of the storm let us have one star.

Struggle, Oh anvils, and help her.
Weave with your wool. Oh winds and skies.
Let your iron and copper help,
Oh dirt of the old dark earth.

Wandering oversea singer,
Singing of ashes and blood,
Child of the scars of fire,
Make us one new dream, us who forget.
Out of the storm let us have one star.

Carl Sandburg, *Smoke and Steel*, 'IV.
Playthings of the Wind, 12. Prayers
After World War,' 1922

One

'Remember that not getting what you want is sometimes a wonderful stroke of luck.'

The Dalai Lama XIV

In all the years since my diagnosis, I've never played the cancer card. I confess to being tempted when Paul was waffling over an opportunity to spend his sabbatical in the Bahamas. Came close when his responsibilities as chair of the Naval Academy math department made him second guess our decision to revisit friends we'd met during his faculty exchange year with Britannia Royal Naval College. But after decades of marriage Paul was tuned into me – almost eerily so. I'd just been *thinking* I'd toss back my hair in a Scarlett O'Hara kind of way and drawl, 'Oh, dah'link, I hope ah can get back to England some day before ah die,' when he fixed me with those bottomless-cup-of-coffee eyes and sucked the thought clean out of my head.

'Of course we'll go to Dartmouth,' he said, brushing his lips against my cheek. 'Start packing.'

In recent years, I'd begun hinting about owning a retirement cottage on the water. Shamelessly. I'd left brochures out on the coffee table, circled waterfront homes advertised for sale in the back pages of *Chesapeake Bay* magazine, clicked through to virtual tours on online realtor listings and even dragged Paul along to Sunday open houses in order to 'familiarize ourselves with the market.'

'Dream on, Hannah,' he'd say, holding tight to his wallet, but agreeing to tag along on these outings simply to humor me.

On one such Sunday the previous winter, an agent from Barfield and Williams near Salisbury, Maryland had taken us to tour a three-bedroom, two-bath bungalow perched high on a bluff overlooking the Wicomico River, a property with a waterfront view that made both our hearts sing. Unfortunately, both the listing price and the state of the stock market at the time sang woefully out of tune.

I'd drooled over the open concept living room, dining room and kitchen area, waxed poetic about the screened-in porch and oohed and ahed over what the realtor's listing described as a charming colonial, thoughtfully updated throughout with crown moldings and windows affording a breathtaking sunset view.

'It's my dream house,' I'd gushed to Paul.

With a sideways glance at Caitlyn Dymond through a fringe of long lashes, he'd elbowed me in the ribs. 'Shhhh.' But it was too late. Caitlyn already knew she'd hooked a couple of live ones, so as time went on and the property didn't sell, the agent emailed us periodically:

'It's a buyer's market.'

'Motivated sellers!'

'Make an offer – all they can do is refuse.'

Still, we'd balked.

The following spring, shortly after we'd sprung forward into Daylight Savings Time, I came home from an evening out with my grandkids at Chick-Fil-A and movies at the mall to find Paul sitting at our kitchen table with reams of paper spread out before him. As I closed the kitchen door, Paul looked up, a Cheshire Cat grin lighting his face. 'I think we can do this, Hannah.'

'Do what?' I asked, tossing the car keys on the counter.

'Buy that house on the Wicomico.'

I took a deep breath, considered what part the three Miller Lite empties lined up on the sideboard had played in his decision and said, 'You're serious?'

'Perfectly.'

'How come we can afford to do it today when we couldn't afford to do it last week?'

Paul raised an index finger. 'Ah, well you may ask. Connie's been offering to buy me out and, as you know, I'd resisted. But while you were at the movies tonight I called my sister and took her up on her offer.'

Paul's sister raised rare breed cows and decorative gourds on the Ives family farm with her husband, Chesapeake County police lieutenant Dennis Rutherford. That Paul was willing to sell his half of the farm that he and his sister had inherited from their mother took me completely by surprise. I gaped, breathing slowly through my mouth.

'I was only holding on to it out of sentiment,' my husband explained. 'We haven't been down to south county for months.'

3

I pulled out a kitchen chair and plopped down next to him, trying to catch my breath. 'Are you sure?'

He reached for my hand and folded it into his own. His was ice cold and damp from the beer bottle he'd been holding. 'I hope the house will make you as happy as it will make me. It'll be a perfect place for the grandkids. Sailing, kayaking, swimming, fishing. And that long pier . . .' He paused, his eyes unfocused, dreamy. 'Crabbing. Tie a chicken neck to a string, attach it to the dock and ease it into the water. Takes me back. I'd like them to experience that kind of carefree childhood, too.'

Lost in some childhood memories of my own that didn't involve creative use of poultry, I didn't answer right away. After a moment, Paul said, 'So, are you with me?'

I ruffled his tight salt-and-pepper curls and kissed his forehead. 'Is the Pope Catholic?'

Paul picked up the phone and made an offer that night: ten percent under the asking price. Caitlyn responded by showing up on our Annapolis doorstep the following morning, her abundant red hair tied up in a low ponytail, documents in hand. 'Good news,' she said as I invited her inside. 'They've accepted your offer.'

'I can't believe we're doing this,' I said ten minutes later as we sat down with the agent at our kitchen table. I signed my name at the bottom of the contract and added the date, then slid the document over to Paul.

'What's next?' Paul asked after he'd signed the contract himself and reached for his checkbook.

Caitlyn smiled. 'We wait for the check to clear, then set a closing date.'

Which explains why, a week later, I was sitting in our basement office, prowling the Internet, searching for curtains at bedbathandbeyond.com when the phone rang. I was busy comparing tabs to grommets so I cursed the interruption, but the phone cut off in mid-ring so I figured Paul had picked it up. 'If it's Ruth,' I yelled, 'tell her I've already got all the feng shui remedies I need.'

My sister, Ruth Gannon, owns Mother Earth, a New Age shop on Main Street in Annapolis. Our Prince George Street home already looked like an auxiliary showroom for Mother Earth with all the wind chimes, water features, mirrors and candles she'd brought over.

'Three *baguas* are two too many, if you know what I mean.'

I had selected a bright island floral for the guest bedroom windows when I felt Paul standing behind me. 'It wasn't Ruth,' he said quietly.

'Who, then?' I asked, clicking the mouse to select eighty-four inches.

'It was Caitlyn Dymond. The deal fell through.'

'What?' I swiveled in the chair to face him, looked up into his troubled eyes. 'How can that be?' I sputtered. 'They accepted our offer! We signed a contract! Paid the deposit!' I waved a hand at the computer screen. 'I'm even ordering curtains!' An awful thought occurred to me. 'Don't tell me the check bounced.'

'No, the money is all there. Apparently there was another, earlier contract, one that Caitlyn knew nothing about.'

5

'Offer them more money!' I said.

Paul shook his head. 'It won't work. Already tried. Apparently the other contract pre-dates ours.'

I glared at my husband, silently seething. 'I don't understand. Why didn't Caitlyn know about the prior contract? Isn't that what multiple listing databases are for?'

'Well, we'll find out in a few minutes. Caitlyn's on her way over to explain.'

'It had better be good,' I grumped, as I consigned the curtains sitting in my virtual shopping cart to oblivion and stomped up the stairs after my husband.

Fifteen minutes after her phone call, Caitlyn arrived, ashen-faced. We showed her into the living room. I was so pissed off I didn't offer her anything to drink.

'I'm so sorry,' she began as she settled into an armchair, dropping her oversized handbag on the carpet next to her feet. 'I'm as unhappy about this as you are.'

'Were we gazumped?' I asked, referring to a practice I'd learned about in England where buyers could be outbid, even after an offer has been accepted.

She shook her head. 'No.'

From his spot on the sofa, Paul leaned forward, forearms resting on his knees. 'Well, *what*, then?'

'As I explained to Paul on the phone, there was an earlier contract that I knew nothing about. The sellers decided to go with the earlier offer.'

'But, but . . .' I stuttered, trying to collect my thoughts. 'Was that offer higher than ours?'

Caitlyn shook her head. 'No, the same amount.'

'Two contracts on the same property,' I mused. 'Is that legal?'

'It's not illegal.'

Paul made a time-out with his hands. 'Wait a minute. Wasn't the Wicomico house a Barfield and Williams listing?'

'It was,' Caitlyn said.

'The company you work for.' It was a statement, not a question.

She nodded miserably.

Paul pointed an accusatory finger. 'Then how come *you* didn't know about the earlier offer?'

'Kendall Barfield was the listing agent, not me,' Caitlyn said obliquely.

Paul flopped back in his chair. 'Ah, I see.'

'See what?' I asked.

'So, if we got the house rather than these other folks, whoever they are, Kendall would have to split the commission with you. Am I right?'

'Correct.'

'But if *she* sells the house . . .'

Light dawned and I finished the sentence for him. 'Kendall gets to bank the full six percent.'

'Right,' Caitlyn said.

Angry tears pricked my eyes. I'd never met Kendall Barfield, only seen her photograph – all fluffy white-blonde hair and toothy, demonic grin – staring out at me from an advertising placard attached to the shopping cart I was pushing through the Acme Supermarket. 'How bitchy.'

'I'm furious, too, Hannah,' Caitlyn confided. 'This is the third time Kendall's pulled a stunt like this. If she weren't the biggest realtor on

7

the Eastern Shore, swear to God, I'd quit.' She bent over, picked up her handbag and set it in her lap. 'But, I have another listing here that I think will appeal to you and Paul. A waterfront home on Chiconnesick Creek, just outside of Elizabethtown.'

'I doubt it,' I said, swiping at my nose with the back of my hand. I'd never heard of Elizabethtown, so how good could it be?

Paul snatched a tissue out of the box on the end table and handed it to me. 'Give Caitlyn a chance, Hannah.'

I dabbed at my nose, thinking murderous thoughts as I watched Caitlyn rummage through her bag.

'This listing just came on the market, and it's my exclusive.' Caitlyn grinned. 'The owner's a friend of mine. No way Kendall can screw up *this* sale.' She handed me a printout.

As I studied the photographs on the listing, my spirits gradually lifted. 'I feel like I'm back in Dartmouth, Paul. The house looks like an English cottage, rose arbor and all. And the price is certainly right.'

'It's an estate sale,' Caitlyn explained. 'The widow is hoping the house will move quickly.'

I handed the printout to Paul who flipped through it, his eyes scanning it carefully. When he reached the bottom line, he glanced up at Caitlyn, his brow furrowed. 'Looks charming, but it's one hundred thousand less than the place on the Wicomico.'

'Well,' Caitlyn confided. 'It needs a bit of work.'

'How much work?' I wanted to know.

'You said it looked like an English cottage, Hannah. That's because it *is* an English cottage. The main part of the house was built in 1765. Maryland was still a British colony then. It's been added to over the years, of course, but with some sense of style and respect for the home's historic origins.'

'Sounds intriguing. When can we see it?' Paul asked.

Caitlyn pulled an iPhone out of a side pocket of her handbag and tapped a few keys. 'How about tomorrow after lunch?'

After we'd agreed, figured out where Chiconnesick Creek was – Tilghman County, just north of the border Maryland shares with Virginia – and Caitlyn had left, I fixed two glasses of iced tea and joined Paul on the back patio. I settled into a lounger, took a long sip of tea and said, 'I wish Naddie were still writing murder mysteries instead of dabbling in watercolors.'

Paul turned his head and studied me over the top of his sunglasses. 'Why?'

'Because I have a victim for her.'

Paul laughed, then closed his eyes as if deep in thought. 'Let me guess. For a novel called *Final Closing*?'

'I'm sure that title's already taken, but yes.' I stirred my tea with an index finger, then dried it on my shorts. 'Kendall Barfield slumped over her desk with a knife sticking out of her back. I would pay extra for that. It would totally ruin the cut of her Ralph Lauren blazer, of course.'

9

Paul snorted into his glass. 'You're a hard woman, Hannah Ives.'

'Well,' I said, sipping my tea, 'it'd be cheaper than a therapist.'

Two

'Fortune is like the market, where many times, if you can stay a little, the price will fall.'

Francis Bacon, *Essays, Civil and Moral*, 'XXI: Of Delays,' 1909–1914

Following a relentlessly healthy breakfast of yogurt, granola and whole wheat toast, washed down with mugs of robust French roast coffee, Paul and I climbed into his elderly Volvo and set off for Maryland's eastern shore. Using the address Caitlyn had given me, I programmed the GPS, a Tom-Tom device that Paul had nicknamed 'Stella' because her voice reminded him of his high-school girlfriend. I tried not to be grumpy as I suction-cupped Stella to the windshield.

'According to Stella, the trip will take two hours and thirteen minutes,' I announced as Paul took the exit off Rowe Boulevard and merged with the heavy traffic on Route 50 heading for the Bay Bridge. 'We should be able to pick up a bite of lunch in Elizabethtown before it's time to meet Caitlyn, assuming they have restaurants in Elizabethtown, that is.'

'Several,' Paul said. 'I Googled around this morning. There's a bakery on High Street that sells designer coffee. Just across the street is a family-run café called the High Spot, kind of a local watering hole, I gather. Used to be a hardware store. There's a pub called the Crusty Crab and a more upscale restaurant on the town wharf we could investigate today, too, if you like. It's called the Boat House, as I recall.' He hiked a thumb, indicating the back seat. 'Printout's in the canvas bag.'

'Excellent,' I said, after reaching for the bag and shuffling through the pages Paul had printed, checking out the sample menus. 'The Boat House sounds perfect. According to this,' I said, waving the printout, 'they serve world-famous crab cakes.'

'Boat House it is, then.' After a moment, he said, 'I visited the Barfield and Williams website, too, and printed out the complete specs for the cottage. It's stapled at the back.'

But I'd already found the PDF describing the property and was reading through it. 'I regret to inform you that the cottage has a name.' I paused for effect. '*Legal Ease*. Must have belonged to an attorney.'

Paul groaned. 'Ya think?'

I read on. 'Waterfront, two acres, so far so good.' I looked up. 'Boat dock, it says. I wonder if there's enough water for Connie and Dennis to tie up their sailboat?'

'The Chiconnesick is pretty shallow, two to three feet at mean low water. I doubt it could accommodate *Sea Song*, even at high tide. Her draft is four and a half feet.'

'Oh,' I said, disappointed.

'But if this all works out,' Paul continued brightly, 'we can certainly look into buying a small power boat for zipping around the Bay. And for fishing, too, of course.' He caught my eye and winked before turning to concentrate on merging into the EasyPass-only toll lane at the entrance to the bridge.

'Wish we could just toot over from Annapolis in a boat,' I said about ten miles further on, thinking about the long drive still ahead of us.

'Wouldn't save all that much time, sweetheart,' Paul pointed out as he eased to the right and took the exit where Routes 50 and 301 part ways at the Queenstown Outlet Mall. 'And it'd be a long, wet ride, particularly in a chop.'

'Or if it's raining,' I muttered. 'Wishful thinking, I guess.'

While Paul drove south keeping an eye out for the county's notorious speed traps and his cruise control set to fifty-five, I studied a map in the eastern shore guidebook I'd picked up at the Ivy Bookshop on Falls Road on a recent visit to Baltimore with my younger sister, Georgina, who lived nearby. In the section describing Tilghman County, I learned that Elizabethtown, its county seat, was named after Elizabeth of Bohemia, the 'Winter Queen,' the only daughter of James I of England to survive into adulthood. Her brothers, Henry and Charles, had Capes in Virginia named after them, so it seemed only fair. 'Did you know that Chiconnesick means "land where the blue-birds sing?"' I asked my husband. 'Bodes well for birdwatching, if you're into that sort of thing.' I turned a few pages, read on. 'The early settlers apparently bought the land from the Piscataway Indians in exchange for six Dutch blankets.' Thinking about the asking price for *Legal Ease*, I sighed and added, 'Those were the good old days.'

I closed the guidebook and tucked it into my tote bag.

A fender-bender on the Choptank River bridge just north of Cambridge delayed us long enough that I saw all hope evaporate of getting lunch at the Boat House in Elizabethtown before meeting with Caitlyn. As we waited, engine idling, at the head of a long line of vehicles for the tow truck to clear away the mess and haul it away to the body shop, I reached for the emergency power bars I'd packed in my handbag, unwrapped one and handed half of it to Paul, who polished it off in two bites.

On the outskirts of Salisbury, where Route 301 peels off to Ocean City and the beach towns along the Atlantic shore, we joined Route 13, the backbone that bisects the Delmarva peninsula – what the native Americans had called 'Nassawadox,' the land between the two waters – with bucolic towns and villages scattered along either side.

I'd almost forgotten about the GPS until shortly after passing the turnoff for Pocomoke City, when Stella came to life and said, *In one mile, make a right turn.*

We obeyed, winding along a two-lane state road for several miles until the fields of corn and soybeans gradually gave way to the houses of Elizabethtown, a prosperous-looking colonial town with a single traffic light. As we waited at the intersection of High and King for the light to turn green, I counted only one empty storefront along the block, a former pharmacy with Wm Chase & Sons spelled out in black and white tiles on the sidewalk out front. A sign posted in its display window read *Blue Crab Art Galley – Coming Soon*, so apparently the town had the vacancy situation well in hand.

Stella directed us through the traffic light, past another block of shops, left over a small wooden bridge and down a deeply shaded street lined on both sides with lovingly restored, high Victorian homes. At the edge of town, the cornfields resumed. After about five miles, Paul slowed when Stella confidently directed us down a dirt track – two ruts with grass growing tall along the hump in the middle. 'Is she *serious*?' he asked, applying his foot firmly to the brakes.

'Caitlyn said it was out of the way,' I reminded him.

'*This* out of the way?' Paul leaned forward, checked Stella's display and frowned suspiciously. 'I'm betting it's further along.'

As Paul crept forward along the paved road, I peered through my window, scanning down the long rows of corn. Almost immediately I spotted Caitlyn's lime-colored VW bug on the far side of the field. 'There's Caitlyn's car, so I think we're in the right place.'

'Hold on to your teeth,' Paul joked as he backed up, turned right and steered cautiously and bumpily down the road with tall grass *whoosh-whooshing* against the undercarriage.

Caitlyn's VW was parked on a gravel drive next to the most charming cottage I'd ever seen outside the Cotswolds. If Jane Austen had greeted us at the front door, complete with dark ringlets and frilly cap, I wouldn't have been surprised. Instead, it was Caitlyn who awaited us, dressed in white jeans and a floral T-shirt, leaning against a white picket gate, her thumbs rapidly stabbing a text message into her cell phone. When she caught sight of our Volvo she smiled, made a final stab and tucked the phone back into her handbag. 'Well, what do you think?' she asked when we pulled up to the gate and stepped out of the car.

'It's lovely,' I gushed as I closed the car door behind me.

Caitlyn grinned. 'I told you so. Great curb appeal, don't you think?'

Behind me, Paul grunted. 'If it *had* a curb.'

I shot him a look, then took several steps backwards to widen my view. I whipped out my own iPhone, aimed and took some photos, trying to capture as much of the scene as I could. The stone wall, yellow with dried moss. The half-timbered stucco. The way the lace-curtained dormers peeked out of the shingled rooftop like friendly eyes. 'It's like something out of a Beatrix Potter illustration, isn't it, Paul?'

'As I'm not Flopsy, Mopsy, Cottontail or Peter, I'm withholding comment until we can see inside,' my husband replied with a grin.

Caitlyn lifted a wrought-iron latch and pushed the wooden gate open. 'No time like the present, then.'

The moment we stepped through the gate, I was a goner. As we strolled along the flagstone path that curved gently up to the dusty red front door, I fell hopelessly in love with the huge oak tree that dominated the yard, including the wooden crutch that propped up one of its low-hanging branches. I was charmed by the plantings along the path, cascading over the rims of blue ceramic pots. I wanted those leaded windows, those shutters, those window boxes where screaming orange begonias bedded down with pink petunias, trailing purple sweet potato vine. I coveted the wooden bench, too, borne on the backs of stone turtles. I pined for the bird bath, even fancied the topiary swan – which needed a trim – but, no matter, I was good with pruning shears.

'Hannah? You coming?' Paul called from the murky depths of the entrance hall while Caitlyn held the front door wide.

Light fixtures like inverted trumpet vine blossoms, green with the patina of age, flanked the door. I wanted them, too.

Inside, an open staircase led directly to the second floor. 'There's a modern bath upstairs with two bedrooms adjoining,' Caitlyn informed us, waving a hand casually upward then chugging on. 'But you'll want to see the downstairs first.'

The claustrophobic entrance hall spit us out into a bright living room with an enormous stone fireplace at one end and a drop-dead view of Chiconnesick Creek at the other. Paul slammed on the brakes and sucked in air. 'Whoa!'

From her spot in front of the wall-to-wall

picture windows, Caitlyn grinned. 'Exactly. This is all part of the original house,' she continued. 'The kitchen and dining room, too.'

I blessed the kitchen – which had modern stainless-steel appliances and marbled granite countertops – but the dining room was dark and pokey, with barely enough room for a table that would seat six. 'Can we knock this down?' I asked, running my hand along the wall that separated the dining room from the kitchen. 'And it's not just my aversion to flocked wallpaper, either,' I grinned, although it featured acid-green flowers that even a Victorian housewife would have found hideous.

Paul smiled. 'Hannah's been watching too many makeover shows on TV.'

'You'd have to consult a builder,' Caitlyn said, 'but it seems to me that anything's possible, as long as it's not load-bearing.' We trailed back into the living room after her. 'Through this door here you'll find the master suite addition, which I know you'll adore,' Caitlyn chirped, herding us quickly along. She paused at the door and swept her arm to the side like a game show hostess. 'And the previous owners balanced off the master suite with an office and laundry room addition over there.'

'Everything's so tidy and clean,' I commented as we wandered into a master bedroom dominated by a king-sized bed, which was staged with enough decorative pillows to bed down the entire U.S. Army.

'There will be issues, I'm sure,' Paul said as he peered appreciatively into the walk-in shower

17

that would comfortably accommodate his lanky six-foot-two-inch frame. 'There usually are in a house of this age.'

'Pedigree, my dear,' I corrected. 'Not age.'

'It's not, "Do you have termites?"' Paul expanded on the thought, opening a door that led to a linen closet, peeking in and closing it again. 'It's "How have the termites been treated, and how often?"'

'According to the owner, the house was last tented five years ago, but you'll have an inspection, I'm sure,' Caitlyn interjected as she opened one of the French doors that led from the bedroom out onto the deck.

We followed. Paul rested both hands against the railing, took a deep breath, leaned forward and let it out slowly. 'I could get used to this.'

Below us, the lawn sloped gradually down to the shore where a wooden dock extended about fifty feet into the creek. At the far end a power boat bobbed, secured to the dock with blue and white lines, the ends of which had been neatly coiled on the planking like braided rugs. A splash of neon blue among the cattails and jewelweed turned out to be a kayak, inverted onto a wooden rack.

'The boats convey,' Caitlyn said.

Paul whistled. 'You're kidding.'

'Nope. As I said, she's a motivated seller. *Legal Ease* was always *his* retreat, not hers. She's looking forward to buying a condo in Scottsdale and to spending more time with her grandchildren.'

Paul turned his back on the view, sat back

against the porch rail. 'The asking price. How much wiggle-room is there?'

Caitlyn shrugged. 'A bit, but honestly, I don't think the house will last long at this price point.'

Paul scowled. He hated to be pressured. 'We'll need to factor some renovations into the equation, of course, as well as repairs.'

Caitlyn's smile seemed a bit forced. 'Of course.'

Paul rolled forward onto the balls of his feet. 'My wife and I will have to discuss it, but we could have an offer for you by tomorrow. Can you promise not to schedule any additional showings until then?'

Caitlyn remained silent, studying his face as if gauging his sincerity. 'OK, but if I don't hear from you by noon . . .' Her voice trailed off.

'You will, one way or the other.' Paul checked his watch and switched gears. 'Hannah and I are looking for a nice place to have a late lunch and talk this over. We hear the Boat House is good.'

Caitlyn shook her head. 'Closed on Wednesdays.'

'Where would you suggest, then?' I asked.

'Well, if you want local color, I'd go to the High Spot. You'll run into everyone there, sooner or later.'

While we wandered through the garden waiting for Caitlyn to secure the front door and replace the key in a lockbox hidden in a decorative watering can, I said to Paul, 'We'll have to rename it, of course.'

'What? The cottage?' Paul adjusted a shutter hanging crookedly from a rusty hinge and grinned. 'How about we call it *Crumbles*.'

I smiled back at him. 'Let's just call it home.'

19

Three

'More tears are shed over answered prayers than unanswered ones.'

St Theresa of Avila, 1515–1582

Alas, because of a curriculum planning meeting Paul had forgotten until a colleague called him with a last-minute question, we had to skip the High Spot café and hustle back to Annapolis. Paul could function for days without food, running on diet cola and fumes, but I was faint with hunger, so he took pity, stopping at a Subway just north of Pocomoke City. I dashed in for a spicy Italian foot-long sandwich – half with jalapeños and half without – which we shared as we drove, staving off starvation.

We stopped for gas on the outskirts of Easton and switched drivers. With his hands free, Paul made arrangements with Caitlyn for a quick house inspection, and after the appraiser's report came in later that evening, Paul studied it, did the math and made an offer.

Two days later, we were back on the Eastern Shore. Caitlyn had telephoned that our offer for *Legal Ease* had been accepted, so we agreed to meet her at the High Spot in Elizabethtown to talk specifics and, hopefully, sign the agreement papers.

Losing my dream home because of Kendall Barfield's unethical shenanigans still stung, so I tried to clamp a lid on my excitement by tabling any redecorating plans, at least until the ink on the contract for *Legal Ease* had dried. Yet not even the weather that day – a cool, misty rain – could dampen my spirits.

Parking was plentiful on such a gray morning, so we pulled into a spot on Elizabethtown's leafy town square, scrabbled in the pouches behind our seats for umbrellas and climbed out onto the puddled sidewalk that surrounded the square.

Elizabethtown's town square was dominated by a war memorial, a gray-stone obelisk rising like a miniature Washington Monument from the center of a three-layered concrete wedding cake. But the nearby bandstand, decorated in vibrant colors like a circus carousel, easily stole the show, adding a whimsical high Victorian touch to what was otherwise a rather staid little Georgian town.

We hustled along High Street, past the hotel that used to be a bank and now – according to a sign in the window – served afternoon tea on chintz tablecloths from three to five o'clock in the vault. The office of Barfield and Williams came next, their windows plastered with listings of area homes for sale, including, inexplicably, the one we had so recently 'lost.' I made a rude noise and hurried on. An attorney at law, an antiques store that specialized in restoration hardware – I made a mental note – and . . . I grabbed Paul's arm. We were standing in front of a store called Passionknit. 'Check out the yarn,' I breathed.

Paul frowned. 'Do I have to?'

'No, but I think that bright red merino and silk blend they have heaped in the window would look great on you.'

'Matches my eyes?'

'Hah!' I said.

'I don't need any more sweaters, Hannah. And you have more yarn in the guest room closet than you could knit up in two lifetimes.'

I felt my face flush. Paul was right. I couldn't knit it all up in *three* lifetimes, but whenever one of the mail-order companies I did business with had a bag sale . . . well, just hang a sign around my neck that read *Sucker!*

'Maybe they carry patterns,' I suggested. 'For the yarn I already have. And buttons.'

Paul tugged me away from the window. 'I'm sure they do, Hannah, but there'll be plenty of time to explore that later. Besides, didn't you tell me you were starving?'

'A turtleneck maybe? Irish style, with cables?' When on a mission, I was sometimes hard to turn.

'Hannah . . .'

With Paul's hand firmly grasping my elbow, we moved on.

The High Spot was crowded with men and women dressed in business casual attire – there, I presumed, on a mid-morning coffee break. Wet umbrellas had been tipped into an oversized brass spitoon near the door while raincoats and slickers dripped from hooks along the wall nearby. Several yummy mummies shared an industrial-sized blueberry muffin at a table near the coffee fixings bar, their strollers angled into a corner, the babies they contained blissfully asleep. After depositing our umbrellas in the spittoon, Paul and I dosidoed around two guys wearing red Comcast polo shirts as they hustled out the door, handheld radios crackling, on a mission of mercy for some poor cable television customer or another. We scanned the busy café, looking for Caitlyn.

Caitlyn had already snagged a table for four in a quiet corner near the narrow hallway that led, according to a sign, to the '*Caballeros*' and '*Señoras*,' although there was nothing remotely Spanish about the High Spot's décor, unless you counted the cans of Red Bull I saw chilling in the drinks cooler. She waved us over. 'Coffee?' she asked before we even had a chance to pull out a chair and sit down.

'Please,' I said.

'If it's regular,' she said, pointing to two urns on a table near the back, 'just help yourself. Double soy skinny latte or something fancy like that, you gotta stand in line.'

'Regular's fine with me,' I said. 'Why don't I get it while you and Paul make small talk.' I aimed myself urn-ward. 'But don't say anything important until I get back.'

When I returned, carrying two steaming mugs, with sugar packets and creamer tubs tucked into my pocket, Caitlyn already had papers spread out on the table next to her open laptop. I set Paul's coffee down carefully between two important-looking piles and took a seat. 'This is happening so fast,' I said. 'Doesn't there have to be a title search or something?'

Caitlyn beamed. 'In a small town these things can be expedited. It's all in knowing who to call.' She snapped her fingers. 'I do a favor for someone, they do a favor for me.'

'So, we're good to go?' Paul asked.

'Yup,' she said, offering him a pen.

I cradled the mug between my palms, appreciating its warmth, watching while Paul flipped through several pages of the contract. He read, flipped back, read some more, then turned to one of the pages marked with a red plastic tab. He smoothed the document out on the table. 'Well,' he said at last, reaching for the pen Caitlyn was holding. He caught my eye and waggled both brows. 'Looks like everything's in order here.'

'We're really going to do this, aren't we, Paul?' I said.

'We are.' Paul leaned over the document and signed his name with a flourish, then shoved the papers toward me. 'Your turn.'

I signed the documents, too, in triplicate, on the blank line under my husband's expansive scrawl that looked for all the world as if he'd written *Pralines*. The owner had already signed, I noticed. Her old-fashioned signature would have been perfectly legible even if it hadn't been typed in capital letters below the blank: Julianna Quinn. A notary seal pressed into the document attested to its authenticity.

'There!' I said, pushing the contracts in Caitlyn's direction. 'Are we done?'

'Not quite,' Paul interjected, reaching for the checkbook he'd tucked into his breast pocket.

He'd written the check at home, so all he had to do now was tear it out and . . . He handed it over to Caitlyn. '*Now* we're done.' He reached over, took my hand and held it. 'Looks like my wife and I have bought a house.'

'You have,' Caitlyn said. She handed Paul one of the signed contracts, then tucked our check under the binder clip that held the two remaining copies of our contract for *Legal Ease* together. She slid the whole packet into the briefcase she had balanced on her knees.

But her hand didn't emerge from the depths of the briefcase empty. Paul noticed it first and gave me a nudge. I reached out and took a set of keys from Caitlyn's outstretched fingers. I folded them into my palm, kissed them for good luck and pressed my hand to my heart.

Paul smiled at the melodrama, then turned his attention back to Caitlyn. 'We'll need a contractor. Who do you recommend?'

Caitlyn was prepared with another piece of paper, which she handed to my husband. 'I've written down several names but I wouldn't like to recommend one over another.' She grinned. 'It's a small town. I have to live and work here.'

'I understand,' Paul said. 'But if it were your house, who would you call?'

'They're all reliable, Paul, but if you'll notice, the list isn't in alphabetical order. I'd start at the top. Just sayin'.'

After Caitlyn had left, I examined the keys – *our* keys. There were three on a key ring bearing the Barfield and Williams logo, each tagged with a white disk. I fingered them lovingly, like charms on a bracelet. *Front door. Garage*. And a third surprise addition to the family: *Tool shed.*

Eventually, Paul and I ordered lunch. As the waitress was clearing away our plates, I considered the key ring nestled safely in the handbag hanging by its strap from the back of my chair. The High Spot specialty I'd enjoyed – a Gabby Crabby sandwich – seemed an anti-climax. But that was no reason not to order dessert. We were celebrating, after all.

Four

'Alonso of Aragon was wont to say in commendation of age, that age appears to be best in four things – old wood best to burn, old wine to drink, old friends to trust, and old authors to read.'

Francis Bacon, *Apophthegms New and Old*, 134

The High Spot's bread pudding should come with a warning label. Shot through with raisins and smothered in a sauce of hot buttered rum, you can practically feel your arteries clogging. Even though Paul had the metabolism of a wolverine, I matched him bite for bite.

Paul flagged down the waitress and requested the check while I excused myself to visit 'the *Señoras*.'

26

I had just settled myself when a voice from the adjoining stall chirped, 'Hi, how are you?'

I thought for a moment about ignoring the woman's question, but my mother had taught me better manners. 'I'm fine, thank you.'

'So, what are you up to?' she said.

'Just doing what comes naturally,' I replied, reaching for the toilet paper.

'Can I come over?'

I shot to my feet, re-buttoning my jeans as quickly as I could. 'No! Sorry. Husband's waiting. Gotta run.'

'Listen,' the woman said as I made quick work of washing my hands. 'I'll have to call you back. There's this weirdo in the next stall that keeps answering all my questions.'

She's on the phone. Wiping my hands dry on my jeans, I made a quick escape before the woman could emerge and get a positive I.D. If I were going to live in this town, it wouldn't do to get a reputation as a pervert from day one.

'What's so funny?' Paul asked when I returned to the table.

'Tell you later,' I promised as the waitress appeared with the check.

We were laughing over the incident, lingering over our coffee when Paul set his mug down on the bare tabletop with a solid clunk. 'Hannah, look over there. Isn't that Fran?' He jerked his head in the direction of the cashier where a woman stood, head bowed over her handbag as she rummaged about inside as if searching for small change.

Fran Lawson, my former boss at Whitworth

and Sullivan, had a helmet of hair the color of flat-black patio furniture. This woman was the height and shape of Fran, as I remembered her, but her silver hair was stylishly cut, floating just above the collar of her crisp, white camp shirt like well-behaved cotton candy. 'I don't think so,' I started to say, and then the woman found what she was looking for, handed it to the cashier and turned her head to the left.

I'd seen that chiseled profile thousands of times – talking on the telephone, issuing instructions to the housekeeping staff, presiding over meetings where she was usually cutting funding for one damn fool reason or another. I hadn't seen Fran for more than a decade, not since she'd laid me off – along with half a dozen of my colleagues – in a firm-wide reduction in force.

I ducked my head and whispered, 'Maybe she won't recognize me.'

No such luck.

'Hannah!' a familiar voice shrilled, as irritating as I remembered it.

'Too late,' Paul chuckled, genuinely amused at my dilemma. 'She's heading our way.'

I looked up and forced a smile. 'Fran! Oh, my gosh! Fancy meeting you here!'

'I could say the same thing, Hannah.' She set her mug down on our table, pulled out the chair that Caitlyn had so recently vacated and sat down uninvited. 'I retired from the rat race last year,' she explained. 'Steve and I bought a house on Congress Street, not far from the water.'

'Paul and I just closed on a cottage on Chiconnesick Creek,' I told her, secretly relieved

28

that we wouldn't be close neighbors. If Fran ran her house the way she'd run the office all those years ago, she'd be cutting her lawn a blade at a time with cuticle scissors, measuring the exact distance between tomato seedlings in her garden and bitterly complaining should the pollen from your dogwood tree have the audacity to drift over into her yard.

'Wonderful!' Fran exclaimed. Turning to Paul, she said, 'You're retired now, too?'

'I wish,' he snorted. 'No, I've got a few years left. Hannah and I will be working on the place. *Legal Ease* – maybe you know it?' When Fran shook her head, he continued, 'It's a bit of a fixer-upper, I'm afraid, but at least it will keep us busy and off the streets.'

'Well, if you need work done, you can't do better than Heberling and Son. Dwight converted our garage into a practice studio for Steve, and we couldn't be more pleased.'

Steve Lawson, as I recalled, was a conservatory trained cellist who played first chair with several community orchestras in the Baltimore–Washington metropolitan area.

'So, your husband's still teaching?' I asked.

Fran nodded. 'We have a local symphony in Elizabethtown, too. Small, mostly volunteer – a chamber orchestra, really, but not at all bad.' She paused as a thought occurred to her. 'Say, there's a concert at St Timothy's three weeks from Saturday. They're performing Mozart's *Violin Concerto Number Four in D major* and Mendelssohn's *Italian Symphony*. You should try to attend.'

'We will,' I promised, actually looking forward to the concert. 'If we're going to be spending more time here, I'd like to get involved with the community.'

Fran placed her hands flat on the tabletop. 'I'm *so* glad to hear you say that, because . . .' She paused, looked right and left, then shot a glance over her shoulder as if checking for eavesdroppers. She leaned forward and practically whispered, 'Let me tell you what was found in the county courthouse.'

'Not a body, I hope,' Paul said with a warning glance at me. He'd come close to losing me in a couple of misadventures involving bodies and he wasn't eager to repeat the experience.

Fran chuckled. 'No, not a body, although Elizabethtown is so old that finding a body tucked away in a building as ancient as our courthouse wouldn't surprise me in the least. Not a body at all, but something just as interesting to people who love history the way we do.'

'Now you've aroused my curiosity,' I said, leaning forward on my elbows, hoping to encourage her.

'It's a long story.' She turned a thousand-watt smile on Paul and shoved her mug in his direction. 'Would you mind fetching me a refill while I fill Hannah in?'

Paul stood, shoving his chair back with his knees, seemingly unconcerned about Fran's summary dismissal, perhaps figuring I'd clue him in later. 'Cream? Sugar?'

'Both, please.'

After Paul left, Fran continued, 'Our county

30

clerk retired last December. She'd been in charge at the courthouse for decades. Very old fashioned and not at all computer-savvy, as one might imagine. I was on the search team for her replacement – for my sins.' She laughed, or rather barked, at her own clever turn of phrase.

'After a long search, we eventually hired a young gal named Kimberly Marquis. She worked for the National Archives out in their Greenbelt annex. Not my first choice, mind you, but she's competent enough.' Fran sighed and rolled her eyes. 'What can you expect for the salary the county was prepared to pay, I ask you.'

She paused as Paul returned, then reached out for her refill. 'Thank you, Paul.'

After taking a sip, Fran said, 'Anyway, new broom sweeping clean and all that, Kim was down in the basement clearing things out when she discovered a door marked *Storage*. It obviously hadn't been opened in *years*, Hannah. Rusted lock had to be pried off with a screwdriver. Cobweb city and acres of dust everywhere.' She took another sip of her coffee and considered me over the rim of the mug. Was the woman ever going to get to the point?

'And . . .?' I prompted.

Fran set her mug down on the table. 'When she finally got the door open, Kim found a room full of old records. Leather-bound ledgers, boxes stuffed with file folders, card files, old newspapers and magazines, you name it. Naturally, she called me in. Just a cursory glance, of course, but from what I could tell, some of the papers

31

date back to the early days of the nineteenth century.'

I sat back. 'Wow.'

'Exactly. The present courthouse was built in 1845, and there was an earlier one before that, so who knows what we'll discover down there. The records could have been there since Maryland was a colony still kowtowing to King George the Third.'

'How come nobody knew about them?' Paul asked.

'Oh, Kimberly's predecessor knew, all right. Had to. That storage room is directly under the courthouse bathroom. At some point there was a leak in one of the toilets and many of the records got soaked.'

From long experience as a records manager at Whitworth and Sullivan, I knew where this was going. 'Uh oh. Mold?'

Fran nodded. 'You got it. After the plumbing was repaired, the stupid woman obviously closed the door and put the storage room out of her mind.'

'Are the records valuable?' Paul wanted to know.

Fran shrugged. 'Hard to say until they've been examined. That's where I come in, Hannah. You, too, if you're interested.'

'Examined? What does that entail?' Paul asked.

'Sort, evaluate,' I said, cutting to the chase. 'Make recommendations on what to retain and what to discard. Send some on to the Maryland State Archives in Annapolis, I imagine. Keep or discard the rest.'

'Anything deemed to be of historical value will eventually need to be cataloged,' Fran added, 'so that it can be made available to researchers. And the minute word leaks out about this discovery, genealogists are going to be clambering all over us like untrained puppies, trust me. We'll need to be prepared.'

When I didn't say anything for a moment, Fran gave me a nudge. 'It's right up your alley, Hannah.'

That was certainly true, but I'd worked for Fran before and I wasn't sure I wanted to repeat the experience.

'I don't know,' I said, risking a sideways glance at my husband, who sat as still as a garden gnome, a half smile tugging at the corners of his lips. He was enjoying my dilemma, the rat.

'I have another volunteer,' she said, sweetening the pot. 'You'll like him. He's a local guy named Thomas Hazlett, but everybody calls him "Cap."'

'Is Cap a waterman?' Paul wanted to know.

Fran shook her head. 'No, an army vet. No archival training, *per se*, but he's got local roots that go deep. Also, strong arms and a seemingly inexhaustible supply of energy.'

'I can't give you an answer right now, Fran. With the renovation going forward and all . . .' I shrugged. 'I'm not sure how much free time I'll have.'

Did her lower lip quiver ever so slightly?

I reached for a napkin. Using the company pen Caitlyn had left behind on the table I scrawled down my cell phone number. 'Here's my cell. Give me a call when you have a better idea of how I might be able to help.'

'Thanks.' Fran folded the napkin into carefully creased halves, quarters then eights before tucking it into the coin section of her wallet. 'Have you moved in yet?' she asked as I pushed my chair back, indicating we were ready to go.

'Not yet – we just took possession today, but Paul and I plan to return next week to meet with some local contractors, although we don't have anyone lined up just yet.'

'I'll check my calendar and get back to you, then.' As the three of us stood around the table, Fran reached out and touched my hand. 'It will be just like old times, Hannah.'

Gawd, I hope not, I thought. In spite of my misgivings, I said, 'I'll look forward to hearing from you,' wondering as I heard myself semi-volunteering if working for the woman once again would drive me as crazy the second time around as it had the first.

Fran walked with us to the door of the restaurant. 'Remember to call Dwight Heberling. And tell him I gave you his name. You won't be sorry.'

Five

'Oh, call it by some better name . . .'

Thomas Moore, *Ballads and Songs*, 1841

In the end it was my granddaughter, Chloe, age twelve, who inadvertently started the friendly family argument that led her to win, almost by default, our unofficial 'Name This Cottage' contest. Shortly after we bought *Legal Ease*, Emily telephoned to set up a time when she could drive over with the grandchildren to check out our new place. I could tell from her tone of voice, however, that the trip was primarily to reassure herself that her parents hadn't totally lost their minds.

Fortunately, we hadn't. She was as bewitched by *Legal Ease* as we were.

'Spending my inheritance, I see,' Emily commented with a grin as we gazed out the living-room window together watching Canada geese circle overhead, honking.

'That is our devious plan,' replied her father.

Leading the flock, the head goose, wings spread wide, glided to a landing in the marshland on the opposite bank of the creek. 'Splashdown,' Emily whispered as the rest of the flock followed suit.

'You *are* going to rename it, aren't you?' Emily asked as we watched the geese settle down and begin rooting through the marshland, feasting on eel grass and spartina. '*Legal Ease* is so totally groan-worthy.'

'All suggestions welcome,' I said.

'Your aunt Ruth suggested *Looney Dunes*,' Paul told her.

Emily moaned. 'Figures.'

Chloe, who had been observing the geese with interest, suddenly piped up, 'Where am I gonna sleep, Grandma?'

'There are two bedrooms upstairs,' I told her. 'Why don't you run upstairs and pick one?'

When Chloe reappeared a few minutes later – 'I like the yellow bedroom, Grandma' – she found us in the kitchen, putting groceries away, still trying out names. 'You could name it *Fawlty Towers*,' Emily was suggesting when her daughter entered the room.

I snapped her playfully with a dishtowel. 'You're as bad as your father. If we don't come up with something soon he swears he's going to name it *Base-2*.' I rolled my eyes. 'And they say mathematicians don't have a sense of humor.'

Chloe poked me with a chubby finger. 'I think you should call it *Pooh Corner*, Grandma.'

Timmy screamed with laughter and punched his older brother in the arm. 'Poo! Poo! Grandma's house is poo!'

Jake scowled in a brother-what-brother? sort of way. 'You're stupid.'

'Poo!' Timmy hooted, punctuating the word with a second well-aimed punch.

Jake consulted the referee. 'Mommy, make him stop hitting me!'

'Poopyhead!' Timmy said.

'No, *you're* a poopyhead!' Jake countered.

In time-honored tradition, Emily ignored her sons, turning to me instead. 'Honestly, Mother, sometimes I'm at my wit's end.'

Wit's End. I considered the name thoughtfully, then discarded it, too. 'A little potty humor never hurt anyone,' I pointed out. 'Look, boys,' I said, leaning down to speak at their level. 'Your grandfather is out in the shed. Go find him and ask him to take you to see the crab pots.'

After the children had scampered away with

Chloe in the lead, I said to Emily, 'Back in the day, you were fascinated with the word "tush." You'd even make up songs about it.' I paused for a moment, remembering. '"The wheels on the tush go poop, poop, poop . . ."' I sang after I was sure the children were out of earshot.

Emily laughed. 'Well, it made sense to me at the time,' she said. 'Why else would they call that roll hanging on the bathroom wall tushy paper?'

I laughed, too, then added, 'After "tush" it was "booger." I thought you'd *never* outgrow the booger phase.'

'That must have been high-larious.' She gave me a quick hug. 'The bullshit I put you through, Mom. I'm so sorry.'

I don't think I ever loved my daughter more than at that moment, standing in my new kitchen holding a can of baked beans in one hand, a package of string cheese in the other, tendrils of her fine blonde hair curling softly over her cheeks and forehead. Emily *had* been responsible for a number of my prematurely gray hairs. Following her graduation with honors from Bryn Mawr College, she'd shocked us by eloping with a college dropout named Daniel (please call me Dante) Shemansky. After a quickie wedding at a chapel in Las Vegas, they'd become dedicated Phish Heads, following the popular rock band all around the southwest before settling down in Colorado where Dante trained as a masseuse and Emily worked in a bookstore.

'All's well that ends well,' I quoted after a moment, thinking about the posh spa they now

37

owned and operated on the shores of the Chesapeake Bay near Annapolis. Spa Paradiso had recently been featured in *SpaLife Magazine*. Mr and Mrs Shemansky wouldn't be depending on handouts from us to keep their growing family afloat.

'Is Chloe reading *Winnie the Pooh*?' I asked, wondering what prompted my granddaughter to make the Pooh Corner suggestion.

'That was *ages* ago, Mom, but recently she's been listening to a collection of tunes we downloaded to Timmy's Kindle Fire. Remember that song, "The House at Pooh Corner?"'

'Kenny Loggins,' I said. 'Popular in the early seventies.' I hummed the first line of the ballad to demonstrate that my mind, although aging, was a veritable steel trap. 'They knew how to write songs back then,' I mused. 'Girls, fast cars, heartbreak, momma said, hey, a twangy bit of guitar. Sadly, no more. I don't know what to make of what I hear on the radio these days, Emily. Lady Gaga I can take, but Miley Cyrus? Eminem? And that dreadful rapper – what's his name?' The memory was so horrible that I waved it away.

Emily paused, her arm half in half out of the refrigerator. 'Did you and Dad have a song?'

I looked straight into her astonishing blue eyes, so like my late mother's. 'Oh, yes. It's "Your Song" by Elton John. He still sings it at every concert.'

Emily launched into the oh-so-familiar tune.

'That one, yes,' I confirmed, joining in on the word 'funny.' At the beginning of the second

38

verse I cut her off at the word 'no', my hand raised like a conductor. 'Drumroll, please!'

Emily waited, one eyebrow raised.

'We shall name this cottage *Our Song*. I have spoken.'

'Perfect!' my daughter said, grinning.

'What's perfect?' my husband asked, coming in through the kitchen door.

'Where are the kids?' Emily asked, sounding alarmed.

'Not to worry, Em. I've set them up with the garden hose and some old rags. They're washing the kayak.' He wrapped me in his arms from behind and rested his chin on the top of my head.

'Emily suggested we name the cottage *Our Song* after, well, 'Our Song'. *I hope you don't mind . . .'* I sang.

I felt his chin move. 'I like it. Very much.' He spun me around by my shoulders, took my right hand in his left. Slightly stooped, with his cheek pressed to mine, my husband waltzed me from stove to refrigerator to kitchen sink singing in his gravelly baritone about how wonderful life was with me in his world.

At the kitchen table, he twirled me under his arm and executed a perfect dip, pressing me back against the tablecloth and planting a kiss on my exposed neck.

'Mom!' Emily cried, sounding exasperated and breaking the spell.

I glanced at my daughter over Paul's shoulder. 'What?'

'You're sitting on the grapes.'

Six

'I've often wish'd that I had clear,
For life, six hundred pounds a year;
A handsome house to lodge a friend,
A river at my garden's end,
A terrace walk, and half a rood
Of land set out to plant a wood.'

Alexander Pope, *Imitations of Horace*,
Book II, Satire VI

On the first long weekend we spent at *Our Song*, every day was a treasure hunt. While Paul worked out back in the shed, evaluating the rusting tools and deteriorating equipment that Julianna Quinn's late husband had left behind, I sat cross-legged on the kitchen floor in front of a spacious cabinet, sorting through her pots and pans.

'Chattels,' the contract called them. I had to look it up: 'An item of property other than real estate,' the dictionary explained.

Fortunately for us, when it came to chattels, Julianna had had good taste. I now owned a complete set of All-Clad stainless-steel cookware, for example. At one hundred and fifty dollars upwards for a saucepan – not including the lid – All-Clad was a luxury I could never manage to afford at home, even with a twenty-percent-off coupon from Bed, Bath and Beyond. Now I was cradling a three-quart steamer to my breast and chanting, *You're mine, all mine!*

I'd nested the smaller frying pan into the larger one and was sorting lids, trying them on the saucepans for size, when I heard tires crunch on the gravel outside. I reached up, grabbed the edge of the kitchen counter and pulled myself to my feet, my knees popping. 'After forty it's patch, patch, patch,' I muttered to myself, quoting the embroidery on a decorative pillow I'd also inherited from Julianna.

I leaned over the sink, flipped the curtain aside and peered out the kitchen window. A white Ford pickup with a toolbox in the bed had pulled up out front. By the time I'd reached the side door, opened it and called out, 'Paul! Someone's here!' the truck's driver was already through the gate and standing at our front door, reaching for the knocker.

'You must be Dwight Heberling,' I said stupidly when I opened the door, since *Heberling & Son, Construction* was painted on the door of his pickup in red block letters at least three inches high.

As I spoke, a younger man roared up behind the pickup on a black Harley chopper. He braked hard and dismounted, then engaged the kickstand.

'Yes, ma'am.' Heberling whipped his ball cap off to reveal a sensible graying buzz cut, tucked the cap under his arm and extended his hand. He nodded in the direction of the motorcycle. 'And that there is my son, Rusty.'

Rusty removed his helmet and hooked the strap

41

over one of the handlebars. I guessed immediately where he'd gotten his nickname. His copper hair was drawn back behind his ears and fastened at the nape of his neck in a neat ponytail. He wore a Beatles T-shirt belted into a pair of faded jeans that fit him like a second skin. When he lifted the toolbox out of the Ford, his biceps flexed like an ad on TV for exercise equipment – the 'after' view, not the 'before' – and his pecs rippled impressively all the way from John to Ringo.

Paul suddenly materialized at my shoulder, wiping grease off his hands with a paper towel. 'I was just tinkering with an outboard,' he said. 'Give me a minute.'

'Come in, come in,' I said, opening the screen door wide. 'Please excuse the mess. We're still getting settled.'

Starting in the entrance hall, Paul and I toured the house with Heberling, trailing like bridesmaids after the contractor and his son – who was tapping notes into his iPhone.

Dwight blessed the kitchen plumbing – 'New, I'd say. Last couple of years anyway' – but the plumbing in the bathroom was a different story. 'Copper,' he tsk-tsked, and pointed to the cabinet under the sink. 'Well water in these parts is acidic. See those green spots? Pinhole leaks in the making. Pinholes can cost you big time if they let go.'

Dwight lifted the flush tank lid on the toilet and invited us to look in. 'See those blue-green deposits? Sure sign your copper pipes are corroding.'

As his father explained about pH and extolled the virtues of upflow calcite neutralizers and soda ash feeders, Rusty bent at the waist to photograph the offending pipes. I must have been observing this manoeuver appreciatively because Paul jostled my elbow, bringing me instantly back to a discussion of the merits of PCV piping.

Our Song had no basement, so the breaker box had been installed in the utility room. Since the utility room was a new addition, I was hopeful Julianna Quinn's contractor had rewired the rest of the cottage at the same time. As we clustered around the electrical panel awaiting Heberling's verdict, he peered at the circuit breakers, studied the hand-lettered breaker guide on the inside of the panel door and to my great relief grunted his approval.

The living-room fireplace, however, was another matter. Dwight stood in front of it for a long time, poking experimentally at the stones with a screwdriver. He knelt and peered up the chimney, grabbed hold of the damper handle and tugged. 'Stuck, dammit. Probably hasn't been properly cleaned in years.' He jiggled the handle more vigorously and it suddenly gave up the fight. Before Dwight could pull his arm away a cloud of soot descended and covered his arm.

'Hmmm,' he said, just *hmmmm*, not something you want to hear from either a doctor or a contractor. 'Let's look at it from the outside, then,' he said, leading the way. 'Got a ladder?'

I reviewed my mental list of chattels, came up

blank on 'ladder' and turned to Paul. 'Do we have one?'

'I'll check the shed.' A few minutes later he stuck his head out the door of the shed and called for Rusty to help him lug an extension ladder over to the side of the house. While we waited below, with Rusty steadying the ladder, Dwight climbed and poked at the chimney at various points on the way up with the screwdriver he pulled out of his back pocket. More *hmmmm*s. He examined the roof while we waited below with me trying to convert every 'hmmmm,' 'what-the-heck,' and click of the tongue into dollars and cents.

When he'd finished and returned to ground level, wiping his hands clean on his khakis, I asked, 'How old is the house, do you think?'

Dwight paused, considering. 'See those windows?'

I nodded.

'Six over six. That puts 'em before 1884 when the railroad came and they were able to bring in larger panes of glass. The gambrel roof was popular in this area between around 1730 and 1770,' he continued, 'but it's the chimney that tells the tale,' he said, patting the bricks almost affectionately.

'How's that?' I wondered.

'Around 1770 they began building semi-outside chimneys, like yours. See how it's sunk half into the brick end of the house?'

I did.

'So even if I didn't know that the main part of the house has been around since Josiah Hazlett first settled here in the 1750s, I could date the place to sometime shortly after 1770.'

'Amazing,' I said, impressed with his knowledge.

'So, what's the verdict?' Paul asked after a moment, cutting to the chase. 'On the renovations, I mean?'

Dwight considered Paul soberly. 'Got any coffee?'

'Of course,' I replied. 'Decaf?'

'High octane if you got it.'

'French roast OK?'

'Perfect.'

Rusty had just rejoined us after putting the ladder away. 'How about you, Rusty?'

'Diet Coke, if you've got one.'

Back in the kitchen, I fired up the Keurig, laid out a selection of K-cups and managed to locate a cold Sprite, with which Rusty seemed content. After the coffee brewed, we settled around the kitchen table to discuss the work.

While Dwight ticked off the tasks that needed to be done, Rusty tapped notes into his iPhone using both thumbs. 'I'll be back to you in a couple of days with a written estimate,' Dwight concluded at last.

'No particular rush,' Paul assured him. 'We can manage for the time being, but the sooner you can get started the happier you'll make my wife.'

'I won't take long.' Dwight stood, pulled the ball cap out of his back pocket and, using both hands, adjusted it on his head. 'I heard you made a bid on the Matthews' place.'

'It fell through,' Paul said simply as we walked the contractor and his son to the door.

Dwight grunted. 'Not surprised about that, considering the agency you've been dealing with.'

'Oh, Caitlyn Dymond's been a pleasure to work with,' I was quick to point out. 'It's that other woman, Kendall Barfield, who I'd like to strangle.'

Dwight laughed out loud. 'You'd be standing at the end of a long, long line.'

'It sounds like you know her pretty well, Mr Heberling.'

'Could say that. Used to be married to the woman.'

'Gosh, sorry,' I mumbled. Open mouth, insert foot, as my mother used to say.

'No need, ma'am. When it was all said and done, I didn't like Kendall all that much, either. Best thing to come out of that relationship was Dwight junior here.'

The tips of Dwight junior's ears flushed as red as his hair. I'd been wondering if the young man was intellectually challenged until he addressed me directly for the first time and drove all misapprehension away. 'Just so you know, Mrs Ives, you've gotta watch out for Mom. She's a card-carrying bitch.'

Seven

'Delicta maiorum immeritus lues' –
Undeservedly you will atone for the sins of
your fathers.

Horace, *Odes*, III, 6

When she called a few days later, I agreed to
meet Fran at the High Spot, where we ordered
coffee in paper cups and carried them with us to
the courthouse. Before making any commitment,
I wanted to check out the situation with the
records in the basement personally.

The Tilghman County Courthouse dominated
the town, sitting like a Grand Dame in the center
of the town square. Reminiscent of a Doric
temple, it was constructed in the Greek revival
style so popular in the first half of the nineteenth
century. Four enormous columns marched across
its facade, supporting a triangular pediment on
which Lady Justice stood, holding the scales of
justice in one hand. Lady Justice was blindfolded,
perhaps so that she wouldn't be offended by the
ornate fountain her Victorian successors had
installed on the sidewalk in front of her, over-
flowing with carved marble fruit, fish, game and
other bounty of the Bay. The whole edifice was
topped off, like a candle on a cake, by a clock-
tower with a gold-plated N-S-E-W weathervane.

As we walked up the steps, the tower clock was striking nine.

The day was already warm, so the air conditioning hit us like a blast of arctic wind.

'Morning, Sam,' Fran greeted the uniformed guard, then plopped an oversized handbag down on the table in front of him before easing through the metal detector still carrying her coffee. With a nod to the guard, I followed suit, waiting with Fran on the other side of the security barrier while Sam pawed through the contents of my handbag. I couldn't imagine what kind of trouble they'd be expecting from two mild-mannered senior citizens – dressed as we were in T-shirts and jeans – but in this post 9/11 world you never knew. It paid to be careful.

'Kim's office is down the hall and to the right,' Fran told me once Sam indicated we were free to go.

Although the courthouse was not particularly large, our footsteps echoed along the marble corridor. We passed the courtroom on our left and a library on our right, both with double, elaborately carved wooden doors.

Kimberly Marquis's office adjoined the library. Behind a door with a window labeled *County Clerk* in gold capital letters we found her sitting at her desk, an impressive affair of solid oak. She rose immediately when we entered. 'Fran.' She smiled.

'This is the woman I've been telling you about, Kim. Hannah used to work for me in Washington, D.C. She and her husband have just bought the old Hazlett place.'

'So I heard. I don't usually dress like this for the office,' Kim explained with a grin, indicating the T-shirt, jeans and jogging shoes she wore. 'But court isn't in session, and since we'll be mucking around in the basement, I thought I'd better come prepared to get grubby.'

She retrieved a small ring of keys from the top drawer of the desk and led us back out into the hallway. 'We have coffee here,' she said with a grin, indicating the carryout cups we carried. 'For future reference.'

Our first stop was a room labeled *Staff Only*. Inside were three bistro-style table and chair sets, a full-size refrigerator and a microwave. Two well-worn leather armchairs were angled into an alcove, both bathed in sunlight streaming in from lead-latticed casement windows. Kim punched a series of buttons on a state-of-the-art hot beverage machine which began to gurgle and hiss, eventually producing a puff of steam and a perfectly brewed cup of herbal tea. We sat at one of the tables discussing our plan of attack, then tossed our used cups into the trash.

Kim jangled the keys and asked, 'Ready?'

'I feel like we're off on a secret mission,' I said as Kim led us into the hallway. 'Perhaps we should synchronize our watches?'

Kim turned to face me and chuckled. 'You think you're joking, but when you see what's down in the basement you may be sorry you volunteered.' She waggled her eyebrows. 'Remember, if you are captured or killed, the secretary will disavow any knowledge of your actions.'

Just past the restrooms, Kim paused at an

unmarked door, unlocked it with one of the keys and motioned us through.

From a postage stamp landing a narrow stone staircase descended. Although she had flipped a switch at the head of the stairs, the staircase remained dark. Kim swore softly, then started down. 'Where is Frau Blucher and her candelabra when you need her?' she said.

'Frau Blucher!' I hooted, then whinnied like a horse.

Behind me, Fran mumbled, 'I don't get it.'

'It's from a movie,' I explained while gripping the railing and trying not to stumble. '*Young Frankenstein*. It's hysterical.'

'Oh,' she said, not sounding the least bit amused.

The further down the staircase we went, the cooler, damper and mustier the air became. At the foot of the stairs the room opened out, but it was hard to see what it contained as the only natural light came from narrow windows cut, slit-like, into the stone walls near the ceiling.

Kim felt around on the wall like a blind man, muttering about another switch. After a moment, two unshaded bulbs screwed into sockets in the ceiling sprang half-heartedly to life, only marginally improving the visibility. 'Sorry,' she said, squinting at us in the semi-darkness.

'Can't the town afford one-hundred-watt bulbs?' I asked as I strained to see something – anything – in the shadowy corners.

'You'd think,' Kim replied. 'Sadly, I brought these bulbs in myself.' She leaned closer to me. 'Hundred-watters, too.'

As my eyes grew accustomed to the dim light, I noticed that the stone walls had once been whitewashed but were now mottled, shedding paint like skin that's been badly sunburnt. A row of steel shelving ranged along one wall. On closer inspection, I found they were covered with artifacts – pottery shards, glass bottles, coins, rough-cut nails – likely from an historical dig. A stack of poster boards leaned against the wall nearby. Stick-on letters, some of them peeling off, spelled out TOB CCO HO SHEAD A D PRISE. A shelf opposite held economy-sized packages of paper towels and toilet paper, and several boxes of heavy duty lawn and leaf bags. 'The storeroom's over here,' Kim said, making a hard right turn around a tower of nested trash cans.

'When I first came down here,' she explained, 'I couldn't even get the door to the storeroom open. Had to get the custodian to remove the hinges.'

The door looked solid. Six wooden panels secured with an impressive padlock. Kim opened the lock with a key, hooked the hasp of the padlock onto a convenient nail then yanked the door open. 'The custodian cleaned up the hinges, oiled 'em and so on, but they're still a bit stiff.'

As the door swung open, I was hit by an unmistakable smell. Mold.

Like a mother protecting her child, Fran's arm shot out, preventing me from entering the room. 'Wait!' She delved into her handbag and came up with a small box of latex-free vinyl gloves and a Ziploc bag containing surgical face masks. 'Put these on,' she instructed. 'Kim, you, too.'

51

'Where . . .?' I began, accepting the mask. I positioned it over my nose and mouth and looped the strings over my ears.

'Walgreens,' she said, offering me the box of gloves.

Over Fran's shoulder, Kim made a face but accepted the mask and gloves, as I did, with a tolerant grin.

We suited up and entered the room.

Just inside the door, Fran stopped so suddenly that I barged into her. I immediately saw why. The floor was littered with file folders, the papers they had once contained scattered over the floor. Boxes that had been stacked five high in one corner had collapsed, spilling their contents everywhere.

'Is there no humidity control?' I asked.

'None,' Kim admitted, sounding sheepish.

'Jeesh!' I said. 'What moron thought it was a good idea to store documents in here?' I stepped gingerly around a Seagrams 7 carton so damp that mold grew on it like a garden, fuzzy tendrils reaching out, swaying in the air as I passed. I lifted a corner of it gently with the toe of my shoe. 'This box is from a liquor store. Haven't they heard of archival boxes?'

'Sad, isn't it?' Fran commented.

Kim pointed. 'Over there. That's the worst of it.'

Against the far wall, under a run of various-sized galvanized pipes, once-handsome wooden shelves sagged under the weight of several dozen leather-bound ledgers, quietly rotting.

'Oh, no,' I groaned.

'That's where the air conditioning leaked,' she said. 'The stuff over on this side isn't so bad.'

I climbed over two broken desk chairs and circumnavigated a teetering pile of *National Geographic*s in order to take a closer look. The volumes were in no particular order but the spines that remained were inscribed *lien records* and *chattel mortgages*. There was a book bound in red with no writing on the spine and several cloth-bound cross indexes of land transactions. One book of liens, I noticed, was shelved upside down.

'They've shoved the books right up against the damp stone,' I said in disbelief. 'Lord, what a mess.'

I touched one of the ledgers, saddened that its once elegant leather binding had been reduced to red dust. 'May I?'

Kim nodded. 'Of course. Hard to see how you could mess it up any more than it already is.'

Without touching what little remained of the book's spine, I carefully removed it from the shelf then cast around desperately for a place to lay the heavy volume while I examined it.

'You see the problem,' said Fran, scrambling to clear a spot on top of a relatively stable stack of cardboard boxes.

I set the ledger on the spot she had cleared and, as both women watched, opened it to the title page: Tilghman County, Cross Index Land Proceedings.

I turned several pages, stopping about a quarter of the way though. In a neat, perfectly legible hand, some long-ago clerk had written across the page at the head of neat, red-lined columns: Defendant, Nature of Action, Plaintiff, Book and Page. I ran my vinyl-covered fingertips over the rich rag paper, the perceptible ridges of the ink that spelled out the names still as clear and as bold as the day they had been written which was, according to the date at the top of the page, 1852. Most actions, I noticed, were categorized as 'dower.'

'I know what dower means,' I told Kim, 'but what does it mean in the context of "nature of action?"'

'Well, back in the day, a widow had almost no rights in the assets of her husband upon his death, especially second wives. The theory was that all property should descend to the children of the deceased, and it was their duty to take care of the widow.' She laughed. 'You can imagine how well that worked out. Eventually the laws were changed so that a certain portion of the husband's estate was supposed to go to the surviving wife, so if she wasn't happy with the amount left to her in the will, her only recourse was to go to court and claim the statutory share entitled to her by the new dower laws.'

'So, all these dowers, these widows,' I said, scanning down a long column of women's names, 'were simply trying to keep themselves from being thrown out on the street by their good-for-nothing children or stepchildren.'

Kim laughed into her mask. 'Exactly.'

'Does the state of Maryland have copies of these records?' Fran asked.

Kim shrugged. 'It's possible, but nobody

knows for sure. My predecessor hasn't been very cooperative. The only way to find out is to inventory what is here and send the list to the Maryland Archives in Annapolis for comparison.'

'Even wearing masks and gloves, we can't work in here,' I said, stating the obvious.

'I know,' Fran said. 'I'm trying to find a place where we can move the records while they're being inventoried.'

With some reluctance, I returned the book to its place on the shelf, paused, then thought better of it, moving it back to a relatively dry spot near the door.

'Has the air in here been tested?' I asked, my breath hot against the fabric of the mask.

Fran nodded. 'Awaiting results.'

'We're hoping it's not toxic,' Kim said.

Molds grow everywhere – I knew that from experience. Open up a petri dish just about anywhere, wait a few seconds, clap the lid back on, store it in a warm place and three to four days later – *tah-dah* – you've got a thriving colony of fungus. It's what kind of mold you've got that matters. 'Cross our fingers that it's just aspergillus,' I told her.

'Isn't aspergillus dangerous?' Kim wanted to know.

'It could be with prolonged exposure, or for those with compromised immune systems, but otherwise . . .'

Kim blinked, her green eyes looking enormous over the mask, and I worried for a moment that she might fall into that latter category. 'In the meantime,' she asked, sounding a bit desperate, 'is there anything we can do?'

'First off, of course, we need to lower the relative humidity in here, get it down to around fifty percent.' I glanced from wall to wall, silently calculating. 'A dehumidifier from Sears and Roebuck should take care of it nicely, I think, and they don't cost more than a couple of hundred dollars. We can set up a window fan near the door to get the air moving.'

Kim frowned. 'Believe it or not, I don't have the budget for that.'

'I have a dehumidifier at home in Annapolis,' I heard myself volunteer. 'I'll be happy to loan it to you, at least until we get this situation under control.'

'And I can round up a fan,' Fran added.

'That's super, ladies, but what do we do with all the moldy books?'

Fran ran her gloved fingers over a shelf, studied the results and frowned. 'The experts would use a HEPA vacuum system with filters, but I think we can take care of most of the mold by wiping the books down with denatured alcohol.'

'Aseptrol would be good,' I said, following behind Fran as she perused the shelves nearest the door. Boats were mildew magnets. Drawing on my experience helping Connie and Dennis put their sailboat up for the winter, I added, 'Aseptrol can be bought at any boating supply store, as well as desiccant and mildew control bags. Once we get the dehumidifier going, we can scatter desiccant around to soak up the excess moisture.

'The next step, as I see it, is to get this place cleaned up. First, let's get rid of the junk,' I said, indicating the broken furniture. 'And we should definitely pick up all the loose papers that are lying about and get them into clean boxes.'

Then Kim asked the sixty-four-thousand-dollar question: 'When can we start?'

In for a penny, in for a pound, I thought. I squared my shoulders and came to a decision. 'How about now? I seem to remember some empty trash cans out there.'

While Kim retrieved the trash cans and lined them with plastic bags, I started with a pile of magazines. '*Guns & Ammo*?' I said when she returned, dragging a trash can behind her. I checked the date. 'From 1964? Seriously?'

Kim set a trash can next to my right elbow. 'Judge Porter, may his soul rest in peace, used to read them when things got a little slow on the bench, or so legend has it.'

I deep-sixed the *Guns & Ammo*, followed by *National Geographic*, *Criminal Justice* magazine and a single issue of the *Georgetown Law* journal, its cover stained with coffee rings.

While Fran and Kim occupied themselves by clearing space on the drier shelves near the door for material we already knew we'd want to save, I selected a cardboard box more or less at random, squatted next to it and looked inside. Labeled Detention Center 1966–67, the box contained a hodgepodge of manila file folders, their tabs marked with neatly typed labels, striped in a variety of primary colors. As I leafed through the folders, whatever adhesive had held the labels in place over the years since some long-ago secretary had typed them gave up the good fight and fell to the bottom of the box in a shower of confetti.

I sifted through the contents of the folders, looking for dates. Those at the top contained arrest records dated 1967, as advertised, but near the bottom of the same box I found check stubs from the 1950s and, at the very bottom, a packet of letters tied up with string, the top one postmarked from Seattle in 1934. I sat back on my heels and sighed into my mask. 'Looks like we won't be able to trust what's marked on the outsides of the boxes, ladies. There's all kinds of non-Detention Center stuff mixed up in here, and only part of it is actually from 1966 or 1967.' I waved the packet of letters. 'Who knows what treasures lie inside these envelopes?'

Fran wandered over and held out her hand, so I put the letters into it.

'Three cents,' she said, examining the top envelope closely. 'That's what it cost to mail a letter back then. Fabulous stamp. *Whistler's Mother*. "In memory and in honor of the mothers of America." Don't you love it?'

'Do you suppose the stamps are valuable?' Kim wanted to know.

'I doubt it,' Fran said, 'but depending upon who the letters are from, and what they're about, they could be priceless to a family member.' She handed the packet to Kim. 'Put these in a safe place until we have time to look at them.'

'Well, to paraphrase the *Cat in the Hat*,' Kim said, tucking the packet of letters under her arm, 'this mess is so deep and so wide and so tall, we'll never get through it, there's no way at all.'

'One step at a time,' I reassured her. 'As for me, I'm starting with the furniture.'

Eight

'Mark how fleeting and paltry is the estate of man – yesterday in embryo, tomorrow a mummy or ashes.'

Marcus Aurelius Antoninus, *Meditations*, IV, 48

I had just returned from dragging the last scrap of an ancient folding typewriter table out to the dumpster behind the courthouse when the iPhone I'd tucked into the back pocket of my jeans began to vibrate.

I pulled it out and checked the display. Paul.

'Hey,' I said, stepping out into the sunshine to take the call, feeling grateful for the break.

'You're needed at the cottage,' my husband said. 'Rusty's got the tiles laid in the bathroom, but it seems we have a decision to make about the grout.'

'What's to decide?' I asked. 'Grout is grout.'

'You might think so, my dear, but I'm holding a color chart in my hands right now. There's white, of course, but we've also got pure white, antique white, linen white—'

'Darling,' I interrupted, 'white is white. Pick one.'

'Then there's canvas, cinnamon, and silver,' Paul continued as if I hadn't spoken. 'Mauve, rose, wheat, cocoa, cayenne, smoke, cadet blue and something called Navajo.'

'Navajo? What kind of a color is Navajo?'

'Kind of a warm beige. But you can see why I need you here.'

'Paul . . .' I began, thinking about the mountains of refuse we still had to dispose of in the cluttered courthouse basement.

'I'm leaning toward evergreen myself, maybe black,' he continued.

I had to laugh. 'I'm sure. But you're right – we're going to have to live with the grout for a long time. Tell Rusty I'll be home in about twenty minutes.'

Down in the basement, I apologized to Kim and Fran. 'I'll be back as soon as I can.'

'Not a problem,' Kim said, wiping her hands on her jeans. She checked her watch. 'Three o'clock. I'm ready to call it a day anyhow. How about you, Fran?'

Before coming to work that morning, after stopping at Walgreen, Fran had visited Office Depot and purchased several dozen bankers' boxes. 'Not archival quality, acid-free and all that, but they'll do in a pinch,' she'd said with a sniff. She was busily unfolding one now, and looked up with some annoyance. 'I'll just finish assembling the boxes, then. You two go on,' she said, her face behind the gauze a mask of martyrdom.

60

'See you in the morning?' I asked, looking directly at Kim.

'Sure thing,' she said.

I trudged up after her. At the top of the stairs, the county clerk paused, whipped off her mask and said, 'I'll be getting a set of keys made for both you and Fran so you can come and go as you please.'

'That would be terrific. Thank you.'

After thoroughly washing my hands and face, I bid goodbye to Kim in the courthouse ladies' room, lobbed my paper towel into the waste-paper basket just inside the door and headed for home.

The bathroom tiles were a glass mosaic named 'beachy blue.' After spending five minutes in the master bath with Rusty and the grout samples, I consulted with Paul and we agreed on an off-white grout called 'pearl.' 'Go for it, Rusty,' I said, handing back the sample.

Decision made, I checked in with Dwight who was working on the fireplace, then headed out to the kitchen and poured myself a tall glass of iced tea. I was gulping it down like a thirsty camel when somebody screamed. Short, sharp and painful, like a man being bitten by an alligator.

I rushed into the living room, nearly colliding with Paul as he dashed in through the screen door from the porch.

Dwight, his face ashen, pointed. Rusty, who had come running downstairs to help when his father called, looked ill.

On the hearth sat a small bundle of newspapers, brown and brittle with age. 'I found it on the smoke shelf,' Dwight said, his voice quavering. 'I can't believe I touched it.' He stared at his hand as if it were an alien thing.

'What is it?' Paul asked.

'Maybe it's a doll. Like one of those shriveled apple head things they sell at Cracker Barrel.' Dwight poked gingerly at the newspaper with a soot-stained index finger. 'Made out of suede, you know.' He sighed, stood and took a step back. 'But I'm pretty sure it's a baby.'

'Awesome!' Rusty whipped out his iPhone and leaned closer. I heard the simulated whirr of a camera shutter, then another.

Dwight slapped his son on the back of the head with the flat of his hand. 'Show some respect, asshole.'

'Damn,' Rusty said, rubbing the sore spot briskly. 'It's not every day you see something like this, Pops.' He took another picture just to show who was in charge, then tucked his phone away.

'Why would anyone put a doll up a chimney?' Dwight asked.

Next to me, Paul shivered. 'Why would anyone put a *baby* up a chimney?'

Heart hammering, I knelt down for a closer look. Dwight had peeled back the newspapers far enough to reveal what looked to me like the shriveled mummy of an infant, its skin dark and leathery. The features were sunken, but its button nose was intact and each tiny eyelash remained visible where the eyelids closed against its cheeks.

My heart twisted painfully when I noticed two tiny teeth peeping out over the child's shriveled lower lip. 'Oh, Paul,' I said, sagging against his leg. Focusing through a mist of tears, I noted a cloth diaper, folded in a triangle and secured with a tarnished diaper pin, and a white cotton shift, now grey with soot. The baby was nestled in what remained of a flannel blanket. I wanted to pick up this child and hold it to my breast, comfort it by rocking.

'What's a smoke shelf?' Paul asked the contractor.

'It's a shelf just behind the damper. Catches debris, like bird shit falling down the chimney. Helps the chimney draw.'

'And nobody noticed . . .' I began.

'Even if you stuck your head clear up the chimney, Mrs Ives, you wouldn't be able to see the smoke shelf because it's blocked by the damper.'

I looked up at my husband. 'It's definitely a baby, Paul. We have to call somebody, but who?'

Rusty answered me first. 'The sheriff, I reckon.'

'How long do you think it's been there?' Paul asked as Rusty stepped into the kitchen to make the call. His father stood quietly by the door, as if prepared to bolt.

I cocked my head, trying to read the print on the newspaper. It appeared to be part of the classified section – legal notices, jobs wanted, ads for Motorola TVs on sale at Hechts, ladies summer dresses for five dollars. 'It's wrapped in a *Tilghman Tribune* from August of 1951,' I told him.

63

'Good Lord. If it *is* a baby, the poor thing has been stuck up our chimney for more than sixty years.'

I squatted next to the bundle again, looking closely but not touching. 'Somebody loved this child,' I said.

'How can you tell?'

I pointed. 'Look how her hands are folded. How securely she was wrapped.'

'She? How can you be certain it's a girl?'

I looked up at my husband, tears again distorting my view. 'The blanket has rosebuds embroidered on it, Paul.'

While we waited for the sheriff, Paul, Dwight, Rusty and I sat around the kitchen table like zombies at a wake. Rusty left for a few minutes to rescue the grout he'd been mixing up in the master bath and, when he returned, I offered everyone something to drink. Only Rusty took me up on it.

I'd just popped a K-cup into the Keurig to brew Rusty a second cup of Hazelnut when a white Dodge Charger pulled up outside, its light bar flashing. 'Sheriff' and 'Tilghman County' were painted on the doors, the words separated by a jaunty blue racing stripe. A pale green Honda pulled in behind the police car and a middle-aged man dressed in a gray business suit climbed out.

'Sheriff Hubbard,' the officer said, removing his broad-brimmed ranger's hat as he stepped through the front door. 'But everyone calls me Andy.'

Sheriff Hubbard's prominent nose descended in a straight line from his backward-sloping forehead. Except for a tidy fringe of hair around his ears, he was completely bald and his reddened scalp spoke more eloquently than words of many off-duty hours spent in the sun. He turned to acknowledge his companion in the gray suit. 'I've asked Doc Greeley to come along, to verify exactly what we have here.'

I directed the two men to the living room. As we stood around in a semi-circle, Doc Greeley hitched up the legs of his trousers and squatted. He withdrew a slim metal object from his inside breast pocket and used it to explore the bundle lying on the hearth before him, gently prodding, pulling aside each delicate layer.

'It's a baby, all right,' the doctor announced after a minute. 'By the teeth, I'd say six to seven months old.'

'How did she die?' I asked.

'She?' The doctor looked up, an eyebrow raised.

'The blanket,' I said.

'Ah, yes,' he said. 'Observant.' He rose to his feet. 'Hard to say exactly how she died. We'll have to wait for the medical examiner on that.' He nodded at Sheriff Hubbard.

Hubbard pulled a cell phone out of his breast pocket and punched in a number. 'Sylvia? Will you tell Wicks he's needed at the old Hazlett place?' He paused and listened. 'Yeah. Tell him we've got a body.'

Nine

'Tar-baby ain't sayin' nuthin', en Brer Fox, he lay low.'

Joel Chandler Harris, *Uncle Remus and his Friends*, 1892

It's astonishing how small a box you need to pack up a baby.

Paul had ordered some hiking boots from L.L. Bean and they had arrived the day before. The box they had come in sat empty and clean on top of the recycling bin, so when the doctor asked me if we had 'a box of some kind,' I excused myself to fetch it, then handed it over.

While we watched from the sidelines, like mourners at a funeral, he lined the box with one of our pillowcases fresh from the dryer and laid the precious bundle gently inside. As he secured the lid over the child's wizened face, he said, 'I don't imagine it will get top priority, so it may be a while before we know something.'

'She ought to have a name,' I said. 'It seems wrong to keep calling her "it."'

Paul's arm snaked around my shoulder and pulled me close. 'What about Baby Ella?' he said.

Doc Greeley raised an eyebrow. 'Ella?'

'Short for Cinderella,' Paul said simply, his face grave. 'Little girl of the ashes.'

'Wicks' turned out to be the local undertaker. He arrived in an unmarked black limousine, gave Sheriff Hubbard some papers to sign, placed the box containing Baby Ella on the floor of the passenger side of the car and drove away.

'Where's he taking her?' Rusty asked as the limousine disappeared around the corner of the cornfield.

'Baltimore M.E.,' Hubbard said.

Rusty frowned. 'But even if the kid was murdered, the person who did it must be, you know, like really old, or dead. So what's the point?'

I knew that by Maryland law, all unattended deaths within the state had to be reviewed by the Baltimore medical examiner. I wondered if, after all this time, they'd be able to determine a cause of death. And if it turned out that the child had died of natural causes, would the police make any effort to establish who the child had belonged to? Somehow it seemed important to me to find her family.

I thought about all the people who had lived in our house over the past two hundred and thirty-some years. Was the baby Julianna Quinn's? I had no idea how long Julianna and her late husband had occupied the house, but in a house that dated to the 1750s, except for us they were clearly just the last in a long line of previous owners. I decided to call our realtor, Caitlyn Dymond. Caitlyn, I knew, would have ordered a search to establish a clear chain of title before she sold us the home.

She answered her cell in the middle of her son's soccer game. 'The Quinns owned the property for as long as I can remember,' Caitlyn told me over someone – presumably a parent on the sideline – screaming *Pass it! Pass it! Pass it!* 'We have clerks to do the title searches, so I'm not exactly sure how far back they had to go, but it's dead easy to do, Hannah. All the land records are on file at the county courthouse.'

I was due to work in the courthouse basement the following day, so early the next morning, before donning my mask and plastic gloves, I stopped by Kim's office. I told her about Baby Ella and, after she had sufficiently recovered, I asked for help in tracing the ownership of our property.

'We trace deeds back using the liber and folio numbers,' she informed me. 'In plain English, that's the book and page numbers. If you have a copy of your property tax assessment, or the actual deed, the liber and folio numbers will be printed right on it.' Using a pencil, she jotted something down on an index card and showed it to me: *ABC 123 456.*

'The letters are the initials of the clerk.' She grinned. 'In recent years, that would be me, KCM. The numbers that follow are the liber and folio numbers.'

'Ah,' I said, quickly catching on. 'Those were the reference numbers we saw recorded in some of the leather-bound index volumes we examined in the basement yesterday.'

'Exactly.'

'Hopefully my husband kept a copy of our deed here in Elizabethtown,' I said. 'Otherwise . . .'

Kim held up a hand, cutting me off. 'Completely unnecessary, Hannah. Welcome to the twenty-first century. All that information is public record, most of it online.' Kim explained how researchers could type any Maryland street address into the Maryland Department of Assessments and Taxation Real Property Database and find out all sorts of useful information, like the price someone paid for a piece of property and its current value as well as the liber and folio numbers. 'Once you have those numbers,' she continued, 'you have the magic key. Just go to MDLandRec.net. You use the two numbers to pull up a digital copy of the actual deed.'

'No way,' I said, promising myself that I'd never complain again about how Maryland was squandering my tax dollars.

'We keep microfilm copies here, of course, but the Maryland State Archives houses the originals.'

I perked up at that. Our Prince George Street home in Annapolis was about a mile from the Maryland Hall of Records. I was mentally reviewing the route I'd walk – Prince George to College Avenue to St John Street – when Kim added, 'And the beauty? You don't even have to visit the courthouse or the archives to consult the deeds. You can access digital images of them over the Internet from the privacy of home.'

When I explained that we were still waiting for the Comcast cable guys to stop lingering over their coffee at the Hot Spot and show up to install the Internet at *Our Song*, Kim walked me into the law library and introduced me to one of the courthouse computers. 'If you're going to do a lot of searching,' she said as I sat down in front of the terminal, 'you'll want to register with our network and set up a password. That will allow you to save your search results and come back to them later.'

Following Kim's instructions, I created an account, waited for the confirmation email to show up in my Gmail account, then clicked on the link the archives provided to activate it. 'Now you're in business,' Kim said, patting me lightly on the back.

With Kim kibitzing over my shoulder, I navigated to the Maryland tax assessment database, selected Tilghman County and let the database know I intended to search by street. On the following screen, I filled in *Our Song*'s house number and street name, then clicked Next.

'Wow!' I flopped back in the chair, totally awed. Everything you ever wanted to know about our little home away from home – with the possible exception of where I hid the dark chocolate-covered caramels – was suddenly laid out on the monitor before me.

'Magic, huh?' Kim said.

'Darn right. I'm used to government websites that are slow, make you enter the same information half a dozen times, freeze and then kick you offline with a "Sorry, try again." Kudos to whomever designed this one. Not the lowest bidder, obviously.'

Kim tapped the screen. 'Here are the deed

70

reference numbers I was telling you about. You should jot them down.'

I made a note of the liber and folio numbers for our property on a scrap of paper, then navigated over to MDLandRec.net. From there it was a simple matter to type the numbers into the blanks set aside for 'book' and 'page' – *et voila!* – a digital image of the actual deed for *Our Song* filled the screen.

'Excellent!' I said.

'The information you want is down here,' Kim told me, leaning closer, 'after all the "witnesseths" and "in consideration ofs," the paragraph near the bottom where it says, "being the same property conveyed by deed dated May 31, 1968 and recorded among the Land Records of Tilghman County Maryland in Liber 3088 Folio 201 which was granted and conveyed from Charles T. Quinn and Juliana C. Quinn, husband and wife unto the Grantors herein," which would be you.

'Now you navigate back to the home screen,' she instructed, 'but this time you plug in the numbers 3088 and 201. When *that* deed comes up, it will list the previous owners, too. Keep going back and back and back until you've gathered the whole ownership chain, or the documents run out – whichever comes first.'

'That might take a while,' I said with a grin. 'Dwight Heberling thinks our property dates to the mid-1700s. Was King George II or George III on the throne back then?'

Kim grinned back. 'Google it. Might even have been James II.' She checked her watch. 'I'll leave you to it, then. You've got half an hour before Fran shows up.' She winked. 'And if you're very nice, I won't tell her you're already here.'

'What's the report from the courthouse today?' Paul asked when he returned to the eastern shore from Annapolis later that evening.

I eyed the battered briefcase he carried, bursting at the seams with paperwork.

'Why don't you put your briefcase down and I'll fix you a drink. Gee and Tee?'

'Wine, I think.'

'White or red?'

'Whatever's already open, sweetheart.'

'I'll meet you on the porch,' I said as I headed for the kitchen. 'We can toast the Canada geese. They've been super noisy today.'

A few minutes later I joined him on the porch, carrying two glasses of chilled Sauvignon blanc. 'The house goes back to the middle of the eighteenth century,' I said, handing him a glass. 'Just as everyone suspected.' I settled into the lounge chair next to Paul and adjusted a pillow behind my back. 'It was built by a guy named Josiah Hazlett and seems to have remained in the Hazlett family until early 1952 when it and twenty acres of surrounding land was sold to Liberty Land Development Corporation for a pittance, at least by today's standards.'

'Land development?' Paul looked puzzled. 'Why aren't we sitting in the middle of a cluster of waterfront condos, then?'

I shrugged. 'Sewer? Water? Who knows? Whatever plans they had must have gone bust because LLDC held the property for about ten years, then sold it off to an outfit called Heartland Enterprises, Inc. Charles and Julianna Quinn bought the property from Heartland in 1975 for twenty-thousand dollars.'

'Ah,' Paul sighed and took a sip of his wine. 'Those were the good old days.'

'Tomorrow I plan to spend some time at the courthouse, but in the library, not the basement. Kim promised me access to Lexis-Nexis where I hope to find out more about those two companies.'

The following day, Kim was as good as her word. When a search through Lexis-Nexis turned up nothing particularly useful, she directed me to an Internet database called Forbes People Tracker which provided several links, but none that led anywhere. It wasn't until I logged onto the Dialog database and started trolling through Dun and Bradstreet's *Who Owns Whom* that I struck pay dirt.

Heartland was a real estate development corporation based in Hohokus, New Jersey, but Liberty Land Development – now defunct – had once been an indirect wholly-owned subsidiary of Clifton Farms, a chicken processing plant.

In CrocTail, which contained information about corporations and their subsidiaries going back year by year, I found Clifton Farms easily enough, categorized under 'poultry slaughtering and processes' as well as 'food and kindred products.' Its owner was a man named Clifton J Ames. Clifton J Ames had been dead since 1992, but the processing plant he had established was very much alive. I'd bought a package of Clifton Farms boneless thighs at Acme the previous week. They were still in my freezer.

Ten

'The full truth of this odd matter is what the world has long been looking for, and public curiosity is sure to welcome.'

Robert Louis Stevenson, *The Master of Ballantrae,* 1889

Our Song seemed to be in a state of perpetual makeover; we were living through a real-life episode of HGTV. One day it was *Love It, Or List It.* The next, *House Crashers* or *Flip or Flop.* I expected Jonathan and Drew, the *Property Brothers*, to pop out of the woodwork at any moment with another problem that required our urgent attention, and that of our checkbook.

Using sledge hammers, the wall between the kitchen and the living room had come down in a loud and spectacularly pleasing way, opening up the downstairs to space and light. Dwight Heberling assigned his son to clean up the debris in preparation for the new framing while he took a pair of workers up on the roof and got them going on a more careful demolition of the chimney.

Just when I thought we had everything under

control, the water pump stopped working. Dwight pulled the pump out of the well, swore, pointed out a jumper wire some idiot had installed across one set of contacts at the pressure switch, and pronounced the pump D.O.A. A new pump was ordered, but while we waited for it to be delivered via Fedex overnight, we had no water to drink, do the dishes with or flush the toilets. Dwight and his workers improvised, drawing fresh water out of the creek to mix the mortar and clean their tools. Meanwhile, Paul fetched a bucket of water, set it next to the downstairs toilet and we followed island rules: *If it's yellow, let it mellow. If it's brown, flush it down.*

That's why I found myself at the Acme supermarket early that morning pushing a grocery cart full of bottled water through the checkout line. I'd heaved the last plastic jug onto the conveyor belt when somebody called my name. Caitlyn Dymond was pushing a similar cart loaded with boxes of juice, granola bars and fruit rollups. She steered the cart into line behind me. 'Kids in day camp,' she explained, plopping a super-sized box of goldfish crackers on the conveyor belt just behind the plastic bar that separated her groceries from my water jugs.

'Been there, done that, Caitlyn, and I remember it well.' I eyed the piles of snack foods in her basket and asked, 'Just how many kids *do* you have?'

'Three. Two boys and a girl, but the boys are going through a growth spurt right now. They're eating me out of house and home. Speaking of houses,' she continued, dumping a twelve-pack of potato chips in assorted flavors on the belt. 'Any news on Baby Ella?'

I shook my head. 'Sheriff Hubbard said it might be a while.'

Caitlyn's face fell. 'Oh. I thought maybe by now . . .'

'Sorry, no.'

'Has the investigation held up the renovations on your house?' she continued.

I shook my head. 'Not really. The sheriff sent a crime-scene technician to have another look at the smoke shelf in case any clues to the child's identity had been left behind but they didn't find anything, so Dwight's crew has been able to move forward.

'They've finished knocking down the wall between the kitchen and living-room areas,' I told her as I swiped my credit card through the checkout machine and signed the tiny screen as the automated voice instructed. 'You wouldn't believe how much bigger the place looks. Dwight tells me he plans to finish with the fireplace tomorrow. Sadly, the whole thing needs to come down, but he thinks he can save some of the interior brick and use it when he rebuilds.'

While I bagged my purchases and transferred the water jugs from the conveyor belt back into my cart, Caitlyn finished checking out. 'Before I forget! Don't plan anything for the fifth of July.'

'Why?'

'It's the annual Barfield and Williams picnic. Kendall throws one every year for the agency's clients and other local big wigs. I just mailed the invitations today.'

I frowned. 'I think I have to pedicure the cat.'

Caitlyn chuckled at my lame attempt at humor. 'Oh, you'll definitely want to cancel that. Every mover and shaker in the county will be there, Hannah. Food, music, fireworks. It's actually quite fun.'

'Fran Lawson mentioned something about a picnic the other day while we were mucking about in the courthouse basement,' I said, softening my tone. We parked our carts near the customer service desk while I told Caitlyn about the discovery in the courthouse storage room and what our plans were for the records. '*You* have to attend the picnic, I suppose, since you work with Kendall and all,' I continued, 'but *I* certainly don't have to go. I'm not sure I could stand to look at the woman after the way she screwed us over.'

'Don't come for her, Hannah, come for me. It'll look bad for *me* if my clients don't show. Besides, there'll be door prizes.'

'I'm not sure it's worth it to give up a whole day on the off chance of winning a travel alarm.'

Caitlyn laughed. 'Prepare yourself for a surprise, then. Last year, Kendall gave everyone at the party a flat-screen TV.'

'You've got to be kidding.' I stared at the agent for a moment, dumbfounded. 'So that's where all her commission money goes?'

'You'd think, but no. Kendall was rolling in dough even before she started selling real estate. You know MB and T?'

'The bank?'

Caitlyn nodded. 'I always thought the "B" stood

for "bank," but no. It stands for Barfield, Kendall's grandfather.'

I whistled.

Caitlyn grinned. 'Exactly. After granddad sold to Bank of America in the mid-eighties, he bought into real estate big-time and rode the housing bubble into the stratosphere.'

'Dwight Heberling married well, then?'

'You know about that, huh?'

'Dwight mentioned it,' I said. 'I wonder what happened?'

Caitlyn puffed air out through her lips. 'Poor Dwight. I think they were married for about two and a half minutes. Kendall was on the rebound after Dan Frye dumped her. He was captain of the football team. Dwight followed Kendall around like a lost puppy all through high school. Nearly passed out when she asked *him* to take *her* to the senior prom. The rest is . . .' She paused. 'Well, not exactly history, but Dwight junior ensued. Kendall stuck it out for a few years, then dumped both her husband and the baby so she could go off to college. Dwight was granted full custody, so Kendall spent a good bit of time gallivanting until Daddy had a heart attack and called his little girl home. She's been running the family business ever since.'

'Did Kendall ever remarry?'

'Just a series of affairs,' Caitlyn sniffed.

'How about Dwight?' I asked as we pushed our carts through the automatic doors, out of the air conditioning and into the warm summer sun.

'He did. Almost immediately. To a girl as sweet as her name: Grace.'

78

'I don't think I've met her.'

'Unless you've visited the local humane society, probably not. She volunteers there on spay and neuter days, otherwise . . .' Caitlyn shrugged. 'Grace was a stay-at-home mom. Dwight couldn't have done better choosing a stepmom for his son. Grace loves that boy like he's her own, but then she's been raising him since he was a toddler.'

'I don't suppose the Heberlings will be at the party?'

'Should be. Kendall bends over backwards to show everyone what super-duper friends she is with wife number two. Grace is too much of a lady to say anything against Kendall, but I know it drives her bonkers whenever Kendall calls the house on the pretense of asking for a recipe or something. Early on in the marriage, Kendall would telephone and ask to speak with Dwight. "Oh, Dwight,"' Caitlyn simpered in imitation of Kendall. '"My hot water heater's on the fritz. Could you pop over for a moment and have a look at it, pleeeeze?" She ruined Grace's birthday party one year by calling Dwight repeatedly, claiming she had a stalker. Grace finally put her foot down,' Caitlyn chuckled. 'Poor Kendall has to hire her own handymen now.'

I looked both ways and eased my shopping cart into the crosswalk. Caitlyn followed close behind. When we reached my car I popped the trunk and said, 'What does one wear to this shindig? My party clothes are still back in my closet in Annapolis.'

'You've got two weeks to get it together,'

Caitlyn grinned. 'Slacks with a colorful top would be good. Me? I'm wearing a sundress.'

I closed the trunk over the last jug of bottled water, turned to Caitlyn and said, 'Well, you've convinced me that my mythical cat can wait. Food, fun, fireworks. Sign us up.'

'And if we're lucky,' Caitlyn said with a cheerful wave, 'all the fireworks might not be confined to the sky.'

Eleven

'I SAW in dreams a mighty multitude,—
Gather'd, they seem'd, from North, South,
East, and West, And in their looks such horror
was exprest As must forever words of mine
elude.'

Philip Bourke Marston, *Wind Voices,* 'No Death,' 1883

Back at *Our Song*, Rusty Heberling helped me unload the water jugs from the trunk of my car – one for the kitchen counter, one for the fridge and the rest stacked neatly next to the washer on the floor in the laundry room – then returned to the task of shoveling debris out the living-room window where it slid down a chute and into a wheelbarrow.

I had moved the car around to the side of the house where it wouldn't interfere with the comings and goings of Heberling, Son and miscellaneous subcontractors, when I caught a flash of white out on the main road. *Please, please, please,* I chanted, fingers quite literally crossed, willing the Fedex Express delivery truck to turn, and so it did, beginning the bumpy ride down the lane that led to *Our Song*. I met it at the gate, greeting the delivery man like a long-lost brother as he wrestled the carton carrying my new water pump out of the truck and onto the driveway.

Dwight signed for the delivery, took charge of the pump, unpacked it, confirmed it was the right model, then headed to the kitchen for a glass of ice water, saying he'd fetch Rusty and go off to study the manual.

While the Heberlings boned up on water pump installation in the side yard, I pulled weeds from the flower bed bordering the fence, daydreaming about soaking the dirt out from under my finger-nails during a long, hot bath later that evening. I was tugging at a clump of stubborn crab grass, swearing under my breath, when the crunch of gravel on the drive announced the arrival of another visitor, driving the vision of lavender bubbles clear out of my head.

I looked up and swiped sweat off my forehead using the back of my hand.

A statuesque middle-aged woman and a young man were climbing out of a bright blue Chevy Volt. The woman, who had been driving, carried a notebook; the young man opened the trunk, leaned in and came out holding a shoulder-rigged Steadicam.

Reporters. Damn. Somebody had a big mouth.

'Mrs Ives?'

I admitted that I was.

'Madison Powers, *Washington Post*. We're here to ask you a few questions about the body of the baby found in your home the other day. Do you have a minute?'

Although I was certain it would take more than a minute, I agreed.

The cameraman shouldered his camera, but before he got it rolling, I asked, 'We read the *Post*, so I'm familiar with your byline. Didn't you write that exposé on the chicken farming runoff that's polluting the Bay? Won a Pulitzer or something?'

'Guilty,' she said. She pulled a business card out of her handbag and handed it to me. 'I wish the article had resulted in some sensible regulation, but when forty percent of Maryland's agricultural money comes from Big Chicken, it's hard to get politicians to pay attention.' She looped a wayward strand of dark brown hair behind an ear. 'I won't keep you long, as I can see you're busy . . .'

I gestured toward the house with the trowel I'd been holding. 'I imagine you want to see the fireplace?'

'May I?'

As I led Madison into the house, followed by the cameraman, I told her about the discovery, and about my observations as to the child's age and sex. 'We named her Baby Ella,' I said as I pointed out what remained of the fireplace.

'Who made the actual discovery?' Madison

asked, entirely for the benefit of her viewers as she already knew the answer.

'It was our contractor, Dwight Heberling,' I told her.

Madison turned to the cameraman and made a cutting motion with her hand. 'Where might I find Mr Heberling?' she inquired.

'He's probably out by the garage.' I explained about the broken water pump. 'Follow me.'

We found Dwight sitting in a lawn chair in the shade of an oak tree, hunched over a schematic diagram spread open on his knees. Rusty leaned against the tree trunk, punching buttons on his iPhone. Both snapped to attention when we appeared.

I made the introductions.

As the camera rolled, the Heberlings gave their version of the gruesome discovery. 'It looked like one of those Egyptian mummies you see in museums,' Dwight concluded.

'Like King Tut,' Rusty added, grimacing into the camera.

'How long do you estimate the baby had been in the chimney, Mr Heberling?'

'It was wrapped in newspapers from the 1950s . . .' Dwight began before his son interrupted again.

'But ya know, Pops, I've been thinking. People leave newspapers lying around, ya know, so the body could have been a lot older than 1951, or even younger.'

Rusty was right. I hadn't thought about the possibility that a more modern-day someone had wrapped a dead child up in *old* newspaper. Or that someone, upon discovering the little mummy in a suitcase in the attic or somewhere, had panicked and wrapped it up in a *recent* newspaper and hidden it in our chimney rather than contacting the authorities.

Madison Powers turned to face the cameraman. 'County police are waiting on test results from the state medical examiner. Until then, exactly what happened to little Baby Ella and who placed her in the chimney of this eastern shore cottage, and when, remains a mystery.'

Although her cameraman perked up at my invitation, Madison refused a glass of iced tea on behalf of the both of them. 'I've got to get going,' she said as I walked them back toward her car. 'Do you know who owned this house before you?'

I did, back to day one, but I'd worked hard for that information and decided I wasn't about to do her research for her. She could get her own staffers on it. 'The house dates back to pre-Revolutionary War times,' I told the reporter. 'From the style of construction, we know that the chimney was built sometime around 1770 . . .' I paused to do the math. 'That's two hundred and fifty years, give or take.'

'So, until we hear back from the medical examiner . . .'

'All bets are off,' I concluded.

We'd reached the front gate. I was holding it open, waiting for the cameraman to catch up when a black sedan, traveling a lot faster than was prudent on such a poorly surfaced road – if you valued your shock absorbers – ground to a halt in a spray of gravel just behind the Volt. A preppy, college-aged dude slid out of the driver's seat of the Acura and wrenched a rear door open.

'Someone important, I gather?' I murmured in an aside to Madison.

'In his own mind, at least,' she replied as we watched the kid's passenger unfold a pair of long, chino-covered legs and emerge from the car smiling toothily, already in full meet-and-greet mode. 'That's Jack Ames, Tilghman County Council president,' Madison said. 'He's running for U.S. Congress in November. Watched two full episodes of *The West Wing* and thinks it qualifies him to run the government.'

I didn't need Madison to tell me who the guy was. I'd seen his face – and that of his beautiful wife, two point five adorable children and pedigreed chocolate lab – plastered all over a billboard at the intersection of Routes 13 and 113. SHARE THE FUTURE, it proclaimed in letters three feet high.

'What the hell is he doing *here*?' I asked.

Madison shrugged. 'Same as me, I guess. You gotta admit it's not every day you find the body of a baby hidden in a chimney.'

The cameraman had moved to put the Steadicam back in the trunk, but with a barely perceptible nod from Madison he shouldered the camera again, this time pointing it at the politician as he rapidly closed the gap between us.

'Madison.' Ames grinned. 'Fancy meeting you here.' A sudden gust of wind lifted a lock of his perfectly coifed, evenly colored chestnut hair.

Madison snorted. 'Surprise, surprise, surprise.' She turned to me. 'Hannah Ives, meet Councilman Jack Ames. He's stopped by to sweet talk you out of your vote.'

Ames laughed and extended his hand. When I took it, he covered mine with both of his, stared into my eyes as if checking them for cataracts and said, 'Welcome to Tilghman County, Hannah.'

'Thank you,' I replied, thinking even his hair seemed insincere.

As far as trolling for votes went, though, Jack Ames was barking up the wrong tree. Paul and my primary residence remained in Annapolis, firmly in Maryland's wildly gerrymandered third Congressional district, while Ames was running to unseat the Democratic incumbent in Maryland's ninth. I decided not to mention it.

'I heard about Baby Ella, of course,' he said. 'Somebody's tragedy, for sure.' He wagged his head slowly, sadly, sympathetically. 'But that's actually not why I'm here. Word is you've got a bum well pump.' He slipped a thumb and forefinger into the breast pocket of his oxford button-down shirt and pulled out a business card. 'Friend of mine, Hank Daniels, runs a plumbing and heating business in Elizabethtown. Give him my name when you call and he'll fix you right up.'

'I appreciate the recommendation, Mr Ames,' I said, accepting the card, casting my eyes briefly over it just to be polite. 'But, happily, the replacement pump arrived today. I expect we'll have water again by dinnertime.'

His frown vanished as quickly as it had

appeared, replaced by another of his patented perma-grins. 'Ah, yes, well, that's good news, then.'

I smiled back.

Madison smirked.

The cameraman grinned and lowered his equipment.

'Well, this has been fun,' Madison said, 'but I gotta get going. Thanks for your time, Mrs Ives.'

'You're very welcome.'

She nodded at the politician, 'Mr Ames,' but made no move to go.

Councilman Ames handed me a brochure featuring a color photograph of himself posing in a blue suit with a red-and-white striped tie, superimposed over the U.S. Capitol dome. The American flag in full long-may-it-wave mode had been Photoshopped over his head. 'We need stronger leadership in Washington, D.C., Mrs Ives. When you go to the polls in November, I hope you'll consider me.'

'Thanks, I will,' I said.

I'd lost track of the young chauffeur, but when Ames barked 'Tad!' he magically appeared and whisked the councilman away.

Madison made a rude noise. 'Strong leadership in Washington, my foot. What he really means to say is "I've always wanted to see my portrait hanging in the Rayburn House Office Building."'

I laughed out loud. 'Madison, please feel free to come and interview me at any time. Just as long as you leave your cameraman at home.'

Twelve

'Man: *Some dismal accident it needs must be.*
What shall we do – stay here, or run and see?'

John Milton, *Samson Agonistes*, 1671

It was going on three o'clock when Rusty called through the open window, 'Mrs Ives?'

I put down the iron griddle I was scouring with a pad of fine steel wool and peered out.

Rusty stood in the driveway next to his motorcycle, his brow furrowed. 'Have you seen my helmet?'

'Sorry, I haven't.'

'I swore I hooked it over the handlebars this morning like I usually do, but it's not there now.'

Maryland has a strict motorcycle helmet law; it was illegal to ride a bike without one.

'Dad needs some special waterproof tape to secure the wiring to the water pump before he sticks it down the well, so I gotta go into town, but I can't find the damn helmet.'

'Why don't you take the truck?' I suggested.

Rusty gave me a look that let me know he'd rather walk into town barefoot than be seen driving his father's truck. 'Some bastard stole my fricking helmet!' he growled, then disappeared around the corner of the house. Ten seconds later he stomped back. 'Fuck it,' he said, climbed on his motorcycle, revved the engine and roared off.

Rusty's helmet was jet black, decorated with overlapping red and white stars. I vaguely recalled seeing it hanging from the handlebars earlier that day, but it could just as well have been the morning of another day. Rusty wasn't my son, but no mother likes to see a child ride off into harm's way, so I plopped the griddle onto the kitchen counter and went off to look for the missing helmet.

I searched the downstairs, including the bathroom, then made my way out to the shed. No sign of the helmet there, nor in the garage. I was coming back to the house via the compost heap when I noticed a tiny patch of red just behind the woodpile. 'Ah ha, there you are, you rascal!' Rusty must have set his headgear down on the woodpile and somehow, with all the workers to-ing and fro-ing during the day, it'd got knocked down behind it. I retrieved the helmet, turning it over in my hands as I pondered the best thing to do. Odds were Rusty would ride into town and back without incident, but what if . . .

I tossed the helmet onto the passenger seat of my car and took off after him, going as fast as the speed limit allowed.

I had to slow down at the tiny community of Shelton where I'd recently been pulled over for going thirty-five in a twenty-five mile-per-hour zone. The cop who had stopped me was still lurking; I could see the hood of his cruiser peeking out from behind the dumpster in the parking lot of the general store. He'd given me a warning, but I didn't think he'd be so generous with a repeat offender.

As I passed the store, though, the officer himself was just emerging from inside holding a thermos, so I could have been driving a hundred miles an hour and gotten away with it. I pressed down on the accelerator.

About a mile outside of Shelton, on a long straightaway, I caught sight of a motorcycle way up ahead. I eased my car up to forty, but didn't seem to be gaining on him. As the cyclist crested the next hill, I lost sight of him again, but when I popped over the hill there he was, stuck behind a farm tractor hauling a manure spreader, both proceeding at a more leisurely pace. The distance between us was closing.

I was so intent on my quarry that I barely noticed the black car that had been bearing down on me from behind on the narrow, two-lane road. Lean, low and mean, it stalked me like a panther, so close that I couldn't see its license plate. Was his bumper about to bite mine? I clutched the steering wheel in a death grip, having flashbacks to the time when a couple of thugs had run my car off the road and into a pond. I was starting to hyperventilate when the vehicle suddenly whipped out into the southbound lane and zoomed past me as if I were standing still.

'Idiot!' I muttered, thinking where was the cop now that I needed him? Filling his thermos bottle back in Shelton, dammit.

It took only a few seconds for the black car to

catch up with Rusty and the farm vehicle. The driver tailgated for a while; even he seemed reluctant to pass on a double white line.

I was about two hundred yards away when the black car swerved to the left, then to the right, clipping Rusty's motorcycle and knocking it out from under him. As I watched in horror, Rusty flew into the air and tumbled down the embankment, landing at the edge of a grove of trees that paralleled the road.

'No!' I shouted as the black car shot around the tractor and disappeared over the next hill.

Heart pounding, breathless, I screeched to a halt on the shoulder just behind Rusty's capsized cycle, its rear wheel still spinning. I needed to call 911, but where was my cell phone? *Damn!* In my hurry to leave, I'd left my purse at home.

Perhaps I could flag someone down?

But first, I had to check on Rusty. I scrabbled down the embankment.

Rusty lay face down just short of the tree line, his head buried in a small pile of leaves that had accumulated as he slid along the ground. 'Rusty! Rusty!'

He didn't answer. He didn't move.

Please don't be dead, Rusty. Please!

I knelt down beside the young man, carefully swept the leaves away from his nose and mouth. Blood oozed from a wound on his temple, but that was a good sign, wasn't it? Dead men don't bleed.

'Rusty?'

Still no answer. I leaned over, put my ear next to his mouth and was relieved to feel soft, warm breath flutter against my cheek. Rusty was still breathing.

The impact of the crash had undone the band that secured Randy's ponytail. Gently, I moved his long hair aside, pressed my fingers against his neck and found a pulse. Strong and steady.

I looked up and around, feeling helpless. Rusty had a cell phone, I knew, but where was it? I flashed back to earlier that afternoon: Rusty leaning against the oak tree, slipping the phone into the back pocket of his jeans. Hoping the phone hadn't been damaged in the crash, or thrown clear, I checked his jeans and was relieved to see a rectangular outline on Rusty's right hip. 'I need to use your cell phone, Rusty,' I said in case he could hear me. 'I'm taking it out of your pocket now.'

Rusty's jeans were tight. Using my thumb and forefinger, I wriggled the phone free and when I turned it on, the screen glowed bright with text messages. Rusty was a popular guy.

Dude, Crusty Crab after work? texted someone named Luke.

Ken said, *Got it. Stay cool.*

While Laurie, clearly a girlfriend from all the emoticons that followed her text, wrote: *Movie? Ninja Turtles?* ☺ ☎ ♥

Sadly, beer and the movies would have to wait. Praying that Rusty's phone wasn't password protected, I bypassed the messages, swiped the screen and breathed a sigh of relief when the phone icon appeared.

My finger was poised over the screen when someone said, 'I've called nine-one-one.' A man wearing well-worn jeans and a denim jacket over a stained T-shirt was sliding down the bank behind me. 'He's gotta be hurt bad, a fall like that.'

'He's knocked out,' I said, laying Rusty's phone aside. 'And he's got a pretty bad cut on his head.'

'Jackass went sailing by me like a bat outta hell.'

'You saw the accident?'

The farmer nodded. 'Didn't look like no accident to me, ma'am. Asshole swerved sudden-like, run him off the road on purpose.'

I sat back on my heels, breathing deeply, taking this in. Why would anyone . . .?

While the farmer stayed with Rusty in case he came to and started trying to move around, perhaps exacerbating his injuries, I rushed back to my car, popped the trunk and pulled out a couple of beach towels. I tucked one of the towels around Rusty's body, like a blanket, and used the other to put gentle pressure on his wound.

'Rusty? It's Hannah. Stay with me, Rusty. Help is on the way.'

As I waited with the farmer for the ambulance, I massaged Rusty's limp hand, trying to stroke life back into it, and attempted to reconstruct what had just happened. The car was black, I was sure of that. Make and model, who knew? If it didn't have a distinctive hood ornament, or if nothing was inscribed on the car in racing stripes or fancy chrome letters a mile high, I was clueless. It was big, though. Mean. Two doors. Tinted windows, yes! Dark, way too dark by Maryland standards. No way I could see the driver as required by law. License plate? Oh, I wish, but he went by me like a flash. Perhaps the friendly farmer . . .?

Back up on the road, the farmer was diverting traffic, directing it around Randy's fallen cycle. It seemed like hours, but a police car arrived fairly quickly, followed almost immediately by a chartreuse and white ambulance manned by two EMTs from the Elizabethtown Volunteer Fire Department.

As the EMTs tended to Rusty, I explained my relationship with the victim and told them about the helmet. Then I burst into tears. 'But I was too late! If only he'd been wearing it!'

'Ma'am?' The patrolman was speaking to me. Through my tears, I recognized him as the same guy who had pulled me over for speeding through Shelton. When he offered me his hand, I realized I was still kneeling on the ground and, in spite of the heat of the afternoon, I shivered.

He escorted me to my car, opened the door to the passenger side and made me sit down. A bottle of water magically appeared.

'Where are they taking him?' I asked the officer as they loaded Rusty, now wearing a cervical collar and securely strapped to a backboard, onto a gurney. An oxygen mask covered his nose and an IV snaked out of his arm.

'Peninsula Regional in Salisbury,' the officer replied.

As the EMTs loaded Rusty into the ambulance, I dabbed at my eyes with a tissue, pressing hard, trying to discourage the flow of tears. 'Is he going to be all right?'

'Let's just get him to the ER, OK?' Apparently I had made no move to touch the water bottle because he twisted off the cap and placed the bottle firmly into my hand. 'Drink.'

After I'd taken a few sips, he asked, 'Is there anybody we should call?'

'Dear Lord, yes!' How could I have forgotten about Dwight, back at the house, waiting patiently for his son to return with the waterproof tape so that *I* could have a bath that night. 'We need to call his father!'

'Do you have a number?'

'He's still working at my house,' I said, gathering myself together. 'I'll do it. I'll tell Dwight the bad news.'

Thirteen

'And we meet, with champagne and a chicken, at last.'

Lady Mary Wortley Montagu, 'The Lover: A Ballad,' 1748

Two weeks after the accident, with Rusty lying comatose in the hospital, it seemed odd to be pawing through my closet, worrying about what to wear to his mother's fancy garden party. Neither Paul nor I were in a party mood.

'I can't believe she's going ahead with it,' I commented to my husband as I slid plastic hangers along the rod from one side of the closet to the other.

'They aren't allowing Rusty any visitors, Hannah, so I don't see what more you can do.'

'True,' I mumbled into the sleeve of a ragged terrycloth bathrobe. 'I'm *definitely* going to petition Naddie Bromley to bump Kendall Barfield off in her next crime novel.'

'Therapeutic, no doubt,' Paul chuckled.

'Ah ha!' I'd finally located the turquoise sundress I'd bought in Hawaii at a shop called Tropical Tantrums. I swirled it out of the closet like a matador's cape and held it in front of me. 'What do you think of this?'

'Reminds me of a certain night on the beach at Kauai,' Paul said, drawing me close, crushing the dress, still on its hanger, between us. 'You were barefoot then, too, as I recall.'

I kissed him quickly, then shoved him playfully away. 'Shoes. Where are the matching shoes?' I fell to my knees and scrabbled around on the floor of the closet looking for the pair of turquoise beaded sandals the saleswoman at Tropical Tantrums had also talked me into.

Paul patted my butt affectionately. 'You'll be the belle of the ball.'

'Hardly, dah'link, but you will,' I said, moving my butt out of range and struggling to my feet, holding the shoes. 'Why don't you wear the *barong tagalog* Daddy brought you from the Philippines?' I suggested, referring to the sheer white formal shirt that had been hand-loomed from pineapple fibers, then embroidered from mandarin collar to hem with delicate folk patterns.

'With your tan . . .' I fanned my face rapidly with my hand, then reached for a Hawaiian shirt he'd bought but never worn. 'On second thought, wear this. In a *barong* you'd be too dangerous.'

Paul eyed the shirt – bright red with white hibiscus – critically. 'Jeesh, Hannah, I'll look like Magnum P.I. in this getup.'

I gave him a look. 'And your point is?'

'OK, OK. I can tell when I'm outnumbered.' He tossed the shirt on the bed, then headed for the bathroom. 'How is Rusty doing? Any word on his condition?'

'Dwight tells me he's still in the ICU, being kept in a medically-induced coma.' I eased behind Paul – who was standing at the sink, waiting for the water to run hot so he could shave – and fumbled through my ditty bag, looking for my tweezers. Tweezers and magnifying mirror in hand, I sat down on the toilet seat lid and went to work on my eyebrows. 'Rusty's got a depressed skull fracture,' I said, addressing my reflection. 'The CT showed a temporal hematoma, so they had to go in and drain that. Now they're watching for signs of infection and waiting for the swelling in his brain to go down.'

Paul slathered his face with shaving cream. 'Too soon to tell is what you're saying.'

I lay the tweezers down, watched my husband draw the razor slowly along his cheek. 'I ran into Doc Greeley when I stopped by the hospital yesterday, and those were his words exactly.' I drew a deep breath. 'And all I could think of was please Lord, not another one.'

Because of our long association with the Navy,

we knew several young officers who were suffering the long-term effects of traumatic brain injury: personality changes, inability to concentrate, slurred speech, confusion. Medical advances in the treatment of wounded warriors had improved the outcome for many victims of TBI, but the road to recovery could be rocky and long. 'Rusty really needs our prayers,' I said.

Paul held a washcloth under the hot water tap, wrung it out and used it to wipe the remaining shaving cream off his neck and ears. 'Are the police any closer to tracking down the hit-and-run driver?' he asked as he draped the washcloth over the edge of the sink to dry.

'Not that I've heard.' More or less satisfied with the state of my eyebrows, I tucked the tweezers and mirror away. 'Every day since it happened, I've been replaying the scene in my head. The speeding car, the deliberate swerve . . .'

'The driver might not have done it on purpose,' Paul pointed out. 'Maybe he was changing the radio station.'

'Or texting,' I added, although that was strictly against Maryland law, not that anyone was paying attention, from what I could observe. 'Still,' I said after a pause, 'the farmer saw it all in his rearview mirror. I made quote marks in the air, "Asshole swerved sudden-like, run him off the road on purpose." I tend to agree.'

'Why would anyone want to hurt Rusty?' Paul wondered aloud.

'I've asked myself the same question. And when I asked Dwight, he was just as puzzled.'

'Does Rusty have a girlfriend?' Paul asked.

I remembered the brief text message I'd seen on Rusty's phone back at the accident scene. 'Maybe,' I said. 'A girl named Laurie wanted to meet him at the movies.'

'The car you described seemed like a young man's car to me,' Paul said. 'A rival for Laurie's affections, perhaps?'

'Seems a bit extreme in this day and age,' I said. 'Running someone's motorcycle off the road. Cyber-bullying is more the style.'

I cast my mind back to the day of the accident. It had been Grand Central Station around *Our Song* that day. Workmen coming and going, reporters, cameramen, politicians, even the Fedex guy. Was it just bad luck that Rusty wasn't wearing his helmet when he set out for town that day, or was that exactly what one of our visitors had intended? I shivered.

Paul noticed, and welcomed me into his arms.

Kendall's estate, *Tulip Point*, was about two miles downstream from *Our Song*, situated on the point where Chiconnesick Creek met the Chesapeake Bay. Paul was still tinkering with the outboard engine on the runabout – it lay in a hundred pieces on the floor of the garage – so we had to drive the long way around, by land.

At a mailbox festooned with red, white and blue balloons, we turned right and proceeded down a paved avenue lined with ancient tulip poplars, their interlocking branches forming a covered archway over our heads. The alley stretched from the main road all the way down to a breathtaking mansion that dominated the point, surrounded by numerous outbuildings. The house bore the clear imprint of an architect's hand. Five hexagonal pods sprawled over a tastefully landscaped hill, each pod connected to the next by a glass-enclosed passageway. To the left, several tiki-huts on the far side of a decorative iron fence indicated the presence of a swimming pool.

As for the outbuildings, I lost count. Just outside the main gate, a row of six, single-story cottages were arranged in a semi-circle – housing, I presumed, for the field hands and staff it must take to maintain the place. There was a stable for the horses and a barn for the decorator cows presently chewing their cuds in a disinterested way, considering us with soulful, liquid eyes from behind a white rail fence. 'Do you suppose they were hired for the occasion?' I asked my husband as we drove slowly by. 'From Acme Rent-a-Cow?'

Paul laughed. 'Or Cows-R-Us.'

One hundred yards further on, we were directed to park in a vacant field by a teenage boy wearing an orange vest, waving Day-Glo wands like a ground controller at BWI airport. We parked where instructed, locked the car, then followed several other party guests through an enormous, wrought-iron gate adorned with cattails and herons. A control box had been installed on the pillar to the left, but for today, at least, the electrically controlled gates stood wide open. Just inside, another teen, a girl this time, muttered 'Ives, Ives, Ives,' as she pawed through the name tags spread out on the table in front of her. There must have been a hundred of them, arranged in alphabetical order. Perhaps the A-B-C's were a challenge for her.

'Here we are,' I said, helpfully touching my tag, which sat on the table immediately below the pair of nametags intended for Dwight and Grace Heberling.

'Ah ha!' the teen said, handing ours over. 'Paul and Hannah. Welcome!'

'I doubt they'll be coming today,' I said, indicating the Heberlings' nametags.

The girl's face clouded. 'Isn't it just *awful*?'

We agreed that it was.

'Well,' she chirped, 'if they come they come, if they don't they don't.'

I clipped my tag to the strap of my sundress. 'There!' I said, patting the plastic holder. 'We're official.'

Paul and I stood by the table for several moments, looking around, scanning the guests for somebody – anybody – we knew, while the sweet smell of mesquite and barbecued ribs drew us inexorably forward. A jazz combo – sax, trumpet, bass guitar and drums – played on a raised platform in the formal garden which had been decorated for the occasion with Chinese lanterns.

I inclined my head toward Paul. 'There's our hostess. I recognize her from her pictures.'

'Damn!' Paul muttered under his breath. 'Has the woman been Photoshopped?'

Kendall, perfect in every conceivable way, stood next to one of two long buffet tables where uniformed staff were fussing with Sterno tins and chafing dishes. As blustery as it was that day, even the wind didn't dare mess with her impeccably styled platinum hair. She wore a white, ankle-length linen skirt and a white crochet sweater. A silk scarf was looped casually around her neck – Hermes, if I wasn't mistaken – festooned with interlocking Escher-esque horse heads in gray and black. The ends flapped cheerfully in the breeze as she issued instructions to her staff.

'I'll have to be nice to her, I suppose. Fran tells me that Kendall is donating the office space we need to process the documents from the courthouse basement, plus two computers and a telephone.'

Paul, who had been eyeing the buffet tables hungrily, turned to me. 'That's generous of her. Why?'

I shrugged. 'I haven't the foggiest idea. Maybe it's a tax write off? I can't imagine Kendall doing anything out of the pure goodness of her heart.'

'Where is it? The office space, I mean.'

'In town. Directly over the old drug store.'

Paul leaned close. 'Maybe she has a tenant she needs to evict.'

Suddenly he whistled, long and low.

My head spun around. 'If that wolf whistle is for Kendall Barfield, Professor Ives, you're a dead man.'

Paul chuckled, then pointed. 'If I'm not mistaken, that's a classic Cris Craft sedan cruiser, Hannah. What a beauty!'

I followed the line of his arm all the way down

to the far end of the dock where a large cabin cruiser was tied. Even I, who knew precious little about boats and was usually invited on board simply to serve as ballast, was impressed with the vessel's gleaming white hull, the mirror-like varnish on the exposed woodwork. The vessel's name, *Liquid Asset*, was painted in fancy gold script on the transom. Standing watch at the head of the gangplank was a young server dressed in nautical attire. Clearly, the cruiser was meant to be part of the picnic venue because another, smaller bar had been set up in its cockpit.

Paul nudged me with his elbow. 'Let's go check it out.'

'No, you go, sweetheart. I just spotted Caitlyn. While you drool all over the boat I'll have a nice chat with her.'

I watched Paul stride off, long-limbed and lean, appreciating the view. Then I headed for the bar where Caitlyn waited in line, dressed in a sundress splashed with bright red poppies.

'Hi, Caitlyn,' I said, coming up behind her. 'Love the dress.'

Caitlyn turned, smiled and grabbed my hand. 'I'm so glad you came, Hannah.' She squeezed my hand to punctuate the 'so,' then dropped it to adjust one of the straps that had slid off her shoulder. 'Glad you like the dress. What do you think of the manicure?' She extended her hand and waggled her fingers in my direction. Each nail had been lacquered with a red, white and blue American flag.

'Oooh, patriotic!' I gushed.

Caitlyn beamed, basking in my approval. 'What can I get you to drink?'

'Seems like a nice day for white wine.'

'Coming up. Chardonnay, Sauvignon blanc, Riesling, Pinot Grigio or Viognier?'

'An embarrassment of riches.' I chuckled, considered the choices then asked for a Viognier, gently correcting her French. '*Vee-on-yay*. The "g" is silent.'

'Everything is silent in French,' she said with a good-natured grin. 'Take hors d'oeuvres, for example. Crazy language. That's why I took Spanish. Actually comes in handy these days, what with all the migrant workers.'

'Speaking of hors d'oeuvres,' I said, collecting my wine, 'it looks like the appetizer table has just opened up.'

'What are we waiting for, then?' Caitlyn led the way, wobbling a bit on a pair of red high-heeled sandals that poked holes in Kendall's perfectly groomed lawn.

We grazed along the table's length. I piled my plate high with brie on crusty bread, a couple of crab balls, a generous portion of steamed shrimp and – just to show I was being health-conscious – a small stack of cut up vegetables.

'Where's your husband?' Caitlyn wondered, using her fingers to pick up a giant olive stuffed with garlic and pop it into her mouth.

I waved a carrot stick, dangerously dripping ranch dressing. 'Down at the dock, checking out the Cris Craft.'

Caitlyn gazed over my shoulder and frowned. 'That's not all he's checking out.'

Curious, I turned. After a moment I spotted Paul's red flowered shirt. He stood in the cockpit of the cruiser, talking to Kendall Barfield. As I watched, Kendall reached out and laid a hand on my husband's arm. 'I'm counting to five,' I said, skewering a shrimp with a toothpick and dragging it through the cocktail sauce. 'And if she hasn't taken her hand off my husband by then, I'm going to lob this in her ultra-white direction.'

'Ooooh,' Caitlyn said. 'Can I watch?'

Silently, I glared. *One, two, three . . .*

Fortunately for Kendall, by the time I got to four, Paul had slipped out of her grasp. He turned and said something to the bartender, who twisted the caps off a couple of long-necked beers and passed them over. Paul gave one of the beers to Kendall, they clinked the bottles together then each took a sip.

'What the hell are they toasting to?' Caitlyn wondered aloud.

'I was wondering the same thing.' Silently fuming, I watched as Kendall continued to monopolize my husband. I silently cheered when a guy wearing blue Bermuda shorts and a saffron polo shirt joined their little circle. Kendall graced him with an imperial nod, then completely ignored the newcomer until he shrugged and wandered away. 'I'm sure Paul will tell me all about it when we get home.'

'He better,' Caitlyn muttered into her wine. 'Bitch.'

I laughed. 'Paul's a big boy, Caitlyn. He can handle it,' I assured her with absolute confidence.

I should know. Nearly a decade ago, Paul had been totally impervious to an attempt by a female midshipman to seduce him in a case that had nevertheless severely tested our marriage.

'I almost bought that scarf,' Caitlyn said wistfully as a man I recognized as Councilman Jack Ames drifted into Kendall's charmed circle. 'It was a limited edition.' She drained her wine glass and set it down on a nearby tray where it wobbled unsteadily, then fell over. 'They had it in the window at Lulu's.'

'Why didn't you?' I asked. 'Buy it, I mean.'

'Kendall grabbed it first.'

Juggling my plate in one hand and my wine glass in the other was getting to be a challenge. I nodded toward one of the tall circular tables that had been set up around the yard, each wrapped in a white tablecloth, its ends gathered and secured against the wind around the pedestal with red, white and blue ribbon. 'Shall we . . .?'

'Sure,' Caitlyn said. Then, 'Wait a minute. There's somebody I'd like you to meet – Mindy Silver. She runs Silver Farms, one of the few independent chicken farmers left in the county.'

I turned. 'Where?'

'The blonde, standing at one of the tables near the bar. Wearing the red-and-white striped top.'

'Ah,' I said, spotting the woman immediately. 'She kinda looks like a farmer.' Medium height and solid, Mindy Silver was built straight up and down, like a tree. Her skin was deeply tanned and her dark blonde hair hung loose, just touching her shoulders. From the ragged way her bangs

106

marched across her forehead, I guessed she had trimmed them herself.

The combo had just wrapped up a sixties set with a rousing cover of the Beach Boys classic, 'Good Vibrations,' when Caitlyn dragged me over and introduced me to Mindy. Then she waggled her fingers, said, 'Toodle-oo,' and tottered off.

'Pleased to meet you,' I said, feeling slightly abandoned.

'Likewise.'

'Gorgeous day for a picnic, isn't it?'

'Yup.'

I decided to fall back on my stock of inoffensive ice-breakers. 'So, Mindy, do you work outside the home?'

'I raise chickens.'

'On a large scale?'

'Depends on your point of view, I suppose.'

'Ah, so I guess you have to deal with one of the local chicken processors?'

'Used to.'

'And you don't anymore?'

'Life's short.'

Apparently, the only way I was going to pry a conversation out of Mindy Silver was with a crowbar. I was thinking about wandering off to get a refill for my wine when she surprised me by saying, 'Have you heard of Clifton Farms?'

'You bet,' I told her. 'When the grandkids were visiting, I bought a family-sized package of their drumsticks at Acme. Still have some thighs in the freezer, although my husband is much more of a breast man, if you know what I mean.' When she didn't comment, I added, 'So you raise chickens for Clifton Farms?'

'Once upon a time.'

Although I was curious about Mindy's apparently troubled relationship with Clifton Farms, I sensed that she didn't want to go there – at least not yet – so I took a different tack. 'I prefer organic chicken, raised without hormones or antibiotics. For health reasons, I'm careful about the meat I buy,' I told her. 'In the case of chickens, they pump them up with hormones, and what for? So they get big . . .?'

'Breasts!' she said, finishing the sentence for me. 'We are what we eat. End of story. Folks who believe that hormones don't move down the food chain and into our bodies probably also believe that aliens built the pyramids.'

I laughed. 'As a breast cancer survivor, I couldn't agree more.'

'Girls getting their periods at seven or eight!' Mindy screwed up her lips with distaste. 'There's gotta be a connection. I've heard about you, you know,' Mindy said a moment later, tipping her beer bottle in my direction.

'All good, I hope,' I said, setting my wine glass down on the table so I could concentrate on the food still heaped on my plate.

Mindy grinned, exposing impeccably white but slightly crooked teeth. 'Mostly. You're the gal who witnessed Rusty Heberling getting run off the road, aren't you?'

I admitted that I was.

Mindy frowned darkly and shook her head. 'So,

he's in a coma, and his mother's having a freaking party. Disgusting.'

'Well,' I said, 'she's not the one sitting twenty-four seven at his bedside, that's for sure. That would be his stepmother, Grace.'

'Grace.' Mindy delivered the name on a sigh. 'The most selfless person I know. When she's not organizing a fundraiser for the church she's volunteering at the county animal shelter.'

'So, tell me about your chicken farm,' I said, eager to direct the conversation away from poor Rusty. 'Frankly, it sounds like a lot of work.'

'True. Bought the place through Kendall, fourteen, fifteen years ago. Don't know why she keeps inviting me to her shindigs, but once a customer, always a customer, I suppose.

'Speaking of which,' Mindy continued, 'where's our hostess? I've drunk two of her beers, already – good stuff, too – but I haven't seen her yet.'

Since Paul had extricated himself from the woman's clutches, I'd kept my eye on Kendall. 'She's over there,' I informed Mindy. 'Uh, talking to the saxophone player.'

I wouldn't have described what I was observing as 'talking.' From the stiffness of her back and the way her hands were flailing about, Kendall was giving the poor musician a piece of her mind. The sax player opened his mouth to say something, but judging by the speed by which it snapped shut she must have silenced him with a death ray.

'Maybe she got dumped at the prom while that song was playing,' Mindy mused, taking a pull from the bottle. 'Poor sax.'

'Now if *I* were holding that sax . . .' I paused, realizing it might be the Viognier talking. 'Sorry. With my luck, Kendall's probably your best friend.'

'Oh, I can't stand her, nobody can . . . well, almost nobody.' Mindy seized the last morsel of meat on a spicy barbequed rib with her teeth, pulled it off, looked around, chewing thoughtfully, then tossed the bone over her shoulder and into the boxwood. She licked her fingers appreciatively. 'I'm just here for the freebies.'

'Flat-screen TVs, I heard.'

'Last year, yeah. Year before that it was weekends for two at Dover Downs.' She snorted. 'Some freebie that was. Doug blew four hundred dollars on the slots. Thank you *so* much for that.'

I laughed, as I was probably meant to. 'You're good friends with Caitlyn, I gather?'

'BFFs.' Mindy crossed her fingers. 'Like that. Wish I had bought the farm from her rather than Kendall over there, but Caitlyn wasn't in the biz back then.' Mindy leaned forward and lowered her voice. 'Kendall's not happy with my mouth.'

Mouth?

'Neither is Mr Chicken à la King over there.'

I must have looked puzzled. Mindy had begun gnawing on another rib and used it now as a pointer, aiming it at the buffet table. 'Over there, the guy in the blue seersucker suit?'

'The one picking through the fried chicken with the tongs?'

'Yeah. That's Clifton Ames. Owns Clifton Farms. It's the third largest chicken processing plant in the state. Biggest in the county. That's probably his chicken.' She guffawed. 'A little late to do quality control, old man.'

'I've seen his billboards.' I rolled my eyes. 'Clifton Ames to Please,' I said, drawing quote marks in the air. 'Puh-leeze!'

'Groan-worthy, for sure, Hannah, but less likely to be lost in translation if the company ever decides to go global. *Hace falta un tipo duro para hacer un pollo tierno,* you know.'

'Help,' I said, tapping my chest with a thumb. 'French major.'

'Ah, well. You know Frank Perdue, the "it takes a tough man to make a tender chicken" guy?'

I nodded. The poultry cases of grocery stores world-wide were filled with shrink-wrapped packages of tender Perdue chicken parts. Perdue, up in Hurlock, Maryland, would have to be Clifton Farms' biggest competitor.

'Well, I hear tell that the slogan got terribly mangled when it appeared on billboards all over Mexico. Roughly translated, it said, "It takes a hard man to make a chicken aroused."'

I inhaled wine, coughed, then laughed so hard the wine spilled over the rim of my glass and dribbled down my hand.

Mindy laughed, too, whether at my dilemma or her own humorous anecdote, it was hard to say. 'As I said earlier, I used to be a contract farmer for Clifton Farms, twelve years, but no more.'

'Why not?' I asked once I'd caught my breath.

'It's a bum business,' she said. 'A chicken house costs around a quarter of a million to build and we were realizing only about nine thousand dollars a year from it.'

Chicken houses peppered Maryland's eastern shore – long, narrow structures built like miniature airplane hangars. 'I'm not much of a business-woman,' I said, 'but that doesn't sound like a good return on investment to me.'

'It isn't, unless you're in it for the long haul. Believe it or not there are over seven hundred contract chicken farmers in Maryland, but I'm no longer one of 'em.

'Do you realize,' she continued as she snagged two glasses of sangria from a passing server and handed one to me, 'contract chicken farmers don't own anything. The newly hatched chicks are delivered, you feed 'em what they send you – you're not even allowed to know what's in the fricking feed – and seven weeks later, the chicken catchers come and haul 'em away. You own nothing . . . well, except for the dead ones.'

'So how *does* a chicken farmer make money?' I asked, genuinely curious.

'You get paid by the weight gain of the flock.' She drained her glass of sangria in one long gulp and set the empty glass down on the pedestal table. 'But it wasn't just the money, Hannah. I honestly care about the chickens! When my contract came up for renewal, and I balked, Clifton Ames visited me personally. He wanted me to make a hundred and fifty thousand dollars' worth of "improvements" to my chicken houses.' She drew quote marks in the air with her fingers. '"Improvements," my foot. He wanted me to entirely *enclose* them.' She paused, then rocked back on her heels. 'Can you imagine?' She waved a server over and snagged another sangria. 'So I told him to pound sand. My chickens live the way a normal chicken lives, running around outside, scratching in the dirt and eating bugs and grass.'

'So they die happy?'

'Hah! No, they live a long, happy life, for a chicken. I sell eggs. I turned out to be a big disappointment to Clifton Ames,' she added. 'Thought he'd put me out of business, force me to sell out like so many other farmers in the county did. But I called the bastard's bluff,' she said, raising her glass. 'Here's to eggs, poached, scrambled or fried.'

As Mindy Silver talked, I'd been following Clifton Ames as he wandered away from the buffet table to the bar and down the dock, shaking hands with partygoers all along the way. In his light blue seersucker suit, white shirt and white shoes, and wearing a white fedora over his snow-white hair, he was easy to track as he wound his way among his more colorfully attired friends and acquaintances.

'He's limping a little,' I observed. 'Looks kind of frail.'

'Hah! Don't let that fool you. He may be in his seventies but, trust me, nobody . . . nobody in this county messes with Big Chicken. Ooops,' she continued, ducking her head. 'Look out. He's coming our way.'

In spite of his doddering gait, Clifton Ames closed the distance between us in four seconds

113

flat. He extended his hand. 'I have it on good authority that you are Hannah Ives.'

'Guilty.' I gave him my hand but instead of shaking it he raised it to his lips and planted a damp kiss on the back of it. I suppressed a shudder. He acknowledged Mindy with a nod. 'Welcome to Tilghman County, Mrs Ives. I look forward to meeting your husband.'

'He's down at the dock admiring *Liquid Asset*,' I said.

Ames turned his head to look. Something about the man seemed familiar and I realized with a jolt that his profile resembled that of the politician, Jack Ames. Father and son?

'Ah.' Ames's white, flyaway eyebrows did a little dance. 'Much to admire in that. Did you come here by boat?' he asked, indicating the raft-ups of Whalers, Bayliners and other small craft including a couple of jet skis that bobbed along the dock next to *Liquid Asset* like baby ducklings.

'No, the engine is on the fritz,' I explained with a rueful grin. 'Maybe next time.'

'There you are!' a familiar voice chirped. Caitlyn was back. She looped her arm through mine. 'I found your husband. He sent me off to look for you. He says he's hungry, and would you be kind enough to join him for dinner.'

'If you'll excuse me,' I said, feeling guilty for abandoning Mindy with Clifton Ames, although based on our conversation, I was confident she could handle it. 'Mindy, Mr Ames, it's been fun talking to you.'

'Good luck, Caitlyn,' Mindy called after us as Caitlyn led me away through the crowd.

Caitlyn glanced back at her friend. 'Thanks, sweetie.'

'Good luck with what?' I wanted to know, matching my steps with hers.

Caitlyn leaned her head closer to mine. 'Kendall's about to make some announcements. Stick around and see who'll be going to Cancun this year.'

I stopped short. 'You?'

Caitlyn grinned and thumbed her chest. 'Top agent! And don't you forget it!'

Fourteen

'Anger is a weed; hate is the tree.'

Saint Augustine, *Sermones*, 3, 58

Halfway across the garden, Caitlyn released my arm and paused. 'So, what were you and Mindy talking about?'

'Chickens,' I said.

'Ah. No way that wouldn't have come up!'

'Am I correct in assuming that Clifton Ames, the Chicken King, is the father of Jack Ames, the politician?'

'You got it. Jack is Clifton J Ames the third. The J stands for Jackson. At one time Cliftons one, two and three were all kicking around the county, so to avoid confusion he's always gone by his middle name, Jack.'

115

'Jack stopped by our place the other day. *Said* he was there to help out with the busted water pump, but sort of accidently-on-purpose left me with a brochure. Just in case I happened to miss the placards his minions have already strewn all over the countryside.'

'And if you watch TV, he's all over the local stations, too. He's the current county council president,' Caitlyn explained. 'A real horse's patoot, in my humble opinion. Once, just once, I'd like to hear what a candidate would do for us. Is that too much to ask? But, noooo. It's all how horrible the other guy is. In this case, the other guy is the incumbent, Joseph Collier. Decent sort, Congressman Collier, but old, a bit out of touch.' She tapped her temple with an index finger. 'You know.'

Paul was waiting for us at the bar, standing guard over two glasses of Viognier. 'That's no excuse to vilify the man, though,' Caitlyn said, taking the glass from Paul and having a sip.

'Vilify who?' Paul wanted to know.

'Joseph Collier. He's served his constituents well.'

'Is Jack Ames here?' I asked.

'You bet.' Caitlyn scanned the crowd, which had grown by at least fifty percent since we'd arrived. She pointed. 'Over by the pool, talking to Doc Greeley.'

We watched Jack bid farewell to the doctor and glad-hand his way through the picnickers. 'He's always "on," isn't he?'

'With both headlights.'

'How come Jack isn't going into the family

business?' I asked after a bit. 'You'd think his father would be disappointed.'

'Jack has a younger brother and sister,' Caitlyn explained. 'Annette has an MBA from Harvard and she's incredibly sharp, so my money's on her to take over when the old man dies. The younger brother, Colin, is something of a screw-up. The only thing he's ever done for the family is produce four grandchildren.' She gestured with her wine glass. 'There's one of them now. See that guy horsing around on the high dive? That's Tad.'

Wearing a neon-yellow Speedo the size of a Band-Aid, Tad was balancing on his hands at the end of the diving board. As I watched, he launched himself into the air, flipped twice and dove cleanly into the water. Three teenage girls observing from poolside squealed, flipped their hair and clapped their appreciation.

'Show-off,' Caitlyn muttered. 'You met Tina, the daughter, when she handed you your nametag at the gate.

'You know what I think?' Caitlyn said, tilting the rim of her wine glass in my direction. 'I think that Clifton J Ames the Second had political aspirations of his own, but *his* old man wouldn't hear of it. It was cluck-cluck chickens or hit the road. Cliff's donated a ton of money to his son's campaign chest. If what I read in the paper is true, Jack is outspending Collier by ten to one.' She took another sip. 'Like Joseph P Kennedy, you know. Ames won't be happy until his son is in the White House.'

'What are Jack's chances?' Paul asked.

Caitlyn didn't even pause to consider. 'I think he's a shoo-in.' After a moment, she added, 'I have a new system. I call it punitive voting.'

'Oh, yes?' I said, only half listening. Jack was chatting up a dowager and it was fascinating to watch her fluff up, like a Westminster show dog, under his admiring gaze.

'Indeed. Wear a cowboy hat twenty-four seven? Ten points off for that. And photo ops with your wife and four kids, that's a major deduction – fifteen points. Five more off if there's a dog.' She studied me over the rim of her wine glass, her green eyes serious. 'And when it comes to bad toupees, I am brutal.'

I laughed out loud. 'I think you're going to be my new best friend, Caitlyn.'

Eventually, Paul and I left Caitlyn to her own devices and headed off to the buffet table. We were standing at a table chatting with Doc Greeley, tucking into our roast beef, fried chicken and crab cakes when Kendall stepped up on the stage, took over the microphone and silenced the band. After thanking everyone for coming, and for all the good wishes they had expressed for the recovery of her son, Rusty (in that order), she announced the winner of the salesperson of the year award.

It was not Caitlyn Dymond.

In all the hooting and hollering and backslapping going on among the family of the winner, a relatively new guy to the firm, or so I gathered, Paul leaned over and said, 'Are you ready to go?'

'Caitlyn's going to be crushed,' I said, feeling

118

desperately sad for my friend. 'She was confident she'd win that award.'

Paul shrugged. 'You know what they say about counting chickens before they're hatched.'

I gave him a look. 'Do you think losing the sale of the Wicomico house counted against her?'

'After my recent conversation with Kendall, nothing would surprise me. She's a slick businesswoman.' He linked his arm through mine. 'C'mon. I'll tell you all about it when we get home.'

A few minutes later I glanced around the lawn, the pool and the dock, looking for our hostess but not seeing her, so we finished our wine and made our way through the clusters of partygoers to the reception desk. 'I'm so sorry, but we need to leave,' Paul told the young woman I now knew as Tina. 'Have you seen Kendall?'

Tina's face fell. 'But you'll miss the fireworks!'

'Regrettable, but necessary, I'm afraid. But we wouldn't dream of leaving without saying goodbye and thanking our hostess.'

'The last time I saw her, Uncle Jack had her cornered. Probably twisting her arm for campaign support.' She winked.

'I'd feel really awkward leaving without thanking her,' Paul repeated.

'No worries.' The girl smiled. 'She'll never notice.'

When we turned to go, Tina stopped us with, 'Wait a minute. There's a bag here with your name on it.' While she rummaged around under the skirted table, I noticed that Dwight and

Grace's nametags had disappeared. Had they been claimed and we'd simply missed running into them among the crowd, or had somebody, realizing the couple probably wouldn't be attending, thoughtfully taken the nametags away?

I was about to ask Tina when she chirped, 'Here you go!' and handed each of us a gold-and-green shopping bag, the handles tied together with curled gold ribbon.

At first, I thought it was a bag of the usual swag. Mine contained a coozie from a local independent insurance agency, a ball cap embroidered 'JD's Surf 'n' Turf,' a ginormous beach towel that would tell the world how much I enjoyed drinking Budweiser beer, and a keychain – it floats! – from Merchant's Marine. Under the towel, at the bottom of the bag, I uncovered a white box about the size of a hardback novel bearing the Apple logo. IPad mini was printed on the side. 'Gosh,' I said, turning the box over and over in my hands. 'Is this a mistake?'

Next to me, Paul muttered, 'Jiminy Christmas. I've got one, too.'

The young woman grinned. 'Everybody gets an iPad mini. Cool, huh?'

I was too stunned to speak. I looked at Paul; he looked at me. 'Better than a flat-screen TV,' I said.

'Much.'

As I tucked the iPad back into my bag I became aware that the combo had stopped playing. In the sudden quiet, a man began to bellow, 'Help! Help! Somebody call nine-one-one!'

Tina shot to her feet. 'Oh my God, oh my God, just what we need!' and vanished around the corner of the house, punching numbers into her cell phone as she ran.

Without waiting for Paul, I took off after the girl.

There was a commotion at the end of the dock. As the desperation in the man's voice began to register, the guests stopped what they were doing and turned. A few, like me, began to run toward the water.

'Jesus!' said Caitlyn. She had appeared next to me, gripping a wine glass, swaying unsteadily. She grabbed my arm and held on tightly. 'Damn!' she said. She stuck the tip of her little finger between her lips, sucked on it. 'Broke a nail. Just look!'

When she held out her hand, I could see that the Stars and Stripes that had been waving gaily o'er the land of the free and the home of the brave from her fingernail was now just The Stripes. 'Paid a fortune for that manicure,' she grumped, fanning her fingers, examining the remaining nails one by one, checking for further damage. Suddenly she looked up and slurred, 'What's going on?'

'Shhhh,' I told her. 'Somebody's in trouble.'

As we clustered on the grass at the head of the dock, the uniformed staffer I'd seen earlier manning the bar on the Chris Craft was struggling in chest-deep water, moving sluggishly, holding someone up. I recognized the scarf first, then the platinum hair fanned out around her head, swirling in the water as the young man staggered to shore and laid his burden on the grass. Kendall Barfield.

'So, Kendall took a swim!' Caitlyn snorted. 'Serves the lying bitch right.'

'Caitlyn, behave!' I hissed.

'She as good as promised me . . .' Caitlyn began, but I cut her off with a sharp elbow to the ribs.

As we watched, the staffer knelt next to Kendall's body and pulled several weeds out of her hair, almost tenderly.

'Out of my way!' someone yelled. Doc Greeley charged down the dock, arms flailing from side to side, scattering the crowd like Moses parting the Red Sea. 'And someone call nine-one-one, for Christ's sake.'

Doc Greely fell to his knees next to our hostess, felt for a pulse and checked her breathing. But, I knew, from the way Kendall's eyes bulged, red-rimmed, staring at nothing, by her swollen tongue and how deeply the scarf bit into her neck, that Kendall Barfield had hosted her last picnic.

Within minutes, the paramedics arrived, but there was nothing they could do either. They placed her body on a gurney and covered it with a blanket. As they slotted the gurney into the back of the ambulance, the tail end of Kendall's beautiful scarf slipped out from under the blanket.

Fifteen

*'On all the line a sudden vengeance waits,
And frequent hearses shall besiege your gates.'*

Alexander Pope, 'Elegy to the Memory of an
Unfortunate Lady,' 1717

After Sheriff Andy Hubbard and two deputies arrived, nobody was allowed to go home until somebody – perhaps Tina, the young woman in charge at the gate – pointed out that there was a complete guest list.

The main gates to the Barfield estate had been closed, and an officer posted at the end of the dock to prevent anyone who'd come to the party by boat or jet ski from leaving the same way. Paul and I had been herded into the area near the bandstand, supernaturally quiet now, the instruments returned to their cases, the musicians sprawling in lounge chairs around the swimming pool, smoking and talking quietly.

Only the police and the bartenders were busy.

'What were you and Kendall taking about?' I asked Paul as we drank club soda with lime and waited for official instructions.

'She was apologizing for the snafu over the Wicomico house,' he said. 'Laid the confusion right on Caitlyn's doorstep. Blamed it on her failure to communicate. Caitlyn's always going

123

off half-cocked, it seems. This has happened before – she wonders why she even keeps the woman on, yadda yadda yadda.'

'Did you believe her?'

'Not for a moment,' Paul replied. 'All the time she was talking to me, I was studying her eyes. I'd seen that look before, on the faces of midshipmen trying to explain why their papers were going to be late.'

As Paul talked, I'd been scanning the yard. For the first time, I noticed the security cameras – on the top of the main gate, on the corners of the house near the downspouts, behind one of the cabanas overlooking the swimming pool, in a tree aimed at the dock. I pointed at that one, my heart hammering. 'They'll see you talking to her, Paul.'

'But they'll also see that it was an entirely friendly conversation.' Paul smiled, then put on his Humphrey Bogart voice, 'I'd do just about anything for you, sweetheart, but bumping off a pesky real estate agent isn't one of them.'

'I feel bad about all the snarky things I said about her, and now here I am at her party, drinking a dead woman's wine, and I never even talked to her. Not even once.'

'Well,' my husband said reasonably. 'Now you won't have to.'

Eventually, after asking us the briefest of questions: 'When was the last time you saw Kendall Barfield? Did you notice anything unusual?' the police let us go.

As partygoers trickled out the gates, far more somberly than they had come in, Tina stood on one side, ticked names off the list and – incredibly – continued to hand out the bags of party favors. Just past the checkpoint, a deputy passed out business cards, instructing us to call if we thought of anything important.

As we walked together down the drive toward the field where our cars were parked, Paul took my hand. 'Who do you think hated Kendall enough to do that to her?'

'I wasn't serious about wanting Kendall dead,' I said.

'*I* know that, Hannah,' he replied.

I paused and looked sideways at my husband. 'Do you think the police will hear about my rantings and take them seriously?'

'No, I don't. But maybe the next time somebody pisses you off you will be more circumspect when discussing the extent of your displeasure with relative strangers.'

We had reached the parking lot. Stepping carefully over the ruts that countless tires had torn into the turf, we wound our way through the sea of cars, looking for ours. 'Where the heck . . .?' Paul began, then remembered the car keys and fished them out of his pocket. He punched the unlock button and was rewarded with a beep and a flash of headlights from our Volvo several rows away.

'We can safely eliminate Rusty,' I said, returning to Paul's earlier question. 'He's still in a coma. Grace is probably out as well. As far as I know, she's still sitting at Rusty's bedside, and that certainly would be easy to check. Caitlyn has a good motive, but honestly, I talked with her a lot today, off and on, and I don't see how she would have had the time to slip away and strangle her boss, much as she may have wanted to.'

As we walked, I had the creepy feeling I was being watched. Paul was several steps ahead of me by this time, aiming the keys at the trunk, jabbing the button to pop it open. I glanced around uneasily, but all I noticed were other party guests streaming out of the gates, making their way toward their vehicles.

'Did you see Dwight at the party?' I asked as I tucked my goodie bag into the trunk next to Paul's. And then I froze, realizing what had been staring me down, boring into my subconscious with its chrome headlights: a lean, mean, black sports car in the next row over.

I pointed the car out to Paul. 'What kind of car is that?'

'A late-model Mustang. Why?'

I flashed back to the day of Rusty's 'accident.' To the black car that had borne down on me, filling my rearview mirror with menace. This vehicle had tinted windows, too. I lowered my voice. 'That's the car that hit Rusty.'

It wouldn't have taken much force, perhaps only a tap, for a sports car like the Mustang to knock a motorcycle off the road. And the evidence was there, too, if you were looking for it. I moved in for a closer look.

'Are you sure?' Paul asked.

'Positive.' I pointed out the damage to my husband: a dent in the right front quarter panel, a scrape of black paint on the bumper. 'Don't you think it's odd that the car that ran Rusty off

126

the road is parked here at Kendall's on the very day that she gets murdered?'

Paul wrapped an arm around my shoulders. 'But who would want both Rusty *and* Kendall dead?'

'From what I've been hearing, Rusty barely talks to his biological mother . . .' I paused, leaning into him. 'There's a link, I feel it.'

'Find out who owns this vehicle, then perhaps all will be made clear,' Paul said.

All around us people were climbing into their vehicles and driving away. Before long we'd be the only car left in the row. Quickly, before the driver of the Mustang could return and see me doing it, I jotted down the license number.

'I'll be right back,' I said and jogged away, back through the gates of the Barfield estate, looking for Sheriff Hubbard.

When I returned, Paul was waiting for me in the car. 'Success?' he asked as I slid into the passenger seat.

'Step one,' I said. 'Now for step two.' I convinced him to sit in the car with the air conditioner running, hoping to identify the owner of the Mustang when he – or she – left the party.

Twenty minutes later, though, even the van carrying the band had packed up and gotten out of Dodge. The parking lot stood empty of all but the police vehicles and a dozen private cars, including the Mustang. Paul convinced me it was time to go. 'Sorry that hanging around longer didn't answer your question,' he said.

127

'*Au contraire,*' I told him as he aimed the Volvo down the drive toward the main road. 'It tells me that whoever was driving that Mustang was either family, or an employee.'

'Or both,' Paul added.

Sixteen

'O it's broken the lock and splintered the door,
O it's the gate where they're turning, turning;
Their boots are heavy on the floor
And their eyes are burning.'

W.H. Auden, 'O What is That Sound,' 1936

I was surprised on Monday morning when Dwight showed up for work.

'How's Rusty?' was the first thing out of my mouth.

'Stable,' his father told me. He looked like he'd lost sleep. A small patch of stubble under his left nostril made me wonder if he'd crawled out of bed early and shaved in the dark.

'You didn't have to come to work today,' I said.

'Nothing I can do at the hospital, and if I don't work the bills don't get paid.' Dwight set his toolbox down on the porch. 'Besides, Grace is with him.'

'That's good,' I said. Then added quickly, 'I'm so sorry about Kendall.'

He shrugged. 'I feel bad when anyone dies, but

Kendall was dead to me a long time ago, Mrs Ives. I can count the times we've talked over the past two years on the fingers of one hand.'

'I don't suppose you were at the picnic yesterday?'

Dwight looked blank, then said, 'You're kidding, right?'

'Does Rusty stay in touch with his mother?' I asked, quickly changing the subject.

Dwight snorted. 'Hardly. Grace is the only mother he's ever known. She was a stay-at-home mom, you know. Didn't start doing volunteer work until Rusty started school.'

'I don't suppose Rusty is allowed visitors?'

'No,' he said simply, the one word encompassing a world of sadness.

'You'll keep us informed?' I asked.

Instead of replying, Dwight patted the pocket of his work pants and pulled out a small packet of business cards held together by a rubber band. He slid one out from under the band and handed it to me. 'Grace is on this website, Caring Bridge, posting updates.' He tapped a corner of the card. 'The URL is on there.'

I fingered the card and turned it over, filled with admiration for the woman who loved her stepchild so much that she'd designed these cards – featuring a clipart figure of a running quarterback glancing over his shoulder, arms extended, preparing to receive a pass – and printed them out on her home computer.

'I'm familiar with Caring Bridge,' I said truthfully. As a cancer survivor, I had many friends who'd faced the same challenging road to recovery as I had, who'd found comfort and support from social media websites such as Caring Bridge. 'I'll be sure to visit and post a few notes of encouragement.'

'Thanks. Grace will appreciate that.'

I wondered as I fingered the card if I should tell Dwight about the black Mustang I'd seen at Kendall's party, but decided it would be cruel to get his hopes up before the police had had time to track down its owner and investigate.

Dwight trudged off and was working alone, installing copper flashing around the newly repointed chimney, when Sheriff Hubbard and one of his deputies paid us a visit. He left his hat on the entrance hall table I'd recently imported from our home in Annapolis, and followed me into the kitchen where we sat around the table drinking iced tea.

Paul's conversation with Kendall had been observed, but not, as I had worried, by the security cameras. 'I'm amazed Kendall didn't have cameras trained on *Liquid Asset*,' I said. 'It's got to have thousands of dollars' worth of electronic equipment on board.'

'There is a camera aimed at her usual berth,' Hubbard explained, 'but in order to accommodate all the visiting boats they moved *Liquid Asset* out to the end of the dock. We got miles of footage of a couple making out on a jet ski,' he told us with a rueful grin, 'but nothing on the *Liquid Asset* herself.

'When you were talking to Mrs Barfield,' he continued, addressing my husband, 'how did she seem?'

'I really didn't notice anything unusual, Sheriff Hubbard, but then, I'd only just met the woman so what was usual for her . . .' He shrugged. 'She seemed cheerful, not at all preoccupied, not even with the party preparations. Her staff and the caterers had everything well in hand and she seemed relaxed, genuinely having a good time.'

Hubbard's eyes ping-ponged from Paul to me and back again. 'Do you know anyone who had a grudge against her?'

I answered for the both of us. 'We did, actually. I have to be upfront about that. Before we bought this house, we made an offer on another of her listings. The offer was accepted, and then for reasons I still don't clearly understand, we had the rug pulled out from under us.'

'That was one of the things that Kendall and I were discussing on the dock that day, actually,' Paul added. 'Seems it was simply a failure of her staff to communicate. She told me it's all ironed out now.'

'Besides,' I cut in, 'we bought this place and, renovations aside, we couldn't be happier with it.'

'Anyone else?' Hubbard wasn't going to let us off the hook so easily.

'As my husband pointed out,' I replied, 'we'd only just met the woman, but from what folks say around here, Kendall wasn't everyone's friend.'

Sheriff Hubbard blinked, grunted, but made no further comment. Was he staring me down?

Daring me to lie to him? While I debated whether to mention Caitlyn's serious grudge against her boss over the loss of the best salesperson award, Sheriff Hubbard pocketed his notebook, signaled to his deputy that it was time to go, and stood. 'I appreciate your cooperation, Professor and Mrs Ives. You've been very helpful.'

Following their lead, we stood, too. 'Any time,' Paul said.

'Have you been able to trace the owner of the Mustang?' I asked as I walked the officers to the door.

Sheriff Hubbard paused to retrieve his hat from the hall table. As he settled it again on his head, he said, 'We have, but you must know that I can't share that information with you.'

'Can't blame a gal for trying.' I managed a smile. 'Do you know who was driving the car, then?'

'We do. But again . . .'

I held up a hand. 'Sorry, but it seems highly suspicious that the car that ran Rusty off the road is also parked at Rusty's mother's estate on the day she gets murdered. I'm thinking that Rusty and his mother must have shared more than a simple X-chromosome.'

'Well, if that something occurs to you, Mrs Ives, I hope you'll let us know.'

Hubbard was halfway down the walk when he turned back. 'I have some information for you about Baby Ella,' he said, as if tossing a pacifying tidbit my way. 'I spoke with the medical examiner's office this morning, and there seems to be no sign of foul play. The child was a girl, as you suspected, from six to eight months old.'

'Did they say how she died?'

'From the condition of her lungs, he suspects she died of a serious respiratory infection. It's hard to say precisely, but the baby may have had polio.'

Polio! That news stopped me in my tracks. One never thought much about polio these days, the disease having been eradicated in the United States by the late seventies or early eighties, as I recalled, thanks to Jonas Salk's vaccine.

'There was a polio epidemic sweeping the country in the summer of 1951,' Hubbard continued.

'And Baby Ella was wrapped in newspapers from around that time,' Paul observed.

'Exactly so,' Hubbard agreed. 'So, I don't think we have a crime here.'

'Isn't there some law in Maryland about failure to report a death, or unlawful disposal of a body?' I was grasping at straws, I knew, desperate to hold someone responsible for all the years little Ella spent walled up in our chimney.

Hubbard frowned. 'Well, ma'am, maybe there is and maybe there isn't, but in this case, I have absolutely zero inclination to go looking for someone to prosecute for it.'

Seventeen

*'The woods were made for the hunters of
dreams, The brooks for the fishers of song;
To the hunters who hunt for the gunless game
The streams and the woods belong.'*

Sam Walter Foss, *Dreams in Homespun*, 'The
Bloodless Sportsman,' 1897

In the 1960 classic, *I Hate to Cook Book*, Peg
Bracken wrote a chapter entitled, 'Leftovers: Or,
Every Family Should Have a Dog.' The same
might be said for walks in the country. For long
walks back home in Quiet Waters Park, I often
borrowed my daughter's labradoodle, Coco, but
on that particular morning several days later, with
Paul stuck back home in Annapolis, tied up with
some endless government paperwork involving
sexual harassment awareness training, I was dog-
less and on my own.

After polishing off a bagel with cream cheese
and my second cup of coffee, I inverted the mug
over a peg in the dishwasher, exchanged my cozy
slippers for running shoes and set off.

First stop was the end of the dock where I
checked Paul's crab pot, like he'd asked me to.
I hauled the wire cage up by the rope which
attached it to the dock, but all I found in the
one-way trap was a waterlogged chicken neck.

I dropped the trap into the water and continued exploring the flora and fauna along the shore until the ground grew marshy and started sucking greedily at my shoes.

At the surveyor's pipe that marked where our property ended and the neighbor's farm began, I made a ninety-degree turn, sighting along the property line to a small grove of trees where another ninety-degree turn would take me along our boundary to the main road. As I walked, I was grateful nobody had enclosed either property with barbed wire or chain-link fencing; the cornfields on my right delineated our land from the neighboring farm clearly enough for me.

About halfway along, I was surprised by a doe darting out of the corn and bounding across my path, swift as a gazelle. In its turn, the doe startled a wild turkey, which spread its wings and flapped out of the weeds and into the sky. I paused to marvel at them, breathing in the summer air, heavy with the scent of rich Maryland earth and new-mown hay.

At the grove of trees, the cornfield made a curious detour. I wondered why the trees – a cluster of ancient oaks – hadn't been cut down to maximize the land available to crop. I dived under the low-hanging branch of a lone sugar maple and stopped in my tracks. The dense canopy shaded a cemetery about the size of a two-car garage enclosed by a rusted fence of iron piping, looped together with ornamental chains. Eight large headstones were scattered about, tilted at odd angles as the ground around them had settled or been disturbed by hungry tree roots.

That the cemetery was old, I had no doubt. A few of the headstones dated, I was sure, to colonial days. The round-faced angels, their eyebrows and nose carved into the slabs by a stonemason in one deft, U-shaped stroke, told me that. I knelt before one crooked stone and deciphered the first inscription, partly by feel as the years and the weather, as well as the moss had taken their toll on the porous limestone:

Albert Anthony
Only child of
Albert C & Harriet A
Hazlett
Born in Salisbury
Oct 19, 1848
Died at Elizabethtown
May 18, 1851
Aged 2 years &
7 months
Rest, sweet child, in gentle slumber . . .

The remaining inscription had been covered by the encroaching earth. A maple seedling had taken root at the base of little Albert's grave. I pulled it out before it had a chance to send out roots to further disturb his tiny bones.

This was no formal cemetery of modern oblongs lined up in precise rows, yet someone had been caring for the graves. No weeds grew inside the enclosure; what little grass there was had been neatly mowed. A vase of plastic flowers – roses and carnations – their color not yet faded by exposure to the elements, had been placed in front of another headstone which read:

Mary Charlotte Hazlett
1890–1950
Sleep on, sweet Mother, and take thy rest
God called thee home, He thought it best.

This had to be one of the Hazletts mentioned in the land records dealing with the sale of *Our Song* to Liberty Land Development Corporation back in 1952.

Just beyond, my eyes were drawn to a stone planter about the size of a window box, over-flowing with black-eyed Susans, the state flower of Maryland, and very much alive. It marked the grave of a Samuel Hazlett who had shuffled off this mortal coil in 1845. Samuel had rated an urn with a flaming finial, draped with bunting. A half skull peeped out from under a tasseled curtain carved into its base, surrounded by broken columns and a few twists of ivy.

All the residents here seemed to be Hazletts, the family that had originally owned the land upon which *Our Song* and the farms and homes of our immediate neighbors had been built.

To my right were a cluster of three smaller headstones. I cringed: infant graves. Two children had lived only days, the other less than a year. I thought about Baby Ella, who had lain so long in our chimney and had no grave. An epitaph on one child's stone simply read: *II Kings, iv: Is it well with the child? It is well!*

Ugh. Our ancestors were certainly much more sanguine about death than we are. Most of the epitaphs were along the lines of 'Life was tough, now yay! Dead at last.'

Behind the mound where the children lay, another larger headstone caught my eye.

Nancy Hazlett
1934–1952
Beloved Daughter & Sister

Nancy Hazlett had been only eighteen when she died. My thoughts drifted again to Baby Ella. The dates fitted. Was she yours, Nancy? If so, she should have been buried beside you.

I decided to research the people who had once walked over the land Paul and I now owned, whose graves I could visit every day, if I chose. I knew that by the early 1950s, vital records in local Maryland courthouses had been moved to the new Archives in Annapolis, the shining accomplishment of Maryland's first archivist, Morris Leon Radoff, who built the Hall of Records in Annapolis in 1935 and persuaded the counties to transfer their records there for safekeeping. In the days before the construction of the Chesapeake Bay Bridge, this would mean researchers would have to travel long distances to Annapolis from the counties, some by ferry from the Eastern Shore, so the canny Radoff had partnered with the Church of the Latter Day Saints to microfilm the important records and leave copies in the care of the counties.

Thinking about the moldering records that Kim Marquis had found in the courthouse basement, I wondered if they'd been missed in Radoff's general roundup for the Mormons.

I slipped my iPhone out of my pocket and took pictures of the tombstones, being careful to capture the dates on the inscriptions. The next time I visited the courthouse, I'd see what I could find out about them. I wanted to check out the county library, too.

But first, we had work to do. Now that Kendall Barfield was dead, Kim feared that the rental on the office space wouldn't be renewed. Before the lease expired, Fran and I needed to clear out the storage room so that the mold could be abated and the room thoroughly cleaned, ready to welcome back the records Kim had decided to keep to their forever home.

Eighteen

'Whenever I hear anyone arguing for slavery, I feel a strong impulse to see it tried on him personally.'

Abraham Lincoln, 'Address to an Indiana Regiment,' March 17, 1865

When I arrived at the courthouse the following day, Fran was already at work wiping mildew off items with alcohol and storing them in clean boxes. After I suited up, I grabbed a rag and a bottle of alcohol and pitched in.

Around nine-thirty a.m., Kim showed up in the storeroom, a man in tow. From my crouched position on the floor, he looked exceedingly tall. He wore a short-sleeved plaid seersucker shirt tucked into a pair of dark gray jeans held up by neon yellow suspenders.

'I've got good news and bad news,' Kim said.

Glad for any distraction from the box of shabby file folders I'd been packing, I wiped sweat off my brow with the back of my gloved hand and said, 'Good news first.'

'The county has agreed to thoroughly clean, repair and repaint this space.'

From behind her mask, Fran beamed. 'Great! So what's the bad?'

'It means we'll need to clear everything out by the end of next week.' Even in the relative dark of the storage room, I could see Kim's frown.

Looking at the chaos around me, I groaned.

'Sorry, but to make up for it, I've brought Cap along to help.'

I remembered that the first time I'd talked to Fran in the High Spot café, she'd mentioned a volunteer nicknamed 'Cap.'

'Welcome to hell,' I said, handing Cap a face mask and the box of rubber gloves.

'Kim said it was a mess, but I never dreamed it'd be this bad.' Cap pulled on the gloves, snapping them over his wrists like a pro, then adjusted the face mask over his nose and mouth.

I handed him a folder I'd wiped clean of mildew and showed him how to place it with the others

140

in the bankers' box. After we'd filled half a dozen boxes, I helped Cap carry them upstairs and load them onto a book truck. Once outside, we stripped off our protective gear and together we pushed the truck across the street to the office space the late Kendall Barfield had acquired. We rode the elevator up to the third floor and unloaded.

After working without air-conditioning in the summer heat, sweat had soaked the underarms and gone through the back of my T-shirt. Cap's shirt clung damply to his back, and his cafe-au-lait skin glistened with sweat. A case of bottled water sat on the floor near the office door. I handed a bottle to Cap, then took one for myself and unscrewed the lid.

'Thanks for your help, Cap,' I said after taking a few refreshing swigs of water. 'Is the "Cap" short for something?'

Cap paused in mid-sip, half standing, half sitting against the edge of one of the three metal desks in the room. '"Captain." It's a military thing.'

'What did your momma call you when you were born?' I asked, pulling up a chair.

'Tommy,' he replied. 'Unless I was misbehaving, and then it was Thomas Edward Hazlett you cut that out right now!'

'Hazlett! My gosh, are you related to the Josiah Hazlett who owned the old Hazlett Place? We've just moved into the cottage there.'

'Hardly, ma'am. My ancestors were Hazlett's slaves.'

I felt my face flush. 'I'm embarrassed. I should have figured that out.'

Cap grinned. 'We *could* be related, of course. No telling what mischief old Josiah was up to with the house slaves back then. But never had the time or the inclination to have one of those DNA tests done to find out for sure.' He grinned. 'Assuming, of course, that the white side of the Hazlett family was inclined to cooperate with the experiment.'

'I took a walk around the property the other day,' I told him. 'There are a lot of Hazlett gravestones in a little cemetery near our place. I stupidly assumed they were descendants of Josiah Hazlett himself.'

The corners of Cap's eyes crinkled in amusement. 'Not for over one hundred years. That land had been in *my* family ever since our great, great grandparents were freed by Samuel Hazlett's will back in 1846.'

'He sounds like a good man,' I said, 'especially for a plantation owner back then.'

Cap snorted. 'Depends on your point of view, I suppose.'

'Are you the one who's taking care of the graves?' I asked.

Cap nodded.

'Did you hear about the baby we found in our chimney?' I asked cautiously.

'Everybody did.'

'After Dwight found the baby in the chimney, I did a little research . . .' I began, picking my words carefully. 'From the newspaper the child was wrapped in, they figure she was born around 1950 or 1951.'

Cap's dark eyes bore into mine. 'And . . .?

142

'Well, one of the tombstones was for a Nancy Hazlett who died in 1952, so naturally I wondered . . .' I let the sentence die.

'Nancy was my sister.' The desolation on his face tore at my heart.

'I was afraid of that,' I said. 'I'm so sorry, Cap.'

'Nancy drowned in 1952, Mrs Ives. The police ruled it a suicide.' He made quote marks in the air. '"While the balance of her mind was disturbed." I've never gotten over it.'

'Had she been depressed?' I asked.

'Honestly? I really don't know. I enlisted in 1946 when Nancy was still in junior high. When I left for the army, she seemed like a happy kid to me.

'While I was serving in Korea in 1950,' he continued, 'I received a telegram that Mom had died of cancer. Soon after that, Nancy lost the farm. I didn't find that out until much later, of course. They told me it was because she didn't pay the taxes.' Cap began pacing from the desk to the window to the door and back again. 'Dammit, Mrs Ives! She was just a kid! I should have been here for her, but that was impossible.'

Remembering the dates inscribed on Nancy's tombstone, I figured she was sixteen – still a minor – when her mother died. 'You couldn't get compassionate leave?'

'Leave?' Cap laughed bitterly. 'Early in the war, my plane was shot down. I punched out in time but spent the rest of the war as a guest of the Chinese in a POW camp near the Yalu River. We were completely isolated, had no idea what was going on in the rest of the world. And when they did give us news . . .' He paused, snorted. 'News. Hah! It was lies, all lies. We were losing the war, our government had abandoned us, our wives were sleeping with other guys . . .'

I swore softly.

'Yeah, well, I survived. Lucky, huh? Forty percent of the POWs didn't.'

Cap placed hands on both sides of his water bottle and crushed it like an accordion, then stared at the label for a long time. He was shutting down.

There was a lot more to the story, I knew, but like other war heroes, Cap seemed reluctant to talk about it. Was it the poet, Robert Frost, who once said, 'Half the world is composed of people who have something to say and can't, the other half those who have nothing to say and keep on saying it?'

In my experience, the vets who preened and strutted and boasted about the war were the guys who shot themselves in the foot at the motor pool. True heroes, like Cap, had experienced horrors and simply didn't talk about it. Was that a good thing? I wasn't so sure.

Paul and I knew Navy pilots, POWs from the Vietnam era, some who'd been isolated, tortured, starved, held in captivity for five years or more. A few had seemed stable and happy after repatriation, and then later, sometimes *decades* later, woke up in a padded room at Bethesda Naval Hospital under round-the-clock observation.

'What do you suppose happened?' I asked. 'With Nancy, I mean.'

Cap took a deep, shuddering breath and lobbed his empty water bottle slam-dunk into a nearby trash can. 'I always figured Nancy couldn't live with herself for losing the family farm.' He paused. 'A baby? Damn. I didn't know about the baby, of course. If she'd had the baby's death to deal with, too . . .' His voice trailed off.

The baby had to have had a father, I thought, and if Nancy wasn't married . . . well, the early 1950s wouldn't have been an easy place for an unwed mother. She was a teenager on her own, with a dead mother and her only brother a POW in a country half the world away. Who could Nancy turn to? Maybe suicide had seemed like the only way out.

A wave of sadness washed over me. 'So you came home to no family and no farm.'

'It wasn't much of a homecoming,' Cap agreed. 'When I was repatriated in July of '53, I was expecting Nancy to meet me at the airport.' He swallowed hard. 'Cliff Ames the Second showed up instead. Broke the news about Nancy. Took me to a bar. We got stinking drunk.' He smiled at the memory. 'Jobs were scarce after the war, especially for black vets like me. Cliff's father was all into "Honor a Hero: Hire a Vet." He looked out for me and two other homecoming vets, although we had to start at the bottom like everybody else, even Cliff junior.'

I raised an eyebrow.

'Cliff got stuck in the office, filing papers, licking envelopes and making coffee.'

I tried to imagine the Chicken à la King struggling with Maxwell House coffee in a can and an old-fashioned office percolator. 'I would have paid good money to see that,' I chuckled.

'Me? I went to work for Clifton Farms as a chicken catcher,' Cap continued. 'It's hot, dirty work. A bit like slavery, I imagine. Round up the chickens and stuff 'em in cages. Did that for a few years, then ended up working for Ames as a supervisor.

'About ten years ago,' Cap continued, 'Ames junior outsourced the chicken catching to a labor contractor in North Carolina who brought his own people in, paying them half the rates he previously paid to Maryland workers.'

'How much does a chicken catcher get paid?' I asked, genuinely curious.

'It's piece work, Mrs Ives. We used to get paid five dollars and eighty cents per thousand.'

'Per thousand?' I tried to picture myself trying to round up even ten chickens – flapping in panic, squawking, talons digging into my arms – and failed.

'They pay the contract workers two bucks thirty per thousand,' Cap continued. 'I figured that was God's way of telling me it was time to retire.'

Less God and more Clifton Ames, I mused, wondering if Cap felt betrayed by his old friend.

I drained my water bottle and tossed it into the trash can after his. 'So how do you spend your time now, Cap, other than helping out here?'

'About twenty-five years ago my late wife and I bought a little farm that backs up onto the state park. The army was good to me, Mrs Ives. VA loans and other benefits kinda fell into the laps of POWs like me. The army gave us a dollar a day for every day we spent in captivity, plus twenty-six dollars a week for six months to help us get back on our feet. Since I had a job, I was able to save most of it.'

'Do you have a picture of Nancy?' I asked.

Cap reached into his back pocket and pulled out his wallet. From the credit card section, he selected an old black-and-white Polaroid. A petite, light-skinned girl wearing a Sunday go-to-meeting dress and carrying a bouquet of spring flowers beamed out at me from behind the plastic laminate. 'Your sister was beautiful,' I told him. I studied her face, trying to see a family resemblance to the man perched on the windowsill in front of me, the afternoon sun highlighting his tight salt-and-pepper curls.

'You're thinking she looks white,' Cap said after a moment.

I flushed. 'Not really,' I said, although I was. By the way his mouth quirked up in amusement, I didn't think Cap was fooled by my denial.

'Our daddy was white,' Cap continued, 'but he died in the bombing of Pearl Harbor. He was a gunner being trained on the U.S.S. Utah when it was hit.'

'December seventh, 1941. A day that will live in infamy,' I said, quoting Franklin Delano Roosevelt. 'But,' I continued, trying to phrase my question carefully, 'your mom was a Hazlett.

Did she keep her maiden name when she married your dad, or was he a Hazlett, too?'

Cap snorted. 'They never married, Mrs Ives. Couldn't.'

'Couldn't?'

I felt five kinds of stupid when Cap explained, 'Anti-miscegenation laws. Until 1967, it was illegal for blacks to marry whites in the state of Maryland or anywhere else in the south, for that matter.'

'Ah.' I paused to let the terrible significance of that fact sink in.

'While my father was alive, he sent money home. After he died . . .' Cap shrugged. 'No marriage, no widow's benefits. Nothing for us kids, either. Mom went to work cleaning houses.'

The wrongness of his mother's situation brought tears to my eyes.

'That's why I joined the army, actually. A steady paycheck, money to send home.' He flashed a rueful grin. 'An allotment of fifteen dollars a week went a lot further back then.'

I handed Nancy's photo back. 'I'm so, so sorry, Cap.'

Cap tucked the photograph of his sister back into his wallet. 'Thanks. It's OK, really. It was a long, long time ago.'

Nineteen

'Lost Angel of a ruin'd Paradise!
She knew not 'twas her own; as with no stain
She faded, like a cloud which had outwept its
rain.'

Percy Bysshe Shelley, *Adonais*, 1821

When the Tilghman All-County High School moved to a sprawling new campus a mile outside of Elizabethtown, the public library took over the 1940s-style brick school building not far from the courthouse and, after extensive renovation, moved their collection in. In recent years, the facility had expanded to include community meeting rooms, a small movie theater and a computer room that was always busy with patrons – mostly senior citizens – surfing the Internet.

After signing up for a library card at the check-out desk, a helpful librarian wearing an I.D. badge that said 'Kathy Harig – Reference' escorted me to the glassed-in room which housed the library's historical collection of newspapers and magazines, plus several glass-fronted shelves featuring books – both fiction and non-fiction – written by local authors.

'The yearbooks are shelved over here,' Kathy told me. 'I'm pleased to say that we have them going back to the 1920s.'

'I'm looking for Tilghman High School, late 1940s, early 1950s,' I said, thinking back to Nancy's teenage years.

'Black or white?'

'I beg your pardon?'

'Black or white? Schools were segregated in Maryland back then.'

Because of our Navy father, I'd been educated largely on military bases. I'd always attended school with kids of other races, so school segregation was foreign territory to me. As I gaped at the librarian, whose tawny eyes were staring me down, waiting patiently for an answer, a fact floated up from the place in my brain where old high-school civics lessons were stored. 'But wasn't there a Supreme Court decision in the early 1950s that outlawed school segregation?'

'Brown versus Board of Education, yes, in 1954. The ruling struck down the doctrine of "separate but equal" and ordered the states to desegregate schools "with all deliberate speed." Maryland, I'm afraid, had a rather loose interpretation of how speedy "deliberate" was. In this county, for example, it was practically glacial.' She selected a key from the loop clipped to her belt and used it to open one of the glass-fronted cabinets. 'After the Civil Rights Act passed in 1964, Maryland finally had to get its act together. Magnet schools, busing. Fortunately, we had no massive resistance like when Governor Faubus called out the Arkansas National Guard to prevent nine black students from enrolling in a Little Rock high school.' She stood with her back to the open bookcase, hands folded in front of her.

'Orval Faubus,' Kathy said, drawling like a hill-billy in a television sitcom. 'With a name like that, you gotta know the guy's a moron.'

'Dad was stationed in Norfolk back then,' I said. 'I remember that Prince Edward County in central Virginia chose to close all its public schools rather than integrate. The white kids were able to enroll in private schools that excluded blacks, but until the Supreme Court stepped in two years later, the black kids had nowhere to go.'

'Shameful.' Kathy wagged her head. 'So,' she chirped more brightly a heartbeat later, 'do you know which high school you're looking for?'

'Black, I think.'

Kathy pointed to a short row of tall, narrow, red-bound volumes. 'Harriet Tubman H.S.' was embossed on the spines in gold letters. Graduation dates – 1948, 1949, 1950 and so on – had been affixed to the lower edge of the spine by someone on the library staff using black pen on a white label covered with clear tape.

'You planning a reunion or something?' she asked.

I had been studying the bindings and only half heard what she said. 'I beg your pardon?'

'There's been a flurry of interest in the old yearbooks recently. I just wondered if someone was planning a reunion.'

'Not that I know of,' I said, and left it at that. If I looked like I might be organizing a reunion for a black high-school class from the early 1950s, I should probably schedule a facelift and get serious about the SPF in my sunscreen.

'Well, let me know if you need anything,' Kathy added before returning to the short line of patrons waiting impatiently for her at the reference desk.

Left on my own, I plopped my handbag down in a nearby study carrel, dug around for my notebook and pen and got started.

Based on the information I'd gleaned from Nancy Hazlett's tombstone, I figured she would have been a high-school freshman in 1947 or 1948, so I reached for those volumes first.

After browsing through the yearbooks covering 1947 through to 1950, scanning class after class of smiling black faces, it was clear that Nancy Hazlett had not attended Harriet Tubman High. Had she gone to school at all, I wondered, or had she dropped out after junior high, perhaps to help her mother?

I returned the volumes to their proper place on the shelf, then turned my attention to the section where the white yearbooks were shelved.

The Tilghman County High School yearbooks were tall, bulky volumes, bound in blue buckram. In 1932, someone had decided to change the binding to a dirty tan, but apparently thought better of it because, the following year, they'd reverted to blue.

Tiger Tales 1947–1948 had been embossed on the front cover of the first volume I selected, the title arched over an image of a tiger, the school's mascot.

It didn't take me long to find Nancy, smiling out of a one-by-one-and-a-half-inch black-and-white photo, bookended between John Haley and Mary Hendricks.

I flopped back in my chair. Well, well, well. Miss Nancy Hazlett had been passing for white.

As I leafed through the yearbooks, I watched young Nancy mature from a gawky fourteen-year-old into a beautiful young woman. In the tiny photograph allotted to each freshman, Nancy wore bangs and the rest of her hair had been scraped back from her face and gathered into two high, stubby ponytails. Two years later, as a junior, a larger image showed that she was parting her hair on the side in a shorter do, and giving free rein to the curls that massed over her ears and cheeks. She was strikingly beautiful – today, we would say she had movie-star quality – and I could understand why any young man might fall, hard, for that sweet smile and those pale blue eyes – or were they green? It was hard to tell from the black-and-white photographs.

Nancy had been a member of the Future Homemakers of America and the French Club, and she'd sung in the Glee Club. One of the club photos showed her standing in front of the group, dressed in a choir robe. Eyes closed, head thrown back, she clutched a microphone and I could almost hear the solo she must have been belting out when the photographer pressed down on the shutter.

As I browsed through the pages, a familiar face leapt out at me: Clifton Ames in his pre-chicken à la king days. Even without consulting the captions, I would have recognized his photo because of the striking resemblance he bore to his son, Jack.

Clifton Ames had been a year ahead of Nancy in school. In the 1949–1950 yearbook his senior picture showed a fresh-faced, handsome lad with a full head of gleaming blond hair, parted on the right side and slicked back. Cliff's face popped up all over the place – he played football and baseball, was president of the Debate Club, raised a calf with 4H . . . I wondered when the boy had time to study. He played chess with the Chess Club, was in the French Club, served as assistant editor for the school newspaper and . . . I paused, then paged back for a second look at the members of the French Club that year. There he was, two rows above Nancy, posing in the back row along with three other boys, all sporting goofy adolescent grins.

Clifton Ames and Nancy Hazlett were pictured together no fewer than three times, participating in the school activities they both must have enjoyed. As I stared at a photo of the two attractive teens posing side by side for the *Oklahoma!* cast photo – Cliff's Curly to Nancy's Laurey – the chemistry between them seemed unmistakable. Still, reading anything more into the relationship was somewhat of a leap.

By 1950, though, Cliff had graduated and Nancy had dropped out of school, presumably to have her baby. 'Oh, Nancy,' I thought sadly as I ran a finger gently over a photograph taken – according to the caption – at a talent show in her junior year. Nancy was dressed in gingham as Dorothy in the *Wizard of Oz* and singing – I could almost hear it now – 'Somewhere Over the Rainbow.' She was surrounded by a chorus of

154

Munchkins. They wouldn't have been smiling, I mused, if they'd known she was black.

I swallowed hard and began leafing idly through the remaining pages of the yearbook, hoping to stumble across other candid shots of the pair. Perhaps there was an index? I flipped quickly through a large section of ads from local sponsors – Quality Star Auto Parts Congratulates the Class of 1950! – until I reached the back, and there it was. An alphabetical list of students at Tilghman High, the page numbers where their pictures appeared and – incredibly! – their home addresses.

I sat back, stunned. How times had changed.

I quickly located the entry for Nancy Hazlett and was surprised to find not the address that I knew so well because it was my own, but a street and house number in Sturgis, a seaside village about twenty-five miles to the east. Carrying the yearbook, I returned to the reference desk where I stood in line behind a woman inquiring loudly about the Cape May–Lewes ferry schedule. When she moved on – *Forty-five dollars! Highway robbery!* – I quickly took her place.

'More like piracy,' I said.

'Agreed. It can't be highway robbery if you're on the high seas.' Kathy grinned and ran fingers through her silver bangs. 'Did you find what you were looking for?'

'I did.' I laid the yearbook, open to the index, on the desk in front of her and turned it the right way round to face her. 'I can't believe they published the students' home addresses,' I told her.

'Kids were safer then,' she said in a voice tinged with nostalgia. 'Mom used to turn me loose after lunch and I wouldn't come home until she rang the bell for dinner. Sometimes not even then.' She grinned. 'But then I'd get my ass whupped.'

'Do you have any old criss-cross directories?' I asked.

Her eyes widened in surprise. 'Gosh, nobody's asked for one of those in years. Nowadays reverse lookups are all online.'

'I'm curious who is listed at this address in 1949 or 1950,' I said, tracing Nancy's entry in the book with my index finger.

'I'm not sure that the directories for Tilghman County go back that far,' she said, 'but let's have a look.'

I followed Kathy through an unmarked door into a room crowded with desks and carts piled high with books in various stages of processing. Metal shelves at the far end of the room held ancient reference books double-shelved, one row in front of the other, to save space. I recognized most of them from their bindings – *Contemporary Authors, Science Citation Index, Book Review Index* – a format that had been made obsolete, first by microfiche or microfilm, then DVD databases, and finally by the Internet. Kathy knelt, ran her hand experimentally over a series of dusty books on one of the bottom shelves, said, 'Ah ha!' and produced a Polk's Directory for Tilghman County, Maryland from 1952. Carrying the squat, fat volume, she crossed the room, cleared a pile of newspapers off a nearby computer table, set the book down and gestured for me to join her.

Standing beside her, I watched as Kathy leafed through several sections of colored pages, each marked with a tab before selecting the section that was arranged alphabetically by town, street and house number: Sturgis: Oysterbay Road: 308: Ronald and Bernadette Nightingale.

In 1952, according to the demographic data, Ronald and Bernadette were twenty-eight and twenty-six years old, respectively.

'Here's something interesting,' Kathy said. 'House numbers 310 through 312 are listed as belonging to the Free Methodist Church.' She glanced up at me over the top of her reading glasses. 'Do you suppose Ronald Nightingale was its pastor?'

'I'd like to think that Nancy was taken under somebody's wing after her mother died,' I said as I jotted down the information in a notebook I'd brought with me. 'She was only sixteen. A minister and his wife.' I grinned. 'What could be better than that?'

Kathy flipped to another tabbed section and ran her finger down a dense column of numbers. 'Won't do you much good today, I'm afraid, but their phone number back then was TRinity 87. Isn't that a hoot?'

While Kathy had been searching for the phone number, I did a quick calculation. If the Nightingales were still living, and that was a Big If, they'd be in their mid-eighties. And as a pastor, Ronald would long since be retired.

'I wonder who lives at that address now?' I asked the librarian.

Kathy turned to the computer keyboard, tapped

a few keys. 'Your wish is my command,' she said as she waited for the screen to refresh. 'The county pays for access to a whole range of business-related databases.' She paused, leaned closer to the screen. 'Well, how about that?'

'What?' I said.

Behind her glasses, her brown eyes flashed amber. 'Seems like the Nightingales are still living there!'

Kathy hit a key. A printer on the far side of the work room beeped and after a few seconds, a screen print spewed out. 'Thank you,' I said when Kathy handed the printout to me.

'All in a day's work,' she said. 'Are you going to pay them a visit?'

My heart was trying so hard to escape from my chest that I didn't answer. What *was* I going to do with this information?

Kathy picked up the yearbook and handed it back to me. 'My advice? Just drop by.'

Carrying the yearbook clutched to my chest, I followed Kathy out of the work room. When I asked, she directed me to a photocopier where I slotted in my Visa card and made copies of the yearbook pages that featured Nancy. The last photocopy plopped, face up, into the paper tray – Nancy's junior class picture. Wearing a dark cardigan with a white lace-trimmed Peter Pan collar, Nancy's head was tilted up and to the left, away from the photographer; she was smiling at something just out of camera range.

It seemed unthinkable that such a beautiful and vibrant young woman had had only one more year to live.

Twenty

'Often, while contemplating works of art . . . I have felt entering into me a kind of vision of the childhood of their creators. Some little sorrow, some small pleasure of the child, inordinately inflated by an exquisite sensibility, become later on in the adult man, even without his knowing it, the basis of a work of art . . . Genius is nothing but childhood clearly formulated, newly endowed with virile and powerful means of self-expression.'

Charles Baudelaire, *Artificial Paradises*, 'An Opium-eater, VI. The Genius as a Child,' 1860

By the time I got back to *Our Song* from the library, it was after three – too late to pay a visit to the Nightingales, as much as I wanted to. I considered telephoning and had actually picked up my cell phone to do so when it began to vibrate in my hand. I checked the caller I.D.: Fran.

'Steve and I were wondering if you and Paul would like to come back to the house for a drink after the concert tonight,' she said.

Concert? What concert?

'We should wrap up at St Timothy's around eight or eight-thirty,' she continued.

'Right,' I said as the light slowly dawned.

Dang! Did I have to purchase tickets in advance?

'I've arranged for comp tickets. They're holding them at the door,' she barreled on before I'd had a chance to embarrass myself by admitting that the event had completely slipped my mind.

'Thanks, Fran,' I told her, 'but I'll need only one. Should have told you that Paul wasn't able to come this weekend. Teaching sailing to the plebes.'

'No problem,' she said. 'See you later.'

'Can I bring anything?'

'Oh, no,' Fran said. 'It's all taken care of.'

I'll bet, I thought as I hung up the phone. My brownies probably wouldn't have passed her rigid ten-point inspection anyway – color, texture, moisture level, quality of nuts and who knows what else.

I took a quick shower and changed into something more appropriate – a sundress with a lightweight jacket – although I wasn't completely sure what the citizens of Elizabethtown would consider appropriate for a seven o'clock Saturday evening concert.

At six-forty, I parked in my usual spot behind the county courthouse and walked the two blocks to the church, a classic brick colonial with an impressive white wooden steeple. St Timothy's sat well back on a generous lot with mature trees and well-trained boxwood hedges that only two centuries of loving attention can achieve.

The pews were three-quarters full when I entered the sanctuary and the usher told me they were already out of printed programs.

160

Would I mind sharing? I wandered down the aisle looking for a seat next to someone I knew, close enough to hear the music but not so close that I'd be blasted out of my seat by the trumpet section. Frantic waving up front near the baptismal font caught my eye – Caitlyn Dymond, dressed in black jeans, a white shirt and a festively embroidered Mexican vest was trying to attract my attention. She pointed to an empty spot in the pew next to her and mouthed, *For you.*

Rather than crawl over the ten concertgoers already comfortably seated in the pew, I headed up the side aisle to join her. 'Thanks,' I said as I slid into place next to her. 'I was hoping there'd be someone here that I knew. They ran out of programs.'

'Golly,' she said, 'I think the whole town is here.'

Caitlyn was right. Once I got settled in I realized there were many familiar faces in the crowd. Councilman Jack Ames, for example, arm stretched lazily over the back of the pew behind his beautiful wife, Susan. 'Sit any closer,' I said, indicating the pair, 'and he'd be past her.'

Caitlyn snorted, then handed me the program.

As Fran had promised when she first told me about it, the concert opened with Mozart's Violin Concerto No. 4 in D major, a piece in three movements being performed that evening by a soloist named Thomas Glass, an eighteen-year-old freshman at the local community college. The piece was only twenty-five minutes long, so there was no intermission before the Mendelssohn, only the longish pause for extended applause while young Thomas took four well-deserved curtain calls.

'The program says that Mozart wrote that concerto when he was only nineteen,' I commented in the break between pieces. 'And the Italian Symphony was begun when Mendelssohn was only twenty. Factor in our eighteen-year-old violinist, and do I detect a theme?'

'Prodigies,' Caitlyn whispered. 'It's scary. When I was nineteen all I worried about was clothes and makeup and whether the captain of the football team was going to ask me to Homecoming.' She squeezed my arm. 'He was *gorgeous*!'

While the conductor waited in the wings for the orchestra to retune, I noticed that Jack Ames and his wife were taking the opportunity to glad-hand up and down the pews. 'Tacky,' I whispered. 'And where are their children, I wonder? And the dog?'

'I don't know about the dog, Hannah, but there's a nursery in the church basement,' Caitlyn said. 'My kids are down there now, probably running their teenage sitters ragged.'

Dwight sat in a front pew with Grace, of course, as the concert was a benefit for the humane society shelter. I was glad to see them; they certainly deserved a break, and Rusty would not be lacking for caregivers at the hospital. Kim Marquis and the young man who must be her steady boyfriend, Will, gave me a wave, as did Penny, the cashier at the High Spot.

I craned my neck to take in the rest of the

sanctuary. At the back, leaning against a rack of pamphlets, arms folded across his uniformed chest, stood Sheriff Hubbard.

'I wonder if they're any closer to finding out who strangled Kendall?' I whispered to Caitlyn.

'Half the people in this room had a motive.' She grinned. 'You. Me.' She jerked her head in the direction of the Ames. 'Jack, too.'

'Really?'

'Oh, they look all lovey-dovey now, him and Sue, but last year at the real estate office there was a huge blowup.'

'Oooh, tell me about it.'

'Well, Kendall's got this tract of land north of town. It's zoned agricultural, but if she could get the city council to zone it commercial, she'd make a killing. She's been contributing heavily to Jack's campaign. You scratch my back and I'll scratch yours, you know. She told me a couple of weeks ago that the zoning was in the bag.'

'The blowup?' I reminded her.

'Oh, yeah. Well, Jack had been spending a lot of time with Kendall at the office. One night I was working late putting up new listings in the front office window when Sue barged in breathing fire.' Caitlyn leaned in and lowered her voice even further. 'Jack was with Kendall in her office with the door shut.'

'Were they having an affair?' I asked.

She shrugged. 'Who knows? But I hardly think they'd be screwing in there with me in the next office with my ear pressed to the wall. So to speak.' She paused. 'I think they used to have a thing going, but that was way back in high school,

163

before Jack even met Susan. I honestly don't know how she did it.'

'Did what?'

Caitlyn smiled wickedly. 'Kendall had the knack for staying on friendly terms with all her ex-boyfriends. Me? I loathe my two exes, not that I ever married either of them. Boyd is my one and only.'

'Is he here? Boyd, I mean?'

'My husband? Sadly, no. He's in the National Guard training recruits up in Elkton this weekend. And there's another of Kendall's conquests,' she said, indicating with a sideways jerk of her head the Chicken à la King who had just entered the church and had stopped to chat with Sheriff Hubbard.

'Whoa, Nellie! Are you saying that Kendall and Clifton Ames were once an item?'

'It's common knowledge, Hannah. Happened not long after Dwight started dating Grace. But if Kendall hoped to make Dwight jealous, she failed miserably. Grace was, *is* a treasure and Dwight knew it.' She snapped her fingers. 'He married Grace just like that. And just look at them,' she continued. 'See the way he looks at her when she's talking, like what she's saying is the most important thing in all the world, like The Sermon on the Mount or something.'

But I was looking in the other direction, toward the rear of the sanctuary where Clifton Ames seemed to be pointing out something in the program to the sheriff. How come *he* got a copy and I didn't? I thought sourly. 'Is Sheriff Hubbard a music-lover?' I asked Caitlyn.

'Andy? Nah. Not sure why he's here.' She nudged me with her elbow. 'Expecting trouble from the brass section, maybe?'

'Maybe he's keeping his eye on a suspect,' I suggested.

'Well, I think he's interviewed pretty much everybody in town. Half of them are in this room tonight, you'll notice.'

'He interviewed you, too?'

'Oh, yeah. They even asked for a DNA swab – for purposes of elimination.'

'You gave them one?' I asked.

'Sure. Why not? I didn't kill the stupid bitch.'

Nobody had asked Paul or me for a DNA sample, but I didn't tell Caitlyn that. Fortunately, I was saved from having to think of a way to gracefully change the subject by the conductor's return to the podium. Within seconds, the orchestra was off and running with the Mendelssohn.

When the concert was over, Caitlyn and I followed the crowd out to the meditation garden on the east side of the church where a table had been set up to serve lemonade and assorted cookies and cakes donated by the Women's Fellowship. My hand was hovering over the platter of chocolate-chip cookies with the hope of landing on the one having the most chocolate chips when Sheriff Hubbard approached us.

'Caitlyn Dymond, may I speak with you for a moment, please?'

Caitlyn laughed. 'My, how formal we're being this evening, Andy. Have some lemonade,' she added, gesturing at the table with her acrylic glass. 'You've been working too hard.'

Hubbard didn't smile and made no move toward the lemonade.

'What?' Caitlyn said, her face suddenly ashen. 'It's Boyd, isn't it? Something's happened to Boyd!'

With her free hand, Caitlyn grabbed my arm and squeezed. 'Oh, Hannah, if something's happened to Boyd, I'll just die!'

'It's not Boyd, Mrs Dymond. Is there someplace we can go where we can talk?'

Caitlyn stiffened. Lemonade sloshed over the rim of her glass and dribbled over her hand, but I don't think she noticed. 'Andy Hubbard, you tell me now or I'm not moving from this spot!'

Hubbard flushed; sweat beaded his brow. 'Caitlyn Dymond, I am arresting you for the murder of Kendall Barfield.' As if on cue, Hubbard's deputy materialized out of the boxwood, a pair of handcuffs dangling from his hand.

'Noooo!' she moaned as Hubbard read Caitlyn her rights.

'You have the right to remain silent. Anything you say can and will be used against you in a court of law. You have the right to an attorney. If you cannot afford an attorney, one will be provided for you.'

I grabbed Caitlyn by the arm and pulled her close. 'Do not say anything, Caitlyn, you hear me? Tell him you want to call your attorney. Tell him now.'

'I don't have an attorney, Hannah,' she croaked. The acrylic glass she held cracked and fell to the lawn in pieces as the deputy gently turned her around and, looking up at me apologetically, handcuffed Caitlyn's hands behind her back.

'Do you understand the rights I have just read to you?' Hubbard said.

Caitlyn nodded.

'Yes or no? I'm sorry, Caitlyn, but you have to say it.'

Her voice wavered, but she managed a quiet, 'Yes.'

The chit-chat in the garden had died down. The burry chirp of an evening grosbeak filled the sudden silence; a car somewhere in the distance tooted its horn. 'I can't say anything to you without a lawyer present.' Caitlyn's eyes locked on mine. 'My children! What about my children!' she shouted into the crowd of concertgoers as they parted to let the officers dragging Caitlyn weeping and stumbling through.

'Someone from Social Services . . .' Hubbard began.

'You'll do no such thing!' I shouted. I lurched after Caitlyn. 'I'll pick up the kids, don't worry. When you get to the station, call Boyd. You hear me? Tell him that I have the children. He'll know what to do.'

'I didn't do it, Hannah,' she wailed. 'Honestly, this is all a huge mistake!'

'Couldn't this have waited until Monday morning?' I snapped at the sheriff's heels as his deputy folded Caitlyn into the back seat of the police vehicle and closed the door. 'I can't think of anyone who is less of a flight risk than Caitlyn. You know that as well as I do.'

'The warrant came through at the end of the day and I didn't want to wait until morning to serve it,' the sheriff explained.

I knew the tactic. Arrest the suspect late on Friday and let them languish in a cell over the weekend, breaking down their resistance while waiting to be arraigned when the court convened again on Monday morning. It seemed a dirty trick to play on the mother of three young children whose husband was a Weekend Warrior sacrificing family time to serve his country.

Caitlyn had slumped in the back seat of the patrol car, her head bowed as if trying to make herself as small as possible. I rapped on the window to attract her attention, pressed my fingers against the glass. 'I'll make some calls. Stay quiet. Stay cool.'

On the other side of the glass, Caitlyn, with tears streaming down her face, pressed her fingertips to mine.

The sun had not yet risen the following morning before there was a knock at my front door. I crawled out of bed, staggered to the bedroom window and pulled the curtain aside. In the gray light of dawn I saw a Honda Pilot parked in the drive. I opened the window and called out, 'I'll be right down,' to whomever might be standing on the porch below.

I crawled into a pair of jeans, threw a T-shirt over my head and padded barefoot down to the front door. I opened it a crack and peered out.

'I'm Boyd Dymond, Mrs Ives,' my visitor said, although I hardly needed the introduction.

Caitlyn's husband was dressed in rumpled camouflage fatigues and combat boots caked with dried mud. 'I'm here to pick up the kids.'

'Come in, come in,' I said, holding the door wide. 'They're still asleep upstairs. By the time I got them tucked into the sleeping bags we use for the grandkids, it was kind of a late night. Let's not wake them up just yet.' I studied his swollen eyelids, the ravaged, unshaven face. 'Looks like you could use a cup of coffee.'

'Frankly,' Boyd said, stepping into the entrance hall, his camouflage cap crushed in one beefy hand, 'I'm all coffeed out, but I could sure use a glass of ice water.'

I got Boyd settled in the kitchen with a tall glass of ice water, then made myself a cup of coffee and joined him at the table. 'How's Caitlyn?'

'She's still at the county jail,' he told me. 'She'll be arraigned on Monday.'

'On what possible evidence?' I asked.

Boyd pressed a thumb and forefinger to either side of his nose and massaged his tired eyes. 'Stupid, stupid, stupid!'

'What?'

'Caitlyn was pissed, *really* pissed about that salesperson of the year thing. The guy who won the trip?'

I nodded, encouraging him to continue.

'Caitlyn had trained him, for Christ's sake.'

'I saw how upset she was at the picnic,' I told Boyd. 'But going from upset to murder is quite a leap.'

'Oh, Caitlyn didn't kill Kendall, Mrs Ives. She wouldn't kill anybody. We've got three kids! She couldn't . . . wouldn't do that to them.'

'On what evidence are they holding her, then?'

'Apparently they have witnesses. One of the musicians was on a break, having a smoke by the pool. He claims to have seen Caitlyn on the patio by the swimming pool, yelling at Kendall in front of one of the cabanas. Some kids hanging around the pool claim to have seen it, too.'

'Are the witnesses sure it was Caitlyn?' I asked.

'There was no mistaking my wife, not in that red poppy sundress she was wearing.'

'Right. I see.'

'Anyway, Caitlyn admits to a lot of shouting and arm waving, says she told Kendall she could take her job and shove it where the sun don't shine, but that's all.'

By this time I'd stopped breathing altogether. 'And?' I prodded.

'According to this drummer's story, in the middle of all the shouting, Caitlyn grabbed Kendall's scarf. Caitlyn denies this, of course.'

'Ouch!' I said. 'But did this drummer actually *see* Caitlyn strangle Kendall?'

Boyd bowed his head and spoke into his hands. 'No. His break was over. He got called back to the bandstand so he doesn't know what happened after that.'

'I'm no expert, Boyd, but I honestly don't see how they can charge Caitlyn with murder based on such circumstantial evidence.'

170

'That's what I told the cops, but unfortunately there's more.'

'More?'

'They found one of Caitlyn's fingernails caught up in Kendall's scarf. They matched it to Caitlyn's DNA.'

I flashed back to the picnic, to Caitlyn's ruined patriotic manicure. 'Damn.'

'What am I going to do, Mrs Ives?'

'Well, first, you can start calling me Hannah.' After a moment, I asked, 'Do you have a good lawyer?'

Boyd nodded. 'Caitlyn's father has connections. The guy left a dinner party in Baltimore to drive over here and meet with her. He's there with her now.'

'Excellent. I'm sure he'll be able to get Caitlyn out on bail.' I stood, walked behind his chair and rested a comforting hand on his shoulder. 'I'll bet she'll be home by dinnertime on Monday.'

Boyd studied me with sad eyes. 'I hope you're right.'

'Of course I'm right. Now, you're going upstairs to wake up those children and tell them they're going out for breakfast.'

'Breakfast? Where?'

'Where else? McDonalds.'

Twenty-One

*'Did that woman, could that woman,
somehow know that here before her very eyes
. . . sat a Negro? Absurd! Impossible! White
people were so stupid about such things for
all that they usually asserted that they were
able to tell and by the most ridiculous
means: fingernails, palms of hands, shapes of
ears, teeth, and other equally silly rot. They
always took her for an Italian, a Spaniard, a
Mexican, or a gipsy. Never, when she was
alone, had they even remotely seemed to
suspect that she was a Negro.'*

Nella Larson, *Passing*, Knopf, 1929, pp. 18–19

With three unfamiliar children in the house, it
had been a long, restless night. After Boyd belted
his kids into the Honda and drove them off to
McDonalds, I went back to bed, fully dressed,
sleeping through the alarm that would have gotten
me up in time to go to church.

Shortly after noon, I crawled out from under
the covers, dazed and blinking into the sunlight
streaming in through the bedroom window. I
wolfed down a peanut butter sandwich and a
bowl of tomato soup, then checked in with
Paul.

'Boyd came for the children,' I told him. 'And

Caitlyn's father has sent over a hot shot lawyer, so things are under control for the moment.'

After commiserating with me for a minute or two, Paul told me he was going sailing with his sister, Connie and her husband, Dennis.

'I hate you,' I said. 'I hate you all. Tell them I said so.'

Paul laughed. 'What are you planning to do today?'

Before Caitlyn's arrest had thrown everything out of kilter, item number one on my To Do list was interviewing Ronald and Bernadette Nightingale in Sturgis, Maryland. There was nothing more I could do to help Caitlyn, so visiting the Nightingales had just shot back to the top of the list. 'I'm planning to drop in on a couple who almost certainly knew Nancy Hazlett as a teen,' I told him. 'They were in their twenties back then, so that means they're pushing ninety now. If I'm lucky they'll still be at that address and they'll still have, you know, all their marbles.'

In recent years, I'd volunteered in the memory unit at Calvert Colony, a high-end continuing care retirement community near my home in Annapolis. I knew, first hand, what havoc old age could wreak on the mind. 'Time, as they say, may be of the essence.'

'Good luck, then. Be careful, my dear.'

'Always,' I said. I blew a kiss into the telephone and hung up.

The drive from my home to Sturgis took less than twenty minutes. Following the advice of my GPS – in the voice of comedian John Cleese – I entered the town and turned left onto a quiet, tree-lined and curb-less street.

Your destination is ahead, on the right.

I slowed and studied the house numbers. Number 308 Oysterbay Road was a neat, one-story rancher immediately next door to a modest, white clapboard church. An oversized white sign installed on the lawn in front of the church told me in big red letters that I'd reached Bayside Methodist Church. Smaller black letters below invited me to worship there on Sunday at eleven a.m. or, if I preferred, to attend a praise service at seven p.m. on Wednesday night. 'Taste and see that the Lord is good,' read the bottom of the sign and, below that: Pastor John Neal.

Although it was Sunday, church was long over, the parking lot empty. I pulled in, parked, walked the short distance back to number 308 and climbed the front steps. There was no sign of a doorbell, so I opened the screen door and knocked briskly on the solid wood door behind it.

My knock was answered by an apple dumpling of a woman wearing a blue-checked apron dusted with flour. 'Sorry,' she said, wiping her hands clean of flour on the apron. 'You caught me making cookies for the bake sale on Saturday.'

I introduced myself. 'And you must be Bernadette Nightingale.'

'I am indeed. Come in, come in,' she said, stepping aside to let me pass. 'I need a break anyway. Would you care for some iced tea?'

'I don't want to put you to any trouble.'

Bernadette's gray eyes peered at me from

behind a pair of round tortoiseshell eyeglasses. That, plus the no-nonsense, short-cropped hair gave her an old-fashioned scholarly look. 'No trouble at all, Hannah,' she said. 'I've just brewed a pitcher. It'll only take a minute to get it together.'

'I'd love some tea, then,' I told her. 'It's been a hot day.'

'So, how can we help you?' she asked as she led me past the kitchen. My stomach rumbled as the unmistakable smell of warm chocolate and vanilla wafted into the hallway, teasing my nostrils and making me regret my skimpy lunch.

We. That was a good sign. Ronald Nightingale must still be alive.

'My husband and I just moved to Elizabethtown,' I told her as she opened the screen door leading to the back porch and we stepped through.

'Are you looking for a church home, then?' she asked, smiling. 'Although Sturgis is a bit out of the way for Elizabethtown, isn't it?'

I smiled back. 'We already have a church home, I'm happy to say. Saint Timothy's in Elizabethtown.'

'Ah, yes. Episcopalians.'

'Dyed in the wool,' I said.

'My husband is retired now, but he used to be the minister at the Methodist church next door, back before the merger. We were EUB in the old days.'

'EUB?' I'd never heard of that denomination.

'Sorry. Evangelical United Brethren Church. We merged with the Methodists in 1968.'

'This was the parsonage, I gather?'

'Yes. When they built the new parsonage – perhaps you saw the fancy brick house around the corner? – the church allowed us to buy this one.' She smiled. 'A love gift, really. Except for the years we spent doing missionary work, we've lived here since our twenties, so we were very grateful.' She gestured toward a wrought-iron chair. 'Won't you have a seat?'

'Paul and I just bought the old Hazlett place on Chiconnesick Creek,' I told her as I scooted the chair out from under the table and sat down in it. 'Perhaps you know it?'

Bernadette stared at me for a moment without blinking. Then she closed her eyes, took a deep breath and blew it out slowly through her lips. When she opened her eyes again, it was to say, 'I knew this day would come.'

'Do you want to tell me about it?' I asked.

She chewed her lower lip, then said, 'It's a long story.'

I smiled in what I hoped was a friendly, non-confrontational way. 'I'm not in any hurry.'

Inexplicably, her face brightened. 'I'm sorry, I promised you some tea! I'll be right back.'

I shot to my feet and said, 'Can I help?' Now that I'd come so close, I didn't want to let the woman out of my sight.

She raised a cautionary hand, chuckled, said, 'No, no. It'll only take a minute. I'll be right back,' and disappeared into the kitchen.

I passed the time by admiring the beautifully manicured lawn and her well-tended vegetable garden, surrounded by chicken wire fencing to protect it, I assumed, from hungry deer. Tomatoes, peppers, cucumbers, carrots – I was constructing a mental salad when Bernadette called out, 'See, that didn't take long,' and reappeared with a tray holding a pitcher of tea, three glasses, a plate of cookies dusted with confetti-colored sugar, and an elderly man I took to be her husband.

'Ronald Nightingale,' the man said, extending his hand. Pastor Nightingale wore a white polo shirt tucked into a pair of green-plaid Bermuda shorts that ended just north of two knobby knees. From his tawny complexion I suspected it was Ronald, not Bernadette, who was responsible for the orderly garden.

Bernadette glared at her husband. 'Hat!'

Ronald's cheeks flushed. 'Be right back,' he said. When he returned, an Orioles baseball cap had been pulled on over his bald head. A few wispy white hairs stuck out of the opening at the back.

Once we were settled around the table with glasses of tea, Bernadette spilled the beans. 'Hannah is here about Nancy Hazlett.'

If Ronald was surprised, his face didn't show it. 'When I read about the baby in the chimney, I was afraid . . .' His voice trailed off.

'There's been no positive I.D.,' I said softly, 'but the child was wrapped in a newspaper from 1951.'

Bernadette stole a look at her husband. 'I told you we should have taken her with us.' There was nothing accusatory in her tone, simply anguish, raw and deep.

Ronald seized her hand and held it tight against

177

his thigh. 'We can't second guess ourselves now, Bernie. It seemed like the right thing to do at the time.'

My attention had been focused on Ronald, so I didn't realize, at first, that Bernadette was quietly crying. She turned her tear-stained face to me. 'Nancy was just starting her senior year and she'd gotten the lead in the school musical,' she sobbed. 'It seemed cruel to drag her away to Angola.'

'Angola?' I was losing the plot.

'In 1951, God called us to the EUB mission station in Quéssua, Angola,' Ronald explained. 'Bernie taught nursing and I ran the agricultural station.'

'We were there for a year,' Bernadette added.

'Was Nancy a parishioner, then?' I asked.

'In a manner of speaking, she was,' Bernadette said.

Ronald returned his wife's hand to her own lap and patted it. 'Let me tell the story, Bernie.

'When we were young, still in our twenties,' Ronald began, 'we got the call to United Brethren here in Sturgis. I was fresh out of seminary.'

Bernadette leaned forward. 'We couldn't believe our luck.'

'Yes,' her husband agreed, then grinned. 'They must have been desperate to hire a newbie like me. Anyway, we needed a person to clean the church and someone recommended Mary Hazlett. Her husband had been killed during the war, you know.'

I nodded.

'Mary came twice a week . . .'

'On Mondays and Thursdays,' Bernadette chimed in.

'On Mondays and Thursdays, yes, and we grew close to her.'

'So, that's how you met Nancy.'

Ronald nodded. 'Mary would sometimes bring Nancy along while she worked. Bright as a button, that little girl was.' Ronald smiled at the memory. 'Wasting away in that dreadful all Negro school down near Pocomoke. A crime, really. Nobody'd put up with it for a minute these days, but times were different back then.' He took several long swallows of tea, his Adam's apple bobbing, then set the glass down on the tabletop. 'Even before we lost Mary . . .' He leaned forward, whispered, 'cancer,' then forged on, '. . . Bernie took Nancy under her wing, tutored her here at the parsonage, mostly in math and science. But Nancy's real talent was music. That was obvious from an early age. She played the piano and sang in our choir.'

'And solos,' Bernadette interjected. She closed her eyes, drifted somewhere far away and began to sing, 'Oh, sometimes I feel like a motherless child . . .'

Ronald squeezed his wife's apron-covered knee. 'It's OK, sweetheart.'

Ronald waited patiently for Bernadette to finish the stanza, her ruined soprano wavering, slowly dying away, before continuing, 'One day, Bernie and I had a long discussion and decided we had to do something about it.'

Ronald's eyes cut sideways. 'Have you seen any photographs of Nancy?'

179

'I have.'

'Ah, well you understand, then.' He coughed and cleared his throat. 'So one day, with Mary's permission, I put Nancy in my car and drove her up to the high school in Elizabethtown. Registered her as my niece from Chicago, my late sister's child. It was a lie, of course, but one I know God will forgive me for.'

'Nancy was such a talented young girl,' Bernadette said. 'She would have languished in that poor black school. "Separate but equal!" What a crock. Rundown buildings, untrained teachers, ancient textbooks, no extra-curricular activities to speak of.'

'They asked for her transcript from the school in Chicago, no surprise, and I told them it was on the way,' Ronald continued. 'The principal telephoned me about her missing records again about a month later, but by that time he'd heard Nancy sing and I don't think it mattered much anymore. Just a freshman, and they gave her the lead in the school musical . . .' He paused to consult his wife. 'What was the show, my dear?'

'Gilbert and Sullivan,' she replied. 'Nancy played Yum-Yum in the *Mikado*.'

'She was making straight As, too,' Ronald added.

'Wouldn't they have written to the Chicago school directly for the transcript?' I asked.

'Oh, they did!' Bernadette glanced sideways at her husband, as if waiting for permission to go on.

He laid a gnarled hand on her arm. 'It's OK,

Bernie. It was a long time ago, and Marilyn's been gone for years. She won't mind. Tell her.'

Bernadette leaned forward and spoke quietly. 'The school secretary, Marilyn Daniels, was one of our parishioners. She figured out what we were doing and confronted me about it after church one day. I panicked!' She pressed a hand to her chest. 'But you know what? She understood. Completely. And she made the whole transcript problem go away. It simply vanished – poof! We never heard one more word about Miss Nancy Hazlett's school records from Chicago, and nobody *ever* suspected she was passing for white.

'And then, just before Nancy's senior year, we left for the mission station in Angola,' she said.

'Bernie wanted to take Nancy with us,' Ronald said, 'but Nancy and I talked her out of it. Nancy planned to finish her senior year and apply for a music scholarship at Peabody in Baltimore, and Marilyn convinced me her chances of that were slim to none if she missed out on her last year of high school.'

'But if Nancy was pregnant . . .' Bernadette choked on the word.

'Did Nancy have any boyfriends?' I asked as gently as I could.

'She had lots of friends,' Ronald said, 'but I don't remember any one in particular.'

Bernadette tapped her temple with an index finger. 'At our age, the hard drive is pretty full. If I could just get rid of all those advertising jingles from the fifties, or reruns of *I Love Lucy*, I'd be able to store more information up here.'

'Nancy was a popular girl,' Ronald said. 'Until

she got her driver's license it seemed I was always picking her up after one extra-curricular event or another.'

'Oh, why didn't she confide in us?' Bernadette wailed. 'We could have *helped*!' She jumped up, threw open the screen door and disappeared into the house.

'Bernie has always blamed herself for Nancy's suicide,' Ronald said softly once his wife was out of earshot.

Feeling like a voyeur, I stood. 'I'm sorry. Maybe I'd better go.'

'No, stay. Please. A nice long cry will do Bernie good. It's been sixty years in coming.'

'Did Nancy continue to live here while you were in Angola?' I asked once I'd retaken my seat.

'Oh, no. There was an interim pastor, a single man. Nancy convinced us that she could manage on her own at the farm and we'd given her our car to drive, of course. She was almost eighteen, after all, and very mature for her age.'

'Her brother showed me a photograph, and I'd have to agree.'

'Ah, yes, poor Thomas, coming home to . . .' He paused. 'Well, to nothing. Three years in a prisoner of war camp can mess with your mind, then to lose your mother, your sister and the family farm all in one fell swoop the minute you step off the plane.'

I shuddered.

'It doesn't bear thinking about.'

'Cap, uh, Thomas mentioned a wife.'

'Tanya. A real prize, that woman. Thomas got

himself a job at Clifton Farms and Tanya worked in the office there. Came into his life at just the right time, Tanya did. Gave him the stability he needed.'

'Did they have any children?'

Ronald shook his head. 'Some medical issue, I understand. Sadly, Tanya's been gone for a couple of years now, but we're all getting old. Some days I wonder how I can keep putting one foot in front of the other,' he chuckled. 'Use it or lose it, as they say.'

Me, too, I thought. We seemed to be straying off target, though, so I guided him back as gently as I could by asking, 'How did you find out about Nancy's death?'

Ronald sighed heavily. 'We wrote to Nancy every week. At first, we'd hear back, but after three months her letters stopped coming. We didn't worry at first. I thought it was just the usual difficulty with getting mail delivered in a third world country. But when I finally got to a telephone and was able to reach Marilyn . . .' His voice trailed off. 'Oh, we simply couldn't believe it! Suicide! No way. Not our Nancy.'

'Passing must have taken a toll on her,' I suggested kindly. 'Always looking over her shoulder, always afraid that someone would find out she was black. How she must have longed to be white.'

'Oh, no, you don't understand at all, Mrs Ives. Nancy didn't want to be white. Nancy just wanted to be free.'

Twenty-Two

'Those who have been once intoxicated with power, and have derived any kind of emolument from it, even though but for one year, can never willingly abandon it.'

Edmund Burke, Letter to a Member of the National Assembly, 1791

Kim and I were sitting in her office, drinking coffee out of proper cups and saucers, discussing my findings in the library and what I'd learned from my visit with the Nightingales when there was a knock on the door behind me. Before Kim could rest her cup in its saucer, the door swung open and Clifton Ames eased into the room, his signature cigarillo clamped between his teeth.

The tip glowed red as he sucked air through the roll of noxious weed. When he removed it from between his lips long enough to say, 'Good morning, ladies, I hope I'm not interrupting anything,' gray smoke curled toward the ceiling.

Kim wrinkled her nose.

I made a production of fanning smoke away from my face.

'You can't smoke in here, Mr Ames,' Kim told the Chicken à la King.

'Oh, yeah. Sorry.' He waved the cigarillo around a bit helplessly. 'Ashtray?'

184

Kim snatched the saucer from under her cup and pushed it across the desk.

Ames snubbed the offending cigarillo out, then grabbed a straight-back chair from the corner, dragged it over next to mine and sat down in it. 'Mrs Ives.'

I was impressed that he remembered my name. It had been several weeks since Kendall's party.

'What can I do for you, Mr Ames?' Kim wanted to know.

'I'll get right to the point,' he said. 'I was talking to Fran Lawson at Kendall's shindig a while back and she told me about the work the historical society is doing in the basement here. Now that Kendall's gone, I'm wondering if you need someone to pick up the tab on the office space, the computers and such.'

I'd been wondering about that, too, and it was, in fact, one of the questions I had for Kim on my list, so I was relieved when she replied, 'I think we're in good shape there, Mr Ames. Fortunately, Kendall paid the rental on everything in advance, so we're good for another three months at least. After that . . .' She shrugged. 'Perhaps after that I'll give you a call. It's thoughtful of you to volunteer.'

Ames rubbed his lower lip, seemingly uncomfortable without his familiar cigar. 'What you got down there anyway?'

Kim smiled warily. 'We're not exactly sure. That's where Fran Lawson and Hannah here come in. It's our very good fortune that they live in Tilghman County and that they're both trained records managers.'

'We're making a complete inventory, Mr Ames,' I explained. 'Once we know exactly what we have we'll share the list with the Maryland State Archives in Annapolis. Some of the material will undoubtedly be transferred directly to them. The rest? Well, we'll see.'

'According to the records retention schedule established by Maryland law,' Kim added, 'most of what we found belonged to various county offices and could have been discarded in the 1960s and 70s.'

'Why didn't they? Destroy them, that is?'

Kim twirled a pencil between her fingers, as if considering how to answer his question. 'In 1975, the courthouse was extensively renovated. The funds became available rather suddenly – end of year money, I suppose – so everyone had to hustle to clear out their offices before the painters arrived. They needed a convenient place to store their files temporarily, so they moved them into the basement. But after the painters left, the records never went back.'

'Can't you just give them back to the various offices now, let them deal with it? What are we talking about anyway? Traffic tickets?'

Kim smiled. 'The historical society would hardly be interested in traffic court records, Mr Ames. No, there are some indexes going back to the nineteenth century that we think will prove invaluable to genealogists. Land records, marriage indexes, chattel mortgages . . . material like that.'

'There are some real treasures in those boxes,' I added. 'We found a packet of letters written home by a local soldier during World War One.'

As I spoke, Clifton Ames's eyes never left my face.

'Some of the material is too water damaged to save, I'm afraid,' I said, shifting uncomfortably in my chair.

He continued to stare. What was the man's problem?

A light flashed in my brain. It flashed on so brightly and with such an audible click that I feared, for a second, that Ames might have heard it, too.

This is all about the early 1950s. Clifton J Ames the Second, the man presently giving me the hairy eyeball, had been young back then. Sixteen, seventeen tops? But what about his father, Clifton J Ames the First? It was he who had set up a shadow company, Liberty Land Development, specifically to buy up land from small, predominately black farmers like Cap Hazlett's mother, Mary Hazlett, land on which the sprawling Clifton Farms processing plant now stood. What if there had been something fishy about those transactions? What if we were, quite literally, sitting over the evidence of his father's shady deals? If they should come to light, it would reflect negatively on the family, and might even put the kibosh on Jack Ames's promising political career.

I shot the Chicken à la King a toothy grin. 'Thank you so much for your offer, Mr Ames. And if Fran and I run into any trouble, you will be the first person we call.'

After he left, another thought struck me like a

bolt of lightning out of the blue. In the early 1950s, Clifton J Ames the Second had been too young to negotiate land deals, but I knew from the Tilghman Tigers yearbook that he had attended high school with Cap's sister, Nancy. He'd starred in a musical with her. What if . . .

I plucked a tissue out of the box Kim kept on her desk and used it to retrieve Ames's cigarillo from the saucer. 'Kim, do you have a paper bag or a box or something I can put this into?'

'Are you out of your mind?'

'I'm in love with the man,' I said, dangling the disgusting object between my thumb and forefinger over the saucer while Kim scrabbled around in her desk drawer. 'I want to keep his cigar forever, in a locket around my neck, close to my heart.'

Kim laughed out loud. 'You are a nut.' She held up a Ziploc sandwich bag. 'Will this do?'

'No, it can't be plastic.'

'Because . . .?'

'I can tell you don't watch enough *CSI*,' I said. 'Because it might spoil the DNA results.'

Kim stared. 'My God, you're serious.'

'Deadly,' I said.

Kim opened a drawer, reached in, and upended a box over her desk blotter. Columns of staples tumbled out. 'This should work, right?' she asked, handing the empty box over.

'Perfectly,' I said, sliding Ames's distinctive Bonnie and Clyde cigarillo into the box. 'Now I just need to convince Andy Hubbard that I'm not a nutcase.'

* * *

188

The Elizabethtown Police Station sat on the edge of town near the railroad tracks, adjacent to the train station that had been restored and converted into a charming florist shop named the Watering Can.

Inside the single story brick building I found myself in a boxy waiting room, with a water cooler in one corner and a gumball machine sponsored by the local Lion's Club in the other. A uniformed police officer sat at a desk behind a glass window on the right, talking on the telephone and taking notes. I waited until she finished the call, then tapped on the glass. 'Excuse me?'

She looked up. 'How can I help you, ma'am?'

'I'm here to see Sheriff Hubbard,' I said. 'Is he in?'

'He's on the phone. Who should I tell him is here?'

'It's Hannah. Hannah Ives.'

A few minutes later, I sat on one side of Hubbard's gray metal desk and he on the other. My makeshift paper evidence 'bag' lay like an exclamation point on the desktop between us.

It's fair to say that Andy Hubbard was not impressed with my sleuthing skills. 'And you want me to have this analyzed, why?'

'I suspect that Clifton Ames was the father of Baby Ella. If you could have the lab compare the DNA on this cigar with the baby's DNA . . .' I shrugged. Even to my ears it sounded lame.

'May I remind you that, according to the medical examiner, the baby died of natural causes.' It was a statement, not a question.

'I realize that. It's not the baby's cause of death that I'm questioning, it's her mother's.'

The shadow of a smile played across Hubbard's face. 'The mother. You mean Nancy Hazlett?'

That caught me off guard, but if I could figure it out, it shouldn't surprise me to learn that the police had, too. 'Ah. You're steps ahead of me, I see.'

'Do you know Thomas Hazlett?'

'Cap? Of course. He's helping us clean up the mess with the records in the courthouse. Nancy was his sister.'

'Exactly. After the baby's body was found, Cap contacted us. He thought it likely that the child had belonged to his sister, so he volunteered to be tested. We performed avuncular DNA analysis and the results showed an unusually high kinship index. We can say with confidence that the child's mother was a close relative of Cap Hazlett. The obvious conclusion is Nancy.'

I leaned forward. Using my index finger, I pushed the cardboard Swingline staple box a millimeter closer to his side of the blotter. 'And I can say with some confidence that the guy who smoked this cigar is probably the baby's father.'

Hubbard breathed in noisily through his nose then let it out slowly. 'Did Cap put you up to this?'

'Cap? Of course not. It's just that I've been talking to an elderly minister and his wife who knew Nancy quite well. They remember that she was pretty sweet on Clifton Ames the Second,' I said, embroidering just a bit. 'Black girl, white

190

boy, a baby. Seems like a recipe for disaster, especially back in those days.'

'I think you and Cap Hazlett need to concentrate on getting the courthouse basement squared away and let me do my job.'

'So you don't think the identity of Baby Ella's father is of any importance?'

'Not particularly. Unless a crime was committed because of it.'

'That's my point exactly!'

Hubbard rolled his chair back a few inches and stretched his legs out to one side. 'Did you have Ames's permission to take this sample?'

'Of course not.'

'A court order?'

'Now you're making fun of me, Sheriff.'

'What I'm trying to tell you, Mrs Ives, is that you are not, as far as I know, a trained specimen collector. And even if you were, the chain of custody on this evidence you're bringing me is crap.' He waved a hand over the staple box as if shooing away flies. 'How will we know this cigar wasn't planted or tampered with?'

'Kim Marquis was sitting right there with me when Cliff . . .'

'Save your breath, Mrs Ives. Courts of law require a strict paper trail. A police officer hands evidence off to the evidence clerk, the evidence clerk to the lab and so on. At each step, someone has to sign a form. The lab won't even accept a sample if it isn't accompanied by the appropriate paperwork.'

'I guess it was naive of me to think that small town law enforcement would be more . . .' I paused, choosing my words carefully. 'More laid-back about crime investigation.'

Hubbard bristled. 'May I remind you that there was no crime here? One day, a long time ago, a child died of polio. Shortly thereafter, her mother committed suicide. Why, we don't know, but we can guess.'

'But what if Nancy Hazlett didn't commit suicide? What if she was murdered?'

This time Hubbard groaned. 'Next thing I know you'll be asking me to get a court order to dig up Nancy Hazlett's body.'

'You must be reading my mind.'

Hubbard stood. 'Not gonna happen, Mrs Ives. Now if you or Cap think of anything else that might be helpful, please do not hesitate to let me know.'

I was being dismissed. 'The cigar?' I asked as I headed for the door.

'You want it?'

'Ick, no.'

'I'll take care of it, then,' he said.

I passed through the doorway, then turned back to face him. 'Baby or no baby, nobody I've talked to who knew Nancy thinks she drowned herself on purpose.'

'Do you know how many times I've heard that?' Hubbard asked as he escorted me through the waiting room to the front door. 'In my experience, it's the people who think they knew them best who find out they hardly knew them at all.'

Twenty-Three

'There is only the fight to recover what has been lost And found and lost again and again . . .'

T. S. Eliot, 'East Coker,' 1940

Dwight arrived at *Our Song* on Monday morning ready for work and positively beaming. 'Have you seen Grace's posting on Caring Bridge this morning?' he called as he paused at my open kitchen window.

I leaned over the sink, tweaked the curtain aside and peered out. 'No. From the look on your face, though, I gather it's good news. I could use some good news about now.'

'Rusty's awake.'

'Gosh, that's great! Do you think I'll be allowed to visit?'

'I wish you would. They had him sitting up in bed last night. He's groggy and a bit confused, but the doctor thinks visits from people he knows would be a good thing.'

'Consider it done,' I said.

On the drive up to the hospital in Salisbury, I stopped at a grocery store to buy a selection of tabloid newspapers. Reading about the improbable lives of the rich and famous never failed to amuse me, especially when they were giving birth

193

to alien babies. As I rolled the tabloids up together and tied them with ribbon, I hoped Rusty would appreciate knowing about the bigfoot who kept a lumberjack as a love slave, or that JFK was still alive, spotted living in a love nest with Marilyn Monroe in Oklahoma.

When I walked into Rusty's hospital room, I found him as his father had described: sitting up in bed, holding a tall cup and sipping from a bent straw. Except for a bandaged forehead, greenish-yellow bruising around both eyes and a badly swollen lip, he looked almost normal.

His stepmother looked up, tried to place me and failed.

'I'm Hannah Ives,' I said, crossing to the door and standing at the foot of Rusty's bed. 'Your husband is doing our renovations.'

Grace's face brightened. 'Oh, I'm so pleased to meet you at last. I usually make a point of visiting all of Dwight's clients at some time or other, but . . .' She shrugged.

'Mom's a one-woman Welcome Wagon, the Lemon Bar Queen of the Western World,' Rusty said through bruised lips.

Grace blushed to the roots of her close-cropped, dark brown hair. I wondered if she'd told Rusty yet about the unfortunate death of his biological mother, and chastised myself for thinking that of all the possible suspects in his mother's murder, Rusty had the solidest of alibis.

'Rusty exaggerates,' his stepmother said. 'But I'm glad you came. It's been a rough day.'

After two false starts, Rusty managed to set his drink down on the bedside table. 'A lot can happen when you're in a coma. Someone can murder your mother, for example.'

Grace reached out and squeezed her stepson's hand, held it tight. 'I considered not telling you, sweetheart, but I knew you'd never forgive me if you found out about it from someone else.'

'I'm sorry about Kendall, of course,' Rusty said, 'but she was never much of a motherly mom, if you know what I mean.'

Grace bristled. 'Kendall gave you that motor-cycle, Rusty. She loved you in her own way.'

Rusty stared at Grace as if she hadn't spoken. 'You look like you could use a break, Mom. Why don't you go down to the cafeteria and get some lunch? And when you come back, will you bring me a Diet Coke? In the meantime, I can catch up with Mrs Ives about the reno.'

'It's a little behind schedule,' I told Rusty after Grace had left the room, 'but honestly, I'm not concerned. Even though he's short staffed, your dad has things under control. How are you feeling?' I asked, genuinely concerned.

'Sore. Stiff. And I've got a helluva headache when the meds wear off.' Rusty shifted on his bed and grimaced.

'Do you remember anything about the accident?'

Rusty tugged impatiently at his sheet. 'I can't wait to get out of here!'

'The accident?' I prodded. 'Do you remember it?'

Rusty frowned. 'I remember pouring milk on my corn flakes at breakfast, then next thing I know, I wake up here and it's ten days later.' He rubbed a hand over the reddish stubble on his chin. 'Being in a coma can be a real out-of-body experience, you know? Part of me thinks I went to Aruba.'

That made me laugh.

'Mom tells me you're the one who found me by the side of the road and called nine-one-one,' Rusty continued. 'I want to thank you for that. If you hadn't come along . . .' He shuddered.

'I saw the car that hit you, but I wasn't able to get the license number or see the driver because of the tinted windows.' I paused, wondering whether to go on, but decided to risk it. 'I think it was a late-model black Mustang. Do you know anybody who drives a car like that?'

Rusty's eyes flicked to the left then back again, but failed to meet mine. ''Fraid not.'

Oh, yes you do, I thought.

'You were riding right behind a manure wagon? Do you remember that?'

'Nuh, uh.'

'The farmer driving the wagon saw the car, too. He's actually the one who called nine-one-one while I was . . .' I swallowed hard, remembering. 'While I was checking on you.'

'What the heck was I doing riding off in the middle of the work day anyway?'

I explained about the need for waterproof tape.

Rusty instinctively reached up to rub his forehead, touched the bandage instead and recoiled as if shocked. 'I don't remember that or anything, Mrs Ives.'

'What is the last thing you *do* remember?'

Rusty closed his eyes and rested his head

196

against one of the pillows that had been plumped up behind his back. 'They say I wasn't wearing a helmet. How can that be? I *always* wear a helmet. I'm not an idiot.'

'When you set off on your motorcycle that afternoon, you couldn't find it. That's why I was driving behind you. Just after you left I went looking for it myself and found the helmet behind the woodpile.'

'What the fu—' he began, then flushed. 'What the hell was it doing there?'

I shrugged. 'I don't know.'

'I don't remember much of anything from that day,' he said again. 'I remember having breakfast, my usual corn flakes, then riding to work . . . after that, literally, nothing.' He passed a hand in front of his face, as if erasing a chalk board.

I smiled in what I hoped was a reassuring way. 'I think they call it retrograde amnesia. It should get better. Give it time.'

'I can't find my, my . . . what do you call it?' He wrinkled his nose and pantomimed using a telephone.

'Your cell phone?'

'Yeah, that. Cell phone. Shit! I can't even remember that!'

'You had it in your pocket, Rusty. I dug it out to call nine-one-one, but the farmer showed up saying he'd already placed the call.' I paused, trying to remember what I'd done with Rusty's phone after that. I'd been holding it, and then . . .

'Didn't it come to the hospital with your things?' I asked.

'No. I asked a nurse to look for it, but she struck out. All my stuff's in a plastic bag over there,' he said, waving in the direction of a tall wooden locker in the corner of the room.

Thinking about the many features on my own iPhone, most of which I never used, I asked, 'Do you have the Find My iPhone app?'

'Check,' Rusty said. 'Got my buddy to try tracking the phone that way, but the battery must have died. He went back to look along the road, too, but he wasn't sure of the exact spot, and I sure as hell couldn't tell him where, so he came up empty.'

'We've had some rain. If it's still at the side of the road . . . Gosh, I hope it's not ruined.' I passed the scene of the accident every day, reran the tape in my head on instant replay. 'Would you like me to look for it?'

'That would be great. Thanks.'

'What's your cell number, Rusty? When I get near the spot, I'll try to call it.'

'That's another thing I can't remember,' he said. 'Grace wrote it down for me. It's on a piece of paper in the drawer of the end table.'

I located the number and tapped it into my contacts list. 'I'll give it a shot, but wouldn't it be simpler to replace the phone?'

Rusty lowered his eyes and spoke to his folded hands. 'There's stuff on the phone I don't want to lose.'

'No backups?'

He flushed. 'Actually, there's things I don't want Mom to see.'

I'd never had a teenaged son, but I could

imagine. 'Texts from your girlfriend?' I teased. 'Naughty selfies?'

'Something like that.' He managed a grin, but I could tell that it pained him.

We chatted for a bit about the general progress of the renovations, talking about the roof repair in particular, when Grace returned with a Diet Coke and I bid them both goodbye.

On the way home, I pulled over at the accident scene, parked and crossed to the opposite side of the road. I could tell why Rusty's buddy hadn't been able to locate the spot where Rusty had been struck. The rain had obliterated all traces of tire tracks from the emergency vehicles that had come to assist the injured man. If I hadn't recognized the stand of poplars I would have had a tough time finding it again, too.

Stepping carefully down the embankment, slipping on the damp leaves, I made my way toward the base of the tree where Rusty had lain. I eased my phone out of my purse and dialed Rusty's number, waited, listened. It rang four times, but I heard nothing before the phone clicked over to Rusty's voicemail: *Hey. At the beep. You know what to do.*

Moving back and forth methodically, I kicked the leaves aside. After several minutes, the toe of my sandal struck something hard. An empty bottle of cheap rum called 'Stagger Lee.' I tossed the bottle deeper into the woods and kept looking.

Five minutes later, I hit pay dirt. 'Tah dah!' I announced in triumph to the trees. I leaned over and picked up the phone. After wiping the case dry on my slacks, I pressed the 'on' button. Again, nothing. The phone was definitely dead.

Back at home, I plugged it into my charger. While I waited for it to recharge, I put the Keurig to work making me a cup of decaf, but after two cups of coffee and an hour's wait, the phone still showed no signs of life. I considered putting it into a slow oven to dry – I was sure I'd heard that tip somewhere – but decided on a more cautious approach. I ran a vacuum cleaner hose over all the sound and plug holes, then pulled a Ziploc bag out of a drawer, filled it with rice and sealed the iPhone inside the bag.

In two or three days Rusty would either be shopping for a new cell phone or I would be discovering exactly what he so desperately wanted to stop Grace finding out.

Twenty-Four

'For God shall bring every work into judgment, with every secret thing, whether it be good, or whether it be evil.'

Ecclesiastes, 13

After a three-day sleepover in the bag of rice, Rusty's iPhone arose, like Lazarus, from the dead.

In the weeks since he'd last turned it on – or I had, rather, as I knelt by his side at the edge of the road – only a handful of people had called.

Not surprising, since nearly everyone in town knew Rusty was hospitalized and in a coma.

Since I was 'just testing' to make sure the phone was in working order – that's my story anyway, and I'm sticking to it – I tapped the photo icon and began to thumb my way through the images in Rusty's photo gallery. Either Rusty didn't take a lot of photographs or he downloaded them routinely to his computer at home. There were only thirty in the folder to choose from. Several photographs of a brunette, attractive in an MTV sort of way, wearing a tank top with more than the usual complement of underwear straps showing. A selfie of that same young girl posing with her head on Rusty's shoulder, in a bar, most likely. The Crusty Crab? I wondered if the girl were the Laurie who had texted Rusty about going to the movies on the night of his accident.

There were 'before' photographs of our living and dining room walls, the brickwork on the chimney and closeups of our bathroom plumbing.

I paged on to a photo of our dock taken looking back toward the house, paged forward again and then gasped, instinctively pressing a hand flat against my chest in an effort to control my breathing: Baby Ella.

I flashed back to an image of Rusty kneeling by her mummified body, aiming his iPhone and clicking away. But there were many more photos of the dead infant than I remembered him taking before his father had aimed a discouraging blow to the back of his son's head. Rusty had managed to photograph the child from every angle, probably when he left the kitchen in order – he claimed! – to check on the grout. The last three pictures were closeups. My heart did a somersault when it occurred to me that Rusty was focusing on the newspaper and not on the mummified baby.

The first closeup was too blurry to read, as was the second. By his third attempt, Rusty had managed to hold the camera steady long enough to focus. From the publication dates printed on the top margins of the newsprint fanned out for his camera, I realized, for the first time, that Baby Ella had been wrapped in three separate issues of the *Tilghman Times*, layer upon layer.

We had all noticed the issue for August 1951 which had been on top. But when the bundle was photographed from the opposite side, one could see that issues for May and November of 1950 had been used to swaddle the child as well.

Rusty's next photograph zoomed in on the May 1950 issue. Tucked between the advertisements for local merchants were several columns of public notices. By tilting my head and squinting I could make out the notice for a public hearing in June on a request to change the zoning on a piece of property from residential to commercial. The next photo showed a list of delinquent tax properties. Using my thumb and forefinger, I swiped the photo to enlarge it, wondering if the Hazlett property was listed as delinquent, but unless there was something I didn't understand about the legalese, it wasn't. Another photo captured the court proceedings of the previous month, May 1950, much to the embarrassment, I was sure, of the town residents who had been cited for shoplifting, drunk and disorderly conduct, discharging a firearm within the town limits, running a red light or speeding. Had anyone I know been one of them? Again, no names that I recognized.

The final photograph, however, caused me to sit up straight. On May 25, 1950, the Tilghman county clerk had issued marriage licenses to three couples.

Dean Kelchner, 39, to Deborah Dutton, 39.

Joe Jacobs, 22, to Alison Markwood, 21, and . . . My heart stood still.

Clifton Ames, 18, to Nancy Hazlett, 17.

Math was not my strong suit. My husband had once given me a T-shirt that read: *4 Out Of 3 People Have Trouble With Math.* But even I could do the math on this one. Using my fingers, I counted forward. If Nancy Hazlett had been pregnant in May 1950, or gotten pregnant shortly thereafter, her child would have been born in February 1951, making the baby around six months old in August of that year when, according to the medical examiner, Baby Ella had most likely succumbed to polio.

That Clifton J Ames the Second had been the father of Nancy Hazlett's baby I now had no doubt. Had being in possession of that information almost cost Rusty his life?

It depends, I thought, on what he did with it.

I'd already violated too much of Rusty's privacy

to start feeling guilty. I snooped on, trolling through his text messages, then his email.

It took only a few minutes to find the answer in his outbox. Rusty had forwarded the photograph of the marriage license notice in the newspaper to his mother – Kendall, not Grace. *What do you know?* he'd written. *I'm sure you can put this to good use.*

Suddenly the significance of one of the text messages that had popped up on Rusty's phone at the scene of the accident hit me like a sledgehammer. It was Kendall – 'Ken' – who had texted her son, 'Got it. Stay cool.'

Sadly for Kendall Barfield, staying cool seemed to have proved fatal.

So much for Rusty's claim that he wasn't close to his biological mother. He hadn't wanted Grace to see the contents of his iPhone. This must have been the reason why. Grace, a woman who was deeply involved in charity work and her church would hardly have approved of Rusty's role in what seemed like a blackmail scheme.

Before I could change my mind, I forwarded copies of Rusty's photos to my own email account, then erased the evidence of my crime from Randy's sent file. One thing was certain: I needed to talk to Rusty Heberling – and quick. The question was what, if anything, the young man remembered?

Twenty-Five

'The past is a foreign country; they do things differently there.'

L.P. Hartley, *The Go-Between*, 1953

When I arrived at the hospital, the volunteer at the visitors' desk informed me that Rusty Heberling had been moved to a rehab facility. A quick call to his father, Dwight, told me where.

Bayview Health and Rehabilitation Center sat on several rolling green acres on the outskirts of town, although there was no 'bay view' that I could see.

I found Rusty in his room, a comfortable single furnished more like a hotel room than a hospital, with a bay window overlooking an ornamental lake.

He was seated in a wheelchair by the window reading a Kindle in a large-size font, but looked up at my 'Hello,' and seemed genuinely pleased to see me.

'Mrs Ives!'

'How are you doing?' I asked.

Rusty closed the Kindle and slipped it between his thigh and the arm of the chair. 'As you see, having a bit of trouble getting the stupid legs to cooperate.'

'I'm sorry to hear that.'

He shrugged. 'The Nazis in the PT department work me over pretty good. I need to get well just to get away from them, you know?'

'How's your mom?' I asked.

'Grace?' Rusty smiled. 'It's spay and neuter day, so she's out at the animal shelter. Sometimes I think she cares more about the animals than people.'

'Actually, I'm glad she's not here because there's something I need to talk to you about.' I reached into my handbag for his iPhone and held it out to him.

'Damn! You found it!' A frown clouded his face as what I had just said sank in. 'What?' he asked, withdrawing his hand without touching the phone. He eyed me suspiciously.

'Your phone had been badly water damaged, but I was able to dry it out,' I began. A spare chair sat at the foot of his bed. I dragged it over so I could sit down next to the wheelchair and talk to him face-to-face.

Without confessing to snooping in his phone, I said, 'I'm worried about you, Rusty. Did it occur to you that whoever was driving that black Mustang intended to *kill* you?'

Rusty seemed to be studying the silver medallions on the wallpaper and refused to meet my eyes.

'You know who it was, don't you?'

He turned his head, sucked in his lower lip and nodded silently.

'For God's sake, who?'

'The only dude I know who drives a badass car like that is Tad Chew.'

I couldn't place the name. 'Who is Tad Chew?' I prompted.

'Clifton Ames's grandson. The youngest kid of his daughter, Annette Chew.'

Ah! I remembered the showoff in the yellow Speedo at Kendall's picnic, the kid who'd told the sheriff he'd seen Caitlyn . . . the Mustang in Kendall's parking lot. I caught my breath. Whoa! So, Clifton Ames was sending his grandchildren out to do his dirty work for him. What rock had he crawled out from under?

'Just because he wears J Crew and Banana Republic and starts at Princeton in the fall, Tad thinks he's hot shit.' Rusty was on a roll. 'Works for his uncle Jack part-time, too. Dude doesn't need the money, so what's that all about, I wonder?'

I flashed back to the day of Jack Ames's visit to *Our Song*, pictured the preppy, college-aged kid who'd slid out of the driver's seat of Ames's Acura. Hadn't Jack called his young chauffeur 'Tad?' So, maybe it wasn't Clifton Ames who wanted to silence Rusty. Maybe it was his son, Jack, the owner of the face smiling out at the world from political billboards all over Tilghman County. If Jack Ames had aspirations to occupy the Oval Office at 1600 Pennsylvania Avenue, a family scandal might very well derail his plans.

'Look, Rusty,' I said, moving on. 'What puzzles me is that you were sharing this information with Kendall. It seems to me that your relationship with your biological mom was a lot closer than you wanted anyone to know.'

'The last couple of years . . .' Randy began,

then he shrugged. 'I guess Kendall was on a guilt trip or something. Calling me up, giving me presents. I didn't want to hurt Mom's feelings. Grace, I mean.'

I set the iPhone on Rusty's knee and held it there. 'You need to show these photos to the police. If what you say about Tad Chew is correct, whatever Kendall did with the information most likely got her killed.'

'I know.' His head lolled against the back of his chair. 'I am such a shit!'

'What *did* she do with it?'

Rusty took a deep breath and blew it out slowly through his lips. 'You were at her picnic?'

I nodded.

'Then you saw that boat, that swimming pool?'

'I did. Pretty hard to miss.'

'Kendall didn't pay for all that like everybody thinks. Cliff Ames did.'

I sat back, stunned. 'But why?'

'About ten years ago, Cliff and Kendall had an affair. She was way younger than him, of course, so I was kinda surprised when she bragged about it one night at the Crusty Crab after she'd had a bit too much to drink. Somehow, while they were still sleeping together, she found out that Clifton's old man had rigged it so that he could buy up a bunch of small farms that were being auctioned off for delinquent taxes.'

'Kendall was already working in real estate by then, wasn't she, so she might have stumbled across records of the transactions,' I suggested. *Just as I had.*

'Anyway,' Rusty continued, 'Clifton junior told

Kendall that his dad got him a summer job at the county tax office so that the kid was in on the ground floor, so to speak. Not sure how they managed it, but Kendall told me that the farms went to auction before the owners knew what hit them.'

'The son of a bitch.' The words just fell out of my mouth. I couldn't help it. That certainly explained why Clifton junior was so interested in what records were stored in the courthouse basement.

'Clifton senior allowed most of the former owners to stay on as tenants, like at your place, but there were a bunch of farms up north of town . . .' Rusty paused. 'That's where Clifton Farms built their processing plant.'

'I see.'

'After they broke it off, Kendall used that information to get "loans" from Cliff, but I don't think any of them were ever repaid.'

That figured, I thought. 'And Cliff's marriage to Nancy Hazlett?'

Rusty's eyebrows shot up under his bandage. 'That was a shocker, wasn't it?'

'Why on earth did you share *that* information with Kendall?'

'Insurance?' He closed his eyes, massaged his eyelids with his fingers then said, without actually looking at me, 'I didn't think she'd actually use it. I'm really sorry about that.'

'Look, Rusty. I think there's a very good chance that either Clifton Ames or his son, Jack, murdered your mother. There's also the possibility that Clifton murdered Nancy Hazlett back in 1952 to stop her from telling anyone about their marriage or the baby.'

'Shit,' Rusty said, stretching the word out into two syllables. 'Are you telling me that Clifton Ames was the father of the baby up your chimney?'

'I believe so, and I think you can help me prove it.'

'How?'

'I want you to promise me that you'll call Andy Hubbard and tell him what you just told me. Got that?'

'Yeah,' he said, sounding like he meant it. 'But how does that prove that Ames fathered that baby?'

'I have a plan, and it involves making Clifton Ames believe that the cops are going to exhume Nancy's body to test it for a DNA match to the baby.'

'Are they actually going to do that?'

'No, they don't have to. Nancy's brother, Thomas Hazlett, submitted a sample of his DNA for analysis. They already have a positive I.D.'

Rusty looked relieved. 'So what's the point?'

'If Nancy didn't die a suicide, then there may be evidence that her neck had been broken, just like Kendall's.'

Rusty lowered his head, wrapped his arms around himself in a bear hug and was silent for a long time. When he looked up again, he said, 'I feel sick.'

I patted his knee. 'I think we all do.'

Twenty-Six

'A female interviewer – a reporter in petti-coats? I am very curious to see her,' Ralph declared.

Henry James, *Portrait of a Lady*, 1917

After leaving Rusty, I headed home, stopping first at the grocery to pick up something for dinner.

When I plopped a couple of rib eyes and a bag of Caesar salad on the conveyor belt, Penny said, 'Have you heard the news?'

'What news?' I asked as Penny dragged my steaks over the scanner.

'Tad Chew has been arrested!'

I'd been rummaging in my handbag, searching for my credit card, but that got my attention. 'What for?' I asked, looking up, although I was pretty sure I knew the answer.

'They say he's the one who ran Rusty off the road. My boyfriend works for the towing company that took Tad's car away to the police garage.'

It was wrong, I knew, to rejoice in anyone going to jail, but the news fit in perfectly with my plans.

After Penny bagged my items, I hurried back to *Our Song* where I stored my purchases in the fridge and went out looking for Paul. I found him at the end of the dock preparing to install the outboard – which he had finally agreed to consign to the care of a professional engine mechanic – on the runabout.

'Quick,' I said. 'What was I wearing the day that reporter came calling?'

Paul considered my question while I admired the greasy black smear on his cheek. 'You're asking *me*?'

'The reporter, Madison Powers, gave me her card. I tucked it into the pocket of whatever I was wearing, but I can't remember what that was.'

Paul looked blank.

'The day the water pump was delivered?'

An eyebrow lifted. 'Ah! I think it might have been your black jeans. I remember admiring the way they stretched over your . . .'

I silenced him with a death ray. 'The dirty clothes bag!' I shouted in triumph, and hurried off to find and rummage through it.

Madison's business card finally in hand, I made the call. It went to her voicemail, of course – doesn't anyone answer their telephones these days? – but when she returned my call fifteen minutes later, she seemed pleased to hear from me. After some small talk – during which I learned it was her birthday – I gave her the scoop about Tad Chew, explained the situation and told her what I wanted.

When the article came out in the Maryland section of the *Washington Post* several days later, I was having a cappuccino with Kimberly at the High Spot.

A suspect has been arrested and charged with hit and run in the accident which nearly claimed the life of a Tilghman County building contractor, Dwight 'Rusty' Heberling. Heberling was on a job-related errand when his motorcycle was struck by a late-model Mustang allegedly being driven by Thaddeus Chew of Elizabethtown, who fled the scene. Chew is the grandson of poultry magnate, Clifton J Ames II and a nephew of Tilghman County Council president, Jack Ames, who is running for Congress in Maryland's Ninth district this fall. A source close to the Ames family said, 'Whatever the outcome, Tad has our full support.'

Heberling remains hospitalized but is expected to make a full recovery.

In a related story, it was Heberling and his father, contractor Dwight Heberling, who discovered the mummified body of an infant girl hidden in the chimney of a Tilghman County house they were renovating.

Responding to reports that state police were planning to exhume the body of a former resident of the house to determine if she was the mother of the dead child, a police spokesman said, 'We continue to explore our options, but no decision has yet been made.'

'I could kiss the woman,' I told Kim. 'This is a masterpiece.'

'It's true?'

'Every word. Tad is cooling his heels in the local hoosegow, isn't he, and as for the other . . .' I flapped a hand. 'The "police spokesman" could be anybody.' I winked. 'Or nobody.'

'Tad was actually arrested?'

'Yesterday, I understand. Everything she says in this article is true, including the unidentified police spokesman. Love it!'

'What do you hope to accomplish?' she asked, handing the newspaper back to me.

'Honestly? I don't know. But if Clifton Ames did murder his first wife, Nancy, and he thinks there's a possibility that Nancy's body will be exhumed . . .'

Kim nodded. 'I see, but you have to admit it's a long shot. The man didn't get to be the Chicken King of the Western World by being stupid.'

'True, but smart men aren't always smart when it comes to using and maintaining their power. Consider Bill Clinton, Elliot Spitzer, or that South Carolina governor who spent so much time "hiking the Appalachian trail."' I made quote marks in the air with my fingers.

'What I *don't* understand,' I said, changing the subject, 'is how the two of them could have married so young without their parents' consent.'

'It's simple really,' Kim explained. 'Each county in Maryland sets their own rules for obtaining a marriage license. Back in the day, Elkton over in Cecil County was a regular Gretna Green for couples wanting a quick, quiet marriage, because until they changed the rules in 1938 there was no waiting period. Lots of famous people

214

got married in Elkton, like Cornell Wilde, Debbie Reynolds, Willy Mays.

'But you still had to meet their age require-ments,' she continued, 'which was eighteen, I believe. In Tilghman County, however, you could get married without parental consent at seventeen, but they weren't very picky about proof of age back then. How old are you? Eighteen? All right, then. And if the girl was over fifteen, and could produce a doctor's certificate proving she was pregnant, granting a marriage license was pretty automatic.'

Kim broke her donut in half and dunked the torn end into her coffee. 'What I don't understand is how they managed to keep the marriage a secret. Tilghman County isn't exactly New York City.'

I'd wondered about that, too, but based on what Cap had told me about his sister, I had developed a theory. 'I think she loved him, but he convinced her to keep the marriage a secret, claiming that he needed time to break the news to his family about the baby, or else he'd be disinherited. So she trusted him. Dropped out of school, had the baby alone. When the baby died . . .' I paused. 'She'd lost her mother, her child and her only brother was fighting a war halfway around the world – a POW who might never come home. Perhaps she felt she had nothing more to lose. Perhaps she threatened to tell his parents, so he killed her.'

'Once Nancy Hazlett was dead,' Kim said, 'there was very little chance anyone would find out about the marriage. The original marriage certificates from that time period are on file at the Maryland Hall of Records, but the indexes for 1941 through June of 1951 are conveniently missing.'

'Couldn't you just visit the Hall of Records in Annapolis and look them up?' I asked.

'You'd think, but the licenses are arranged chronologically by year, then by month, then alphabetically by jurisdiction – that would be Tilghman County – then by the groom's last name.'

'Jeesh. So without the index you'd have to know exactly what you were looking for and, even then, you'd have to go through the file of records pretty much one by one. Too bad the index is missing.'

'*Was* missing,' Kim said.

'What?'

'That red-bound volume you brought up the other day?'

'You're kidding.'

'*Eh voila!*' she said. 'It covers the missing period. And there's something else Cap found and brought up to me. Finish up your coffee and I'll show you.'

On Kim's desk in her courthouse office sat a cardboard container about the size of a large shoebox. She pushed it across the desk toward me. 'Cap found this box yesterday afternoon buried under a pile of continuous-feed computer paper. Look inside.'

The box contained about a hundred business envelopes with the return address of the Tilghman

County Office of Property Tax Assessment printed in the upper left-hand corner. Each envelope contained a typewritten letter folded in thirds so that the address showed through the glassine window.

'Open one up,' Kim said.

I slipped the first envelope out of the box and lifted the flap. The letter was dated July, 1950 and was addressed to a Tilghman County resident who rejoiced in the name Ezekiel Hezekiah Agnew. 'It's a foreclosure notice.'

'Exactly. What else do you notice?'

I scanned the rest of the letter, turned it over then took another look at the envelope. The tax assessors had stamped it with a real stamp, a dingy brown and white one honoring the Boy Scouts of America. 'Three cents,' I said a bit nostalgically. And then I noticed that there was no postmark. 'They were never mailed!'

Kim grinned. 'Thank you, Sherlock.'

My fingers flew quickly through the remaining envelopes, through the Andersons, Duncans, Fraziers and Gordons until I found what I knew would be there: an envelope addressed to Mary C. Hazlett at a house number and street that I knew as well, uh, as well as my own. 'She never got it.'

'No. None of them did,' Kim said.

'Rusty mentioned that Clifton Ames had a summer job at the courthouse. Do you suppose . . .?'

'If so, it'll be in the employment records. They're somewhere down in the basement, too.'

I was about to suggest we go search for the

employment records when the telephone on Kim's desk rang. She picked up and listened. 'But we're not done,' she said. Then, 'I understand, but I don't like it.' She hung up without saying goodbye. Not a good sign.

'That was Ginny over at the county council office,' Kim told me. 'The mold report has come in. I'm afraid it's *stachybotrys chartarum*. We've been ordered to stand down.'

'But . . .'

'They tell me it's the "dangerous kind."'

'All mold is dangerous in its way, but there are ways to abate . . .' I began, but Kim cut me off.

'Out of my hands, I'm afraid. Come on. I may need a bodyguard when we tell Fran. She'll go ballistic.'

Twenty-Seven

'An honest politician is one who, when he is bought, will stay bought.'

Simon Cameron, 1799–1889

I love late summer afternoons, that time of day when the sun casts long shadows, bringing Mother Nature into sharp focus. In a large saucepan, I was bringing turbinado sugar, light corn syrup, dark rum and butter to a boil over medium heat in order to make my mother's fabulous pecan pie. Kim had challenged me to a duel.

218

She planned to enter *her* mother's killer peach pie in the bake-off the following day at the Tilghman County Fair. How could I allow her mother to out-bake my mother?

The telephone rang. Still stirring constantly to prevent burning, I reached for the phone. 'Hello.'

'Hannah, it's Cap. I was passing by the courthouse on my way home when I saw two trucks pull into the parking lot. They had BioClean written all over the sides, so I hung around for a bit to see what they're up to. Sam let one of them in through the back door. The guy was in there for a couple of minutes, and when he came out, the rest of them started climbing into white moon suits. I asked Sam what they were up to. Apparently they've been ordered to clean out the storeroom.'

I dragged the saucepan off the burner. 'Who gave them permission to do that?'

'Kimberly, I guess, but I can't get her on the phone to confirm.'

'Have you called Fran?'

'I tried her home phone, but she didn't pick up.' He paused, and I heard a sharp intake of breath. 'Damn. They're carrying out boxes now.'

'Where are they taking them?' I asked, feeling panicky.

'Hold on. I'll call you right back.'

It seemed like hours, but it was probably only a few minutes before Cap rang again. 'Just chatted with the supervisor. He says that because of the mold, the records are going to be incinerated at the county animal shelter.'

I let that information sink in. Knowing how

hard we had worked on inventorying the county's old records, I couldn't believe that Kimberly had authorized their destruction, especially when our work was only half done. 'I'll get there as soon as I can. In the meantime, stick around and see what you can do to delay them until I can talk to Fran.'

When I reached Fran a few minutes later, it was on her cell phone. I could hear merry-go-round music in the background so I presumed, rightly, that she was at opening night of the county fair. 'Fran,' I said without preamble. 'There's a hazmat team at the courthouse, taking our records away.'

'That's not funny, Hannah.'

'I'm not joking. Cap just called. They're parked behind the courthouse so they'd be less obvious, but they're from BioClean. It's the same outfit that cleaned up the meth lab in Dorchester County last month. Cap says they've been ordered to take everything to the county animal shelter and burn it.'

'Hazmat?' Fran said. 'Shit. First they take away our keys, now they let just anyone waltz in and take away county records before we've even had time to find out what's in them?' She paused to draw breath. 'Who hired BioClean anyway?'

'Kimberly, I suppose.'

'I don't believe that for a minute, do you?' She paused. 'I'll call Kim. In the meantime, you call Grace.'

'Grace? Why Grace?'

'She volunteers at the shelter. Perhaps she can hold them off at that end.'

I reached Grace where one usually reached Grace. On her cell phone, sitting by Rusty's bed. When I explained the situation, she said, 'But we're a no-kill shelter. The incinerator hasn't been used for over six months.'

'Apparently they're going to fire it up. Is there any way it can be disabled?'

Grace paused to think. 'There's a big propane tank out back. Maybe if I shut off the fuel . . .?' Her voice trailed off. 'I'll see what I can do.'

When I arrived at the courthouse, I nearly ran my car into Kim's as she was pulling into the parking lot from the opposite direction. She parked diagonally across the exit, jumped out of her car leaving her driver's side door open and sprinted across the parking lot shouting, 'Stop! What are you doing?'

It answered the question of whether or not she had authorized BioClean's clandestine weekend visit.

Kim cornered one of the moon men as he emerged from the courthouse carrying a box I recognized as containing traffic tickets from 1972–1974. I didn't care much about forty-year-old citations for failure to stop at a red light, but the next worker who emerged to face Kimberly's wrath was carrying a box I'd sorted and labeled myself. *Planning and Zoning, Hearings, 1961–1981* stood out in bold black letters on the outside. I planted myself firmly in the workman's path.

He tried to step around me, but each time I countered his move in a cartoonish parking lot *pas de deux*.

'Who's in charge here?' Kimberly asked, her voice low and menacing.

The worker jerked his helmeted head toward another white-clad alien carrying a second box of records labeled *Time Cards, 1950–1960*. 'Owen.'

'Don't move,' Kimberly ordered, and marched over to confront Owen. 'I'm the court clerk. Who authorized you to do this?'

Owen peered at her from behind his plastic visor. 'We have the hazmat contract for the county.'

'How does that answer my question? Who authorized *this* removal?'

'Who did you say you were?'

'I'm the county clerk, Kimberly Marquis. I work here. And *I* certainly didn't order anyone to take our records away.'

'Paperwork is in the truck,' Owen said. He dropped the box of employment records he was carrying to the tarmac and waddled off in his hazmat suit and booties to get it. A few seconds later he returned holding a clipboard awkwardly between gloved paws and thrust it into Kim's hands.

Over Kim's shoulder I peered at the document on the clipboard. In the blank for contact and billing information was a name I didn't recognize. 'Who's that?' I asked Kim, tapping the name that was typed on the form.

'Ginny's the admin assistant for the county council.'

'Jack Ames's office?'

'Bingo.'

'And is this his signature at the bottom?'

'It sure looks like it.'

How low would Jack Ames stoop to protect himself and his family?

'Is there something in the basement that Jack Ames wants to keep buried?' I whispered in an aside to Kim. 'Or do you think he's ordering this destruction on behalf of his father, Clifton Ames?'

Kim shrugged helplessly.

Owen held out his hand for the clipboard. 'We have a job to do, ma'am. I'd appreciate it if you'd let us get on with it.'

'We have personal items in the storage area,' I told him, thinking quickly. 'We'll need to retrieve them.'

'Make it snappy,' he scowled and pantomimed checking his watch which, if he actually wore one, was hidden under layers of white, non-breathable fabric.

As Kim and I hurried into the courthouse, I glanced back over my shoulder. Owen was on his cell phone, presumably reporting this disruption to his supervisors.

In the basement, we found the door to the storeroom standing wide open, two BioClean employees stacking up boxes inside.

'Out,' Kim said. 'Owen needs to see you.'

After the men departed, Kim and I glanced around. What could we save in the few minutes remaining to us?

'If Jack Ames is behind this, it all has to go back to those land deals his grandfather made in the late forties and early fifties. He can't make the actual land records disappear, of course, but without the indexes they're much harder to find,' she said as she lugged two heavy volumes out of the storeroom and reshelved them behind the paper towels and toilet paper in the main part of the basement. The marriage index with its beautiful red leather binding found a temporary home in a box of pot shards excavated from a dig behind St Timothy's Church. Kim located the packet of letters written home by the World War I soldier and tucked them into the waistband of her jeans.

'Just a bit of petty larceny while we wait for this mess to be sorted out,' she said and reached for another box.

Feeling powerless, Kim and I watched from the front seat of my car as the BioClean workers carried ledger after ledger and box after box out of the courthouse basement and loaded them into their service van. I'd counted fourteen boxes, mostly old time cards and employment records, when Fran pulled up in her lipstick red Neon. She joined us, her cheeks glistening with tears. 'I can't reach anybody. All the offices are closed. Everyone must be at the fair.'

'They picked this weekend on purpose,' I fumed. 'Date and time are specified right on the work order Owen showed me.'

I'd never felt sorry for Fran before, but as the three of us watched our carefully planned project evaporate out from under us, I, too, felt like weeping. There was a lot of junk in the storeroom, true, but who knew what treasures were still buried at the bottom of the boxes we hadn't gotten to when Kim had ordered us to stand down and hand in our keys? And if Jack Ames had his way, we'd never find out. I thought back to the first

224

time I'd met the politician when he'd come to welcome us – or so he claimed – to Tilghman County. He'd given me his business card. Told me to call any time. Did I still have it?

I rooted around in my handbag and finally located the card tucked between my Blue Moon Coffee Shop frequent shopper card – well-punched – and my Anne Arundel County voter registration card. Incredibly, it listed his cell. I dialed the number and got a chirpy recording that infuriated me: *Hello. This is Jack Ames, your Tilghman County Council president. Remember me when you go to the polls in November.*

Like hell I will, I snarled while waiting for his voicemail to kick in. He would be judging prize hogs about now, I figured, surrounded by beaming, fresh-faced 4Hers. After the beep, I told his voicemail, 'Call off the hazmat team, Mr Ames. The jig is up. We both know what they're looking for and they're not going to find it at the courthouse.'

Twenty-Eight

'Politics is almost as exciting as war, and quite as dangerous. In war you can only be killed once, but in politics many times.'

Sir Winston Spencer Churchill, 1903

'We've done what we can,' I told the women after I hung up on Jack Ames's voicemail. 'We've saved a few of the important records, and I took photographs of some of the others.'

We were leaning against the front of Fran's car, its hood still warm against my backside. 'I wish I had a shotgun,' Fran muttered. 'I'd pick them off, one at a time as they come out the door. All that history! Don't they realize that once it's gone it's gone forever?'

I laid a hand on Fran's arm. 'Maybe Jack Ames will get my message and show up. I'd like to believe that when he approved that work order he simply didn't understand the historical significance of what we have here.'

Fran scowled. 'Can he really be *that* stupid?'

I checked my watch, well aware that the clock on our records was ticking down. 'Fran, why don't you stay here with Kim? In the meantime, I'm going to the animal shelter. Fingers crossed I can stop the burning.'

It occurred to me that I didn't even know where the animal shelter was. I could have waited and followed one of the BioClean vans, of course, but for what I planned to do I needed to beat them to the draw. Kim filled me in.

Ten minutes later, following Kim's directions, I pulled into a parking lot on the outskirts of Elizabethtown where a large sign read: *Tilghman County Humane Society. Deliveries in Rear.* A single car was parked in the lot. From the humane society decal on the rear window I figured Grace had arrived.

As I climbed out of my car, I noticed that the property adjoined a vineyard. Rows of vines stood like silent sentinels in the gathering dark.

226

Someone was in the shelter; a light shone in one of the windows.

I parked and tried the front door, but it was locked. 'Good girl,' I muttered. Grace responded to my knock almost immediately, pushed the panic bar and let me in.

'I was right, it is propane,' she told me breathlessly. I followed Grace down a hallway and through two rooms of cages housing dogs, cats and rabbits awaiting reassignment to their forever homes. A droopy-eared spaniel, head on paws, stared out at me through the bars mournfully. Another dog, a terrier, began to bark, setting off a chain reaction. By the time we got to the far end of the room we were accompanied by a canine chorus of barks, yips and howls.

'Someone's already turned the incinerator on,' Grace said. 'Warming it up.'

'Isn't anyone here with the animals?' I asked.

'On weekends, we have staff that come in every four hours during the day to feed the animals and check up on things.' She glanced at the clock on the wall. 'It's eight-thirty, so Sandy, our animal care assistant, will have been and gone.'

The door whooshed shut between us and the dogs. We were standing at one end of a long hallway.

'There it is,' Grace said, pointing to a large gray box installed in the wall at the opposite end. The door to the incinerator was at chest height. I paused, feeling ill, thinking of all the animals that had perished there. I could almost hear their ghostly barks, pitiful meows, their agonized screams.

'The controls are over here,' she said, pointing to a wall panel where several indicators glowed green and orange. 'I can switch it off by pushing this button, but when they get here they'll just turn the gas on again.'

'I'm surprised nobody is here from the shelter staff to supervise,' I said. 'I mean, if you or Sandy didn't let them in, how did the incinerator get turned on in the first place?'

'BioClean has a key,' Grace explained. 'Their contract with the shelter allows them to use the incinerator on weekends. Usually they're getting rid of roadkill for the county. Raccoons, possums, deer. This is going to make you want to barf, but . . .' She cocked an arm, deepened her voice and drawled, 'This baby can process up to eight hundred pounds of euthanized companion animals at the rate of a hundred and fifty pounds per hour.'

Grace was right. I did feel like hurling, especially when she added, 'We charge them twenty-five dollars for every one hundred pounds. Maintaining an incinerator can be expensive. There's more to it than just fuel.'

'Speaking of fuel,' I said, 'where's the fuel tank?'

'Follow me.' Grace put the back door on the latch and flipped on an outside light.

The propane tank sat outside the building on a concrete slab. Pipes led from the bottom of the tank and through the wall into the back of the building. There was an on/off valve at the top but, like the furnace inside, that would be easy enough to turn back on. I knelt and examined the connectors. I tried turning one of the nuts that connected the threaded brass couplers with my fingers, but it wouldn't budge.

I swiveled my head to look up at Grace. 'Do you have any tools? A wrench, maybe?'

'Who are you talking to? I'm a contractor's wife. Dwight keeps a spare toolbox in the trunk.'

Grace came back a few minutes later carrying a wrench in one hand and a pair of vice grips in the other. 'Let's try the wrench first,' I said.

She slapped it into my open palm like a surgical assistant.

I adjusted the wrench, tightened it around the connector and tugged it toward me. After two grunts and three swear words, it gave. I loosened the connector, separating the two pipes until there was a gentle whoosh and the distinctive smell of sulphur filled the air. 'There,' I said, standing up. 'If we're lucky, they won't notice that the pipes aren't quite connected.'

We were heading back into the shelter to turn out the lights when my cell phone rang. Fran. The BioClean vans were on their way.

'If we use both our cars we can probably block the driveway,' I told Grace.

Grace rubbed her hands together. 'What fun! Do you think we'll be arrested?'

Twenty-Nine

'Except for this explosion, the interview was very successfully conducted.'

Robert Louis Stevenson, *The Master of Ballantrae*, 1889

Grace and I parked our cars nose-to-nose at the entrance to the parking lot. If BioClean wanted access to the delivery doors at the back of the shelter they'd have to pry the car keys out of our cold, dead fingers, push our cars aside or have the vehicles towed. Either way, our historical records would gain a few precious minutes of life.

While we waited for their vans to arrive, we sat at a circular picnic table on the back lawn where, Grace explained, on pleasant days staff would gather to eat lunch and supervise the animals as they frisked and frolicked in the galvanized dog runs. As night gathered in around us, a full moon began its slow rise over the vineyard, casting long shadows and gilding the vines and the leaves on the nearby trees with silver.

I tried Jack Ames's cell phone again, but failed to reach a live human being. After that, Grace and I talked, killing time. I told her about my family – my husband, daughters and grandchildren – and she outlined the long path to recovery that Rusty's team of doctors and therapists had designed for him.

'Will he be able to return to work?' I asked, selfishly thinking about the renovation at *Our Song* that had been falling further and further behind schedule. During his absence, out of stubbornness, or perhaps deep denial, Dwight had refused to replace Rusty with a temporary worker.

'Because of his inability to concentrate, he may require a bit more supervision, but, yes, Rusty should be able to go back to work eventually.'

I didn't ask how long 'eventually' might be.

'I'm praying for that boy,' Grace told me. I thought she was referring to her own son until she added with a sigh, 'It can't have been Tad's idea to hurt Rusty. Somebody must have put him up to it.'

Jack Ames stood at the top of my suspect list – both for Rusty's accident and Kendall's murder – but I could always use a second opinion. 'Who do you think it was, Grace?'

'God may punish me for this, but on my bad days, I sometimes think it might have been his mother.'

We sat in silence while I let the significance of what she'd said sink in. Grace was all 'do unto others' and 'turn the other cheek.' But what if she'd crossed over into Old Testament 'eye for an eye and tooth for a tooth' territory? Had *Grace* been angry enough at Kendall to kill her? I hadn't seen her at the picnic, but thinking about the missing nametag, that didn't mean she hadn't been there.

Grace was explaining how repetitive tasks, like installing drywall or painting the siding would help rewire her son's brain, when something caught my eye. A pinpoint of orange, followed by a dark shape moving slowly along one of the rows of grapevines. 'Who the . . .' I started to whisper when the distinct odor of a Bonnie and Clyde cigarillo – burned coffee with overtones of ashtray – wafted our way. I grabbed Grace's forearm and squeezed. 'Shhhh.'

As we watched, the figure emerged from the grapevines and headed in the direction of the shelter's back door.

'Does Clifton Ames have a key to the shelter?' I whispered directly into Grace's ear.

'Somebody on his staff does,' she whispered back. 'They have a huge incinerator for dead birds at Clifton Farms but they use ours from time to time for overflow.'

'Charming,' I muttered.

Suddenly, we were bathed in light. The BioClean vans had arrived, angled into the driveway, spot-lighting our vehicles. The lead van began to honk its horn.

We stayed put, hardly daring to move.

After a minute, when no one had responded to his impatient summons, the driver gave up on the horn. He hopped out of the van, walked around to the front and, silhouetted against the headlights, inspected our cars. I recognized Owen. He swore, unzipped and reached inside the top of his white overalls, then put his right hand to his ear. 'Looks like he's calling someone,' Grace whispered.

232

After a moment, a nearby cell phone began to play, 'Do The Funky Chicken.'

My head snapped around.

The song cut off. Clifton Ames had answered his phone. 'What's up?' we heard him say. The tip of his cigarillo glowed red as he sucked on it, listening.

Apparently, Owen had outlined a plan. The BioClean supervisor disappeared around the front of the building and, one by one, lights inside the shelter were turned on.

When the light at the back door snapped on, Ames headed for it.

I replay the scene often, sometimes in my dreams, sometimes while simply sitting on my back porch, but when the action begins, it's always in slow motion.

Ames heading for the door that Owen is holding open for him. He takes a drag on his cigar, withdraws it from his lips with thumb and forefinger then turns it toward him, considering the tip. He flips the cigar away, and it tumbles end over end over end . . .

'No!' I shouted, but it was too late. There was a flash of light and a deafening *whoosh!* as the lit end of Ames's cigar ignited the invisible cloud of propane gas that had leaked out of the tank and settled over the grass. A wave of heat rolled our way. When we looked again, Clifton Ames lay on the ground, his clothes smoldering.

Owen and I reached Ames at the same time. 'Roll him over!' I shouted. While Owen did as I asked, I used my phone to call 911.

Grace disappeared into the shelter, returning

with some wet towels which she draped carefully over the victim.

I was kneeling beside Ames, feeling for a pulse, when the old man moaned. The explosion had torched his eyebrows and burned off his hair. In the ruined landscape of his face, one eyelid opened. 'Wha . . .?'

'Shhh,' I told him. 'An ambulance is on the way.'

'What the fuck *you* doing here?' Owen growled from behind me.

I swiveled to face him. 'Why don't you send your crew home, Owen? Nobody's going to burn anything more here tonight.'

Thirty

'It is a wise father that knows his own child. Well, old man, I will tell you news of your son: give me your blessing: truth will come to light; murder cannot be hid long; a man's son may, but at the length truth will out.'

William Shakespeare, *The Merchant of Venice*, Act 2, Scene 2

Yogi Berra once said, 'It ain't over till it's over.'

The county records sat in the BioClean vans while Caitlyn's attorney, convinced that they contained evidence that would exculpate his client, managed to obtain a court order preventing their destruction until they could be thoroughly examined.

By that time, two days had passed and BioClean was eager to comply with the order. They unloaded the records in the courthouse parking lot where the law firm of Fletcher and Warner LLP had erected a PVC party tent. If it weren't for the summer interns roaming about in surgical masks and latex gloves like Ebola caregivers, one might think we were throwing a wedding.

Caitlyn, happily, had been released on bail and was home with her family. Her father was footing the bill for the whole shebang, so I figured it was a win-win situation, especially for the Tilghman County Historical Society. Fran and I had been tapped to act as unpaid consultants, which consisted of sitting under the tent on folding metal chairs and directing interns to labeled boxes where they could pack the materials once they had finished examining them. After we surrendered the index volumes we'd hidden in the basement in our effort to keep them out of enemy hands, we couldn't help noticing that only a handful of the ledgers covering land transfers in the county were making it into the box we'd designated for them.

'What I don't understand,' Fran said during a bathroom break, 'is why Clifton Ames showed up at the humane society shelter on Friday night rather than his son, Jack. It was Jack who signed the work order. Jack who you threatened on the telephone.'

'Voicemail,' I corrected as I dried my hands on

235

a paper towel. 'I threatened the voice on the man's answering service.'

'Still . . .' she began, but I made a timeout sign with my hands. 'I have a radical idea,' I said. 'Let's go ask him.'

Fran's face brightened. 'Let's!'

The Tilghman County Council met in a modern, two-story administration building about two blocks east of the courthouse. I located the intern who seemed to be in charge – the one holding the largest clipboard – and told him that Fran and I had an errand to run but that we'd be right back.

Five minutes later, we stood outside Jack's office door. Nobody was manning the reception desk, but we could tell by a voice drifting over the transom that we'd cornered the councilman.

Eventually, the room grew quiet. Seconds later, Jack Ames erupted from his office, caught sight of us and slammed on the brakes. 'Sorry to keep you waiting, ladies, but I'm on my way to visit Dad in the hospital.' He paused as recognition dawned. 'It's Hannah Ives, isn't it?' Jack said. 'You're the one who called nine-one-one.'

'I was.'

I asked the obvious question. It seemed only polite. 'How is he doing?'

'Let's step into my office for a moment,' he said, rubbing the stubble on his chin thoughtfully.

'I called the hospital,' I said as we followed the councilman through the door, 'but they wouldn't tell me anything without the secret password.'

'Sit, sit,' Jack said, indicating two chairs facing his desk. 'The burns on his face and hands are painful but superficial. It's his legs we're worried about. Second and third degree burns. He'll recover, they tell me, but he'll need skin grafts followed by rehab to keep the skin supple as the wounds heal. It may be a while before the old man's up and about.'

'We're here about the order to destroy the county records,' I said, cutting to the chase.

'It was your signature.' Fran popped out of her chair waving a photocopy of the county purchase order under Jack Ames's nose.

Jack snatched the printout from her hands and scanned it impatiently. 'It looks like my signature,' he said after a moment, 'but it isn't.'

Jack scrabbled around on his desk until he unearthed an executive order printed on vellum declaring September the First 'Cat Fanciers Day' in Tilghman County. '*That's* my signature,' Ames said, stabbing an index finger at the scrawl at the bottom of the document, next to an official gold seal. 'My A's look more like O's. Check it out.'

We leaned over the document. Fran and I had to agree.

While we were contemplating the implications of that, a bell dinged and a voice called out, 'Sorry I'm late!'

Jack frowned. 'Ginny, come in here for a minute, will you?'

Ginny's head popped around the door but her smile disappeared the minute she saw us. We weren't smiling either.

Jack handed Fran's copy of the work order to

his receptionist. 'What can you tell me about this?'

She glanced at the photocopy and handed it back. 'You left it on my desk with a Post-it that said "Expedite."'

'I see. Would it surprise you to learn that I knew nothing about it?'

Ginny's face paled. 'But . . . I don't understand.'

'Somebody obviously put it on your desk. Any idea who that might have been?'

'I don't know, Jack, honestly. It was there when I came back after lunch on Wednesday. You were away at that fundraiser in Salisbury, so I assumed you'd left it there on your way out. After we got the mold report, the order made a lot of sense.' She shrugged. 'So I expedited it.'

'Was the office locked?' I asked.

Ginny bristled. 'Of course!'

'So the obvious question is who else has office keys.'

Jack ran a hand through his hair. 'Lord, just about the entire city council. My wife, Susan, of course.'

'Your father,' Ginny added helpfully.

'Him, too. And Tad, my driver, until I fired him and took away his keys.' He leaned forward. 'And that was *before* the boy's arrest, I should point out.'

'Your nephew drove you out when you visited my house that day, didn't he?'

Jack frowned. 'Yes, why?'

'Then I think I know who hid Rusty's helmet.'

'Helmet? If there's a point here, Mrs Ives, I wish you'd get to it.' He made a Broadway production of checking his watch. 'I'm already late for the hospital.'

'OK. Here's the timeline. Rusty rode his motorcycle to work that morning wearing his helmet. You paid us a call and while we were chatting, your driver, Tad, wandered off. You had to call out to him, remember? Later that day, Rusty had an errand to run in town and couldn't find his helmet so he took off on his motorcycle without it. Shortly thereafter, he was run off the road by someone driving a late-model black Mustang registered to Tad Chew.'

Jack paled. 'So you're telling me it wasn't an accidental hit and run?'

'That's what I'm saying. It was an attempt at deliberate murder.' I studied him carefully.

Jack stared at me for so long I felt like I was under a microscope. 'Someone else could have been driving the Mustang,' he said at last.

'Always a possibility, I suppose, but since Tad is under arrest, it's clear the sheriff doesn't think so.'

'Why?' Jack flopped back in his chair, waved an arm dismissively. 'Tad is an idiot! It can't have been his idea.'

'I don't think it was,' I said. 'I think *you* put him up to it.'

I watched his face carefully as his expression morphed from outrage to genuine puzzlement. 'That's bullshit! Why would I want to hurt Rusty?'

'It's because of Baby Ella,' I told him. 'It all started with the baby.'

While I talked, Jack had picked up a pen and was idly twirling it between his fingers, first one way, then the other. 'Andy Hubbard tells me the

239

baby belonged to a black woman named Nancy Hazlett who committed suicide back in 1952.'

I nodded.

'It's sad, but so what?' Jack said. 'If there's a connection, I just don't get it.'

'Nancy was passing for white,' I explained. 'She went to high school with your father.'

From the folder in my handbag, I extracted the photocopy I'd made of Nancy and Cliff performing in *Oklahoma!*. Jack stared at it for a long time. 'She's very pretty,' he said at last. 'Looks exotic, maybe Spanish.'

'Her father was white,' I told him.

Still fingering the photograph, Jack nodded. 'I see. But, what does that have to do with . . .' Suddenly he threw his head back against the headrest of his leather chair, stared up, as if consulting the ceiling. 'Jesus, Mary and Joseph!'

Fran started to say something, but I silenced her with a frown and a subtle shake of my head.

Jack leaned forward, his face grave. 'Is there proof of this?'

'From what we can tell, Nancy and your father were actually married.' I pulled a copy of one of Rusty's iPhone photos out of the folder and pushed it across his desk. 'Rusty took this photograph, realized its significance and then, for reasons I don't quite understand, forwarded it to his mother. To Kendall, not to Grace.'

Jack snorted. 'Doesn't surprise me in the least. Sounds like Rusty wanted to cut himself in on a piece of the action.'

'Action?' Fran looked confused.

'Kendall had my father by the short hairs for

years, but I thought it had to do with dodgy land deals back in the forties. This,' he said, tapping the photo, 'is something else altogether.'

'How far do you think your father would go to keep this information from coming to light? Once this news became public knowledge, your father's reputation would be toast.'

Jack smirked. 'Dad doesn't have much of a reputation to protect.'

'But what if,' I began, choosing my words carefully. 'What if it wasn't *his* reputation he was worried about. What if it were *yours*?'

'Mine? You must be kidding.'

'In this climate of gotcha journalism, one could argue that it'd screw up your chances at the White House.'

'White House!' Jack hooted. 'I haven't even made it into the House of Representatives!'

'Your father likes to think big, I hear.'

'But he doesn't think for *me*. Son of a bitch.'

I leaned forward and spoke quietly so that Ginny wouldn't hear. 'I can think of only one reason why your father would authorize the wholesale destruction of the courthouse records. Only one reason why he showed up at the animal shelter last night. There is something in those records that he doesn't want found, and once Fletcher and Warner finish up under the tent over there, we're going to know what it is, too.'

'It's my fault Dad turned up that night,' Jack said. 'There was a message about hazmat on my machine. There's always some kook calling to complain about pollution from his goddamn chickens. They asked for Mr Ames, so I assumed . . .' His voice trailed off. 'Dad was here when I played back my messages.'

'That kook was me,' I confessed. 'You signed the destruction order, or so we thought.'

'And since you didn't,' Fran said, rising from her chair, 'Hannah and I better get back to the courthouse.'

I stood, too. 'And you'll need to push on to the hospital.'

'Hospital? I don't think so. Not today. Let the old fool stew in his own juice. I have things I need to do.'

Jack Ames wasn't planning to visit his father, but based on what I'd just learned, I sure as hell was.

Thirty-One

'Almighty God created the races white, black, yellow, malay and red, and he placed them on separate continents. And but for the interference with his arrangement there would be no cause for such marriages. The fact that he separated the races shows that he did not intend for the races to mix.'

Judge Leon M. Bazile, Caroline County (Va.) Commonwealth v. Richard Perry Loving and Mildred Dolores Jeter, 1958–1966

It was a perfect day for a hospital visit. A line of squalls had moved eastward across the

Chesapeake Bay bringing rain and high winds, dropping the temperature by twenty degrees.

After breakfast I strolled around the yard, picking up broken branches and stacking them on top of the woodpile. Then I exchanged my wet tennis shoes for a pair of dry dockers, climbed into my car and headed north, feeling just about as gloomy as the weather.

Before we left his office, Jack informed me that Clifton Ames had been transferred from the burns unit at Johns Hopkins in Baltimore to the regional medical facility near Snow Hill. I parked in the multi-story parking garage just off Front Street and checked in at the hospital's information desk, where I received a laminated clip-on visitors badge and was directed to the nursing station on the second floor. The duty nurse first pointed out the alcohol handwash dispenser and, only after I'd disinfected my hands, the directions to the patient.

Clifton Ames's room, I soon discovered, was on the right-hand side at the end of a long corridor. A sign on the door read, 'Only one visitor at a time. Thank you.' Ames's door stood ajar, and I was about to push my way in when I heard voices. Either Ames was busy with his caregivers or he already had a visitor, so I parked myself in an upholstered chair someone had thoughtfully placed just outside the door to wait my turn.

The voices were hushed at first. Then one began to stand out. Sitting quietly, I tuned in.

'Is this what you were looking for?' A man's voice, low and intense.

There was a mumbled response, then, a little louder, 'These aren't the originals, of course.'

This time I recognized the voice: Cap Hazlett.

I sat up straight and, acting casual, leaned closer to the door. Using my fingertips, I pushed it open a few inches more.

'You were right, you know,' Cap Hazlett growled. 'The evidence was all there in the court-house basement. Was, I said, *was*.'

'I thought we were friends,' Cliff whined.

'Friends!' Cap snorted. 'What a joke. I should have been suspicious when you met me at the airport all those years ago. You hardly knew me, yet I fell for all your flag waving and patriotic bullshit about wanting to help a returning vet.'

As I strained my ears to hear Cliff's reply, a nurse's aide rumbled by pushing a cart loaded with medications in clear plastic cups. She was joined by another aide who wanted to discuss whether Doctor Freidman had increased the dose of 'Vicodin for the gallbladder in two-thirteen.'

I wanted to shush them, but gritted my teeth instead. After they moved on, I heard Clifton Ames say, 'My father, not me.'

'Oh, your father bought the property at auction through Liberty Land Development, that's for sure,' Cap agreed. 'But that's not all that was shady about those sales, was it?'

'I don't have the faintest idea what you're talking about.'

'Was this what you were looking for in the courthouse basement, Ames?'

Cap was obviously holding something up. I

longed to see what it was, but didn't want to interrupt their conversation, so I stayed put, hands folded in my lap, staring demurely at a watercolor print of the wild ponies of Chincoteague hanging on the opposite wall.

'This was one of hundreds that never got mailed. See here?' He paused, then continued as if explaining something to a stubborn third-grader. 'Uncancelled stamp.'

The delinquent tax notices.

'That has nothing to do with me,' Ames rasped.

'Oh, no? How about this, then? Recognize it?'

If Ames replied, it was in a voice so quiet that I couldn't hear him.

'Your daddy got you that summer job, I'll bet. How long before he started asking you to do favors for him?'

'Just because I worked for the tax assessment office one summer, Hazlett, doesn't mean I had anything to do with the tax notices.'

'This time card says differently. You worked there exactly then, as a file clerk. What else would a file clerk be doing if it wasn't folding, licking and stamping? And I'm betting,' Cap continued in a slow, measured voice, 'that if we analyzed the DNA on the flaps of those envelopes, your genome would be all over them.'

'That proves nothing.' Ames had rallied, his voice stronger.

'It proves you stole my mother's farm.'

'I told you. My *father* did.'

Cap clicked his tongue. 'Like father like son. You did the dirty work for your father and now Tad is doing it for you, is that right?'

'You're crazy, Hazlett. I'm calling the nurse.'

Cap laughed. 'Go ahead. Do it. I'll even hand you the call button. Here, take it. I'm sure everyone will be fascinated when I turn this information over to the *Washington Post*. I can see the headlines now: "Chicken Magnate Steals Land from Eastern Shore Blacks."' Cap laughed again, but there was not an ounce of humor in it. 'What becomes of the Ames political dynasty then, huh?'

'What do you want, Hazlett?' Ames asked quietly a few seconds later.

'I want you to tell me why you murdered my sister.'

After what I took to be a stunned silence, Ames said, 'Your sister drowned. They said it was suicide.'

'Cut the crap, Ames. You knew Nancy well enough to know that she would never have taken her own life.'

'I didn't know . . .' Ames began, then yelped. 'OK, OK! But I didn't know she was your sister until, until . . .'

'Until what, you lying bastard? Until you married her? Is *this* why you ordered Tad to run Rusty off the road?'

I imagined Cap waving Rusty's photograph of the newspaper notice under Clifton Ames's nose.

'I really loved Nancy, Cap. You have to believe me.'

'You just wanted to get into her pants, didn't you? But if I know my sister, she held out for marriage. Didn't she? *Didn't she?*'

Ames screamed, 'Yes, I mean, no! I wanted to

246

marry Nancy, but then, the baby . . .' The sentence ended in a whimper.

'What about the baby?'

'I just needed time to get my dad around to it. We were really young, and he had, you know, expectations.'

'And then what? You found out that Nancy was a *nee-grow*?' Cap drawled.

'You think I didn't know that? I loved your sister! It didn't matter to me that she was half black.'

'But it mattered to your father,' Cap said, his voice steely.

'I thought he'd come around, especially once he saw the baby. I sent her money, visited as often as I could. Nancy and I were making plans, and then . . .'

'The baby died.'

'Yeah.'

'And Nancy came unglued.'

'Yeah.'

'And you thought you were off the hook.'

'I, I . . .' Ames stammered.

'You stupid asshole. In what state would your marriage to my sister have been legal once they found out she was black?'

'I *told* you! I loved your sister. She was the most beautiful, talented . . .'

'Is that why you killed her?' Cap snapped.

If Ames replied to this bald accusation, I didn't hear it because a nurse wandered by just then. She paused and cocked an eyebrow at me. I smiled, pointed a thumb at the sign, silently praying that she wasn't on her way to Ames's

247

room to take his blood pressure or hand him a bedpan. But she simply smiled and walked on.

'The Chinese at Camp Number Three knew how to get information out of prisoners,' Cap was saying matter-of-factly when I tuned in again. 'Forty-three percent of the POWs died up there. Did you know that?'

I thought I heard a groan.

'Tell me how you killed her!' Cap bellowed so loudly that I was surprised when no one on the hospital staff came running.

'Stop it! Stop!' Ames wailed.

'Tell me, you lying coward!'

Ames cried out again, keening, like an animal with its foot caught in a trap. I shot to my feet and straight-armed my way through the door.

Cap stood at the foot of Ames's hospital bed. His cheeks glistened with tears.

Ames lay on his bed in a tangle of sheets. The IV feed had been torn from his arm; the tubing dangled uselessly from the bag, dripping sodium lactate solution onto the floor. 'I didn't kill Nancy, you've gotta believe me!' Ames blubbered. 'My *father* did! He offered her ten thousand dollars to go away, but Nancy turned him down!'

'Cap?' I said quietly. 'Cap, it's Hannah. You can let go of Cliff's legs now.'

Cap turned his head and took me in without the slightest hint of recognition.

'Cap? Let go of his legs.'

'He's not in Geneva,' Cap muttered as I carefully unwrapped his fingers, one hand at a time, from their vise grip on Clifton Ames's loosely-bandaged calves.

Once free of the pressure, Ames moaned with relief.

'Cap! Cap!' I took my friend by the upper arms and began to shake him. 'You're having a flashback!'

Cap raised his hands, palms out, as if shielding his eyes from a bright light. His eyelids fluttered.

'Cap! It's OK. It's Hannah Ives.'

Meanwhile, Clifton Ames had found the remote and was frantically stabbing at buttons. The television mounted high on the wall turned on long enough for Doctor Oz to offer hints on how to reboot our immune system, then faded to black. The reading light over the metal headboard sprang to life. I held Cap's arms in a death grip and was urging him backwards into the visitor's chair in the corner of the room when the duty nurse barged in.

'How can I help you, Mister Ames?'

Clifton's eyes locked on mine for several long seconds, then flicked back to the nurse. 'I, ah, I'd like some more water, please. The ice in my pitcher seems to have melted.'

'Certainly,' she chirped.

'When you get a minute,' I smiled toothily. 'You might want to check Cliff's bandages. He must thrash around a lot in his sleep.'

'Be right back,' the nurse caroled as she headed for the door carrying Cliff's Styrofoam pitcher. 'Only one visitor at a time,' she reminded us as she passed by, then angled her head back and whispered, 'But this time, I'll make an exception.'

After she left, Cliff lay flat on his back, eyes

closed, lips sucked in to form a firm, hard line. After some serious prodding, I persuaded Cap to accompany me up to the hospital cafeteria where I sat him down at a table, then bought us each a cup of coffee. Cap took a careful sip, then set the cup, clattering and sloshing hot liquid over the rim, into his saucer. 'I don't know what came over me,' he said.

'You were having a flashback,' I said. 'To when you were a POW in Korea, I think.'

'No food, no water, no shelter . . . that wasn't the worst of it. Heated bamboo spears, lighted cigarettes, bottle openers twisted into open wounds . . .' Cap shuddered, setting his cup to rattling again. His dark eyes bored into mine. '"We have ways of making you talk."'

Words seemed woefully inadequate. I reached across the table and covered his hand with my own, squeezing hard and holding it there until the shaking stopped.

'His *father* murdered Nancy!' Cap hung his head. 'What am I going to do now?'

The late Clifton Ames, Senior lay moldering in the local cemetery, way beyond the long arm of the law. He may well have murdered Nancy Hazlett, but that didn't get Junior off the hook for Rusty's accident or the murder of Kendall Barfield. Although he hadn't exactly confessed to it, he hadn't denied Cap's bald accusation either.

But in Cap's present state, there was no use discussing that with him now.

'You're going to go home,' I told him firmly. 'And tomorrow morning, first thing, you're going to call your GP and get an appointment. Tell him

250

what just happened. Talk it over. Do what he recommends.'

Cap nodded. 'I hear you.'

'Do you want me to drive?' I asked.

Cap shoved his half-finished coffee aside. 'No. Thank you, Hannah. I'll be fine.'

'You sure?' I was reluctant to leave him on his own.

'Positive.' He gave me a hug. 'I can see you're worried, so I'll text you when I get home. How's that?'

'Call me instead,' I told him. 'I want to hear your voice.'

I walked Cap out of the cafeteria, rode down to the lobby with him on the elevator, and accompanied him to the parking lot. Only after he'd climbed into his car and driven away did I locate my cell phone and check in with Paul. He had driven over that afternoon and was waiting for me at *Our Song*.

I told Paul what had happened in Clifton Ames's hospital room. 'Cap was completely out of it, Paul. He kept saying, "He's not in Geneva." Geneva?'

'The communist Chinese were barbarians,' Paul explained. 'During the Korean War every rule set out by the Geneva Convention was broken. I imagine his captors kept reminding Cap and the other prisoners of that.'

Even though I was standing in the sun, I shivered. '"Toto, I've a feeling we're not in Kansas anymore,"' I quoted.

'Exactly.'

'Can you drive over to Cap's house, Paul? Make sure he gets in OK?'

251

'You want me to sit with him for a while?'

'Yes, thank you, sweetheart. I'd do it myself but I need to phone Sheriff Hubbard. Then I'm going back to check on Cliff Ames. There's something I need to ask him.'

Five minutes later, I slipped back into the room where Ames lay on his bed, sheets in order, pillow fluffed, IV tubes properly reinstalled. Standing directly next to the bed, I said, 'Tell me one thing, Mr Ames. What was your daughter's name?'

Ames considered me with rheumy eyes. He blinked slowly. Then he rolled away, burrowed his cheek into his pillow and faced the wall.

'Surely it doesn't matter now,' I said, addressing his back. 'Please, tell me. What did Nancy name your baby?'

His shoulders rose and fell, rose and fell, but Clifton Ames never replied.

Thirty-Two

'At length, the bad all killed, the good all pleased, Her thirsting Curiosity appeased, She shuts the dear, dear book, that made her weep, Puts out her light, and turns away to sleep.'

Charles Sprague, 'Curiosity: A Poem,' 1829

Baby Ella came home the way she left, in Wicks' long, black limousine, except this time her body was resting in a tiny wicker coffin, woven from

252

seagrass and decorated with pink ribbons and sprigs of fresh spring flowers.

Before she was buried beside her mother, Cap had been reassured by the undertaker that Ella was still swaddled in the rosebud blanket that had belonged to his sister, Nancy.

I am the resurrection and the life, saith the Lord.

I was distracted from Father Ryan's comforting words by a black Acura pulling onto the shoulder of the main road. A familiar figure climbed out and strode alone through the tall corn, its silk shimmering in the late morning sun. Jack Ames eased through the open cemetery gate and silently joined the tiny clot of mourners huddled around the open grave.

Forasmuch as it has pleased Almighty God of his great mercy to take unto himself the soul of our dear sister here departed, we therefore commit her body to the ground.

Cap scooped up a handful of earth, pressed it tightly into his fist then dribbled it slowly over his niece's coffin. A single tear rolled down his cheek and dripped, unchecked, onto his khaki blazer. I stooped, gathered a fistful of rich Maryland earth and sprinkled it over the casket, too. As I watched Paul do the same, I gulped air and swallowed hard, mourning two lives cut cruelly short.

Earth to earth, ashes to ashes, dust to dust, in sure and certain hope of the Resurrection.

Paul reached for my hand, laced his fingers with mine and squeezed three times: I. Love. You. I leaned into him, drawing strength.

One by one – Kimberly, Fran, Caitlyn, the Nightingales and finally Jack added fistfuls of soil to the growing pile on Baby Ella's coffin.

When the short service was over, I invited everyone to the house for coffee and sandwiches. As we walked back with me leading the pack, Jack Ames fell into step beside me. After several minutes, I broke the awkward silence between us. 'How is your father doing?'

'Still in the hospital under police guard. It's surreal.'

'Prognosis?'

Jack snorted. 'Oh, he'll recover in time for the trial. His attorneys are already fluttering around his bedside like guardian angels.'

We'd reached our gate and he held it open for me. 'Sheriff Hubbard told me your father confessed to everything,' I said. 'Strangling Kendall with her own scarf. Coercing his grandson into scaring Rusty by running his motorcycle off the road.'

'All true, I'm afraid. Although Dad is back-tracking a bit now that his lawyers have gotten their hooks into him.'

While the others trooped into the house behind Paul, I invited Jack to join me for a minute in the garden. After we sat down on the stone bench I asked, 'Did he say anything more about Nancy?'

'It's such a tragic, star-crossed lovers kind of story, I almost feel sorry for the old guy. *Almost*,' he emphasized. 'There is no excuse for what my father did. None.'

'At the hospital, your father told Cap that when

254

your grandfather found out about the marriage he tried to buy Nancy off, but she refused the money.'

Jack nodded. 'That's true. What he didn't say is that Dad was there. He saw the whole thing.'

I sucked in air. 'Good Lord!'

'Dad and Nancy were getting ready to go on a boat ride, down at the end of your pier there.' Jack waved in that direction. 'Apparently, Grandfather came charging down the dock like a mad bull, screaming about how their marriage was null and void, threatening to send the pair of them to prison.'

'Prison? They could do that?'

'In 1952? You bet. As late as 1958 a mixed-race couple named Mildred and Richard Loving were sentenced by a Virginia court to a year in jail for the crime – a felony I should point out – of marrying each other.'

I stared at him, slack-jawed.

'Not only that, but when building the case against the Lovings, the police raided their home at night, hoping to catch them having sex, which was also a crime under Virginia law.'

I felt queasy. 'Tell me you're making this up.'

'I wish, but it's true. Mixed-race marriages weren't legal in all states until 1967 when the Supreme Court overturned the Lovings' conviction.'

'I had no idea,' I said, thinking that the Civics class I'd taken in high school must have been sanitized.

'My grandfather's solution was simple, Hannah. Take the money and go away. But when Nancy refused, he was furious. According to my father, he picked up an oar and smashed it over her head.'

I gasped.

'Then the SOB threatened Dad with the oar, too. Forced him to roll Nancy's unconscious body into the creek.'

I closed my eyes and took deep, steadying breaths. 'According to the newspaper reports,' I reminded him once my breathing had returned to a semblance of normal, 'Nancy drowned.'

'Exactly.'

'So if anyone had bothered to call for help . . .'

Jack Ames completed the sentence for me. 'Nancy might have survived.'

Inside the house, I knew, funeral guests were awaiting my appearance. Paul would be plying them with wine, of course, but if I didn't lay out the ham and egg salad sandwiches soon everyone was going to go home tipsy.

'How is all the negative publicity going to affect your campaign, Jack?' I asked as I led him into the house from the garden.

He waved a hand as if shooing a fly. 'I can't worry about that. My campaign manager is running around with his hair on fire, but it is what it is, you know. If it's not meant to be this year, then maybe two years down the road.'

As the two of us straggled into the living room, Jack melted into the group of mourners, flashing a white-toothed politician's grin. I was thinking sourly, *Once a politician, always a politician* when Jack singled out Cap Hazlett and drew him aside.

'What Granddaddy did . . .' Jack's voice broke. 'I'm sorry.'

Incredibly, Cap Hazlett smiled. 'Thank you for coming, Mr Ames.'

'Call me Jack,' he said. 'Please.' Jack grabbed Cap's hand and pulled him into a bear hug. 'I had to be here,' he said. 'Baby Ella was my sister.'

I was standing at the kitchen sink, buried up to my elbows in suds, when Paul walked up quietly behind me.

'Is everyone gone?' I asked without turning around.

'Just waved the Nightingales down the drive,' he said. 'Nice people.'

I slotted another flowered dessert plate into the dish drainer. 'Grab a towel and start drying,' I said.

'Towel, schmowel,' Paul replied. He wrapped his arms around me from behind and rested his chin on top of my head. 'You were amazing today, Hannah. Keeping it all together for everyone.'

I bowed my head so he couldn't see the tears that were coursing down my cheeks and into the dishwater. Beneath his hands, my shoulders shook.

'Hannah?' Gently, he turned me around to face him. He lifted my chin and used a thumb to swipe away the tears. 'Leave the dishes,' he said, 'and come with me.'

Paul took my wet hand in his, led me out the

back door and down the lawn to a pair of pink-painted Adirondack chairs we'd installed at the head of the dock. We sat there silently, side by side, staring out over the creek. 'I know who put Baby Ella in the chimney,' I said at last.

'I figured it had to be Nancy,' Paul said, swiveling in his chair to face me. 'I saw you having a heart-to-heart with Bernadette Nightingale today. Did she shed any light on the situation?'

I nodded. 'Bernadette told me that they used to have a pet cat, a calico named Snickers. Nancy was quite young, maybe eight years old, when Snickers wandered out to the concrete slab that covered their cistern, lay down in the sun and quietly died. Nancy dressed the cat up in her doll's clothes, swaddled it in a blanket and laid it to rest in a box that a pair of roller skates had come in.'

'Ah. I see. And?'

'Well, after Nancy's mother took her home, Ronald buried the cat in the vegetable garden. Bernadette remembers that Nancy was hysterical when she found out about it. She cried for hours and hours, mourning that cat, worried that the animal would be wet and cold.'

As we watched, a Canada goose stirred among the cattails, stood, stretched and fanned her feathers. I counted eight downy yellow-and-brown-tipped heads sheltered beneath her magnificent wings. The mother bird stepped out. One by one the goslings waddled after her, unsteady on their webbed, too-big feet. Gracefully, she eased into the water, turned her head, black neck stretched tall and proud, watching, waiting until the last gosling, a runty little fellow, was floating in the water behind her. Only then did she turn and paddle off.

'A mother always watches over her children,' I said.

Paul squeezed my hand. There was nothing more to say.